SEX *and* RELATIONSHIPS *in the* 21ST CENTURY

A Transsexual's Point of View

VANESSA MATEO

ISBN 978-1-957582-95-5 (paperback)
ISBN 978-1-957582-94-8 (eBook)

Printed in the United States of America

To God be the Glory!
For without Him, I am nothing.

TABLE OF CONTENTS

INTRODUCTION

"Don't be boring!"--Veruschka

Life after forty. So, the saying is true--life begins at forty. I've never felt sexier and more confident--empowered if you will--in the things I do.

Is it pure Italian wisdom when they say "Italians do it better" or is it merely a catchphrase from a Madonna music video from the 1980s? Fast forward to 2017. Maybe it's time for an upgrade: "Vanessa does it better". For real!

Here, in this latest phase of my life--fortysomething and fabulous--I share with you my recent adventures and latest conquests with passion and pizzazz, conviction and accuracy and of course, absolute honesty.

One saying tells us that life is a "big bowl of cherries." I say life is a big buffet table full of things to experience and relish! But please be reminded that as we go through life, we will encounter the sweet and the sour, the fresh and the rotten as well as the ripe and the unsavory. In this world, we'll meet some very nice people–ready to lend a helping hand when you need them, and they'll treat you with kindness and respect. There are also the bad apples: the difficult, obnoxious and abrasive. And there are those who are simply pure evil; conjuring up chaos and controversy all the time, spewing malice and hate, ready to make your life a living hell. And I'm not talking about some bad presidents out there.

But, of course, one mustn't forget about the people whose main goal in life is to make you feel really good–in the bedroom. They are *my* people–the men in my life. Wonderful human beings who've kept me sane and satisfied all these years.

How I've simultaneously and singlehandedly dealt with these different groups of people with different personalities and agendas for four decades while living as a gay individual first and later as a transgender woman in a tumultuous world, I simply have no clue. But, one thing is for sure: I survived and I am now able to put those experiences–the good, the bad and the bad-to-the-bone–in a book: a tangible source of a feeling of triumph and validation that I will cherish for a lifetime. The world couldn't have come up with a much better representation of a tried and true survivor; one who's had major life and societal issues to tackle, not some bikini-clad contestant tackling tiny little crabs in a beach competition on TV.

One hears about some tell all books that would *end* others. Maybe this is one of them. I offer my readers a narrative that is straight from the heart; raw, uncorrupted and laced with humor at times.

I don't believe in suppressing your true feelings and concealing your honest opinions for the sake of political correctness. In this book, what you see is what you get.

I sometimes think about what I have done in life or in this world to make my good friend and lover, Martin, a fitness guru and former Olympian, say "There will never be another one like you, Vanessa."

Such a bold statement! I am flattered. People might ask "How can Vanessa attest to that?" By me backing it up with real stories of struggle and success, endearing testimonials from those who knew me well and titillating revelations that will give people's lives a little bit of excitement. You also need to grab the world by the balls sometimes in order for you to get noticed and for your voice to be heard. Here's my story.

Chapter 1

ONCE UPON A TIME IN MANILA

STRAIGHT OUT OF TONDO

Tondo, that unique, crowded suburb of Manila, full of fierce and colorful characters–*palaban* in Tagalog–special in its own way; a territory once ruled by the proud and brave chieftains of the Philippines many centuries ago before the advent of the Spaniards. It was the place where I spent part of my young life. How could I forget? Never! Just like in a Madonna song, I live to tell the stories.

Tondo is a small and congested area in Manila, with houses and buildings literally at an arm's length from each other, giving the term "limited space" a whole new meaning. One could literally hear the whispers and silent conversations of the people living next door.

Sometimes you'd be surprised by what one neighbor knows about you and your family. Tondo is literally the "hear-say" capital of the Philippines: Nosy neighbors hear what you talk about inside your house or apartment--due to the small proximity of the surroundings-- and they relay or "announce" it to the rest of the world the first chance they could. That's how it works. That's how people know your *business*. That's how the *chismosa* (gossipmonger)) does her business. One would think Dumbo's got the biggest ears. Nope! The people in the Philippines do! "There's no business like other people's business", I like to say.

That's how people get into trouble, too. But, for a young person like me growing up in this type of environment, the only business I cared about was my bicycle rides and outdoor *laro* or games.

I was a bicycle enthusiast when I was very young and I happily made those tight and narrow Tondo streets my personal bike lanes. I may not be as experienced as Greg Almond or Lance Armstrong, but thank God, I made it through. No crashes and collisions and no bruises on my fabulous legs.

Gone are the days when children like myself–back in the mid-1980s–could easily navigate those tiny, busy streets in Tondo while riding my rented bicycle--three pesos for half an hour--and enjoying the wind in my face as me and my friends made our way through. Surely, Juan Luna Street, a major thoroughfare in Tondo, had seen many of my tire marks. Nowadays, you need to be very careful doing that. There's just too many cars, vendor stalls and bystanders clogging my childhood neighborhood these days.

Also, as a little side note to these "bikeventures" in the early evening (circa 1986), I would borrow my neighbor Alex's sidecar or *pedicab*, an improvised bicycle with a protruding carriage on its right side used for commercial transport. Alex, a quiet and decent guy, was new in the neighborhood at the time, having just been married to my longtime neighbor Marla Han, a former *japayuki* (Filipino entertainer in Japan). Her parents, Onyo and Rosa, were friends with my grandparents.

In hindsight, maybe Alex was just being nice towards me and my family. That's why he'd let me ride his *pedicab* for about 15 minutes as part of my early evening neighborhood gallivanting. If 19th century royals (i.e. Queen Victoria) had their "early evening spin" in an open carriage, that *pedicab* ride was my own version.

An interesting part of the customs and traditions in the Philippines is the unwritten rule that when one moves into a neighborhood, long time residents sort of expect him or her to pay obeisance whether by giving material stuff or a friendly gesture. It's almost like an American custom, albeit the opposite: in America, long-time residents welcome newbies with a "Hi" and some pie. In the Philippines, long time residents' attitude is "You be nice to me now, bitch!"

So, in the ensuing months, Alex, the newcomer on V. Serrano Street was, in essence, on probation. He did, eventually, pass with flying colors. My neighbors seem to accept him without any reservation. I can't really say the same thing for his marriage with Marla.

As the old adage goes, "All things must come to an end." Alex and Marla's marriage was over in less than a year, fueled, allegedly, by the latter's parents' meddling (which stems from the fact that Alex came from a "nobody" family, or so the neighborhood rumors went).

I really believe it was the other way around. Prior to this doomed marriage, Marla had been working in Japan's busy night life as an "entertainer"--I'm not talking about doing live band shows and mini concerts. Being that 80 percent of the Filipino population belongs to the Roman Catholic faith, with strict moral guidelines and religious views, I have a feeling Alex's family disapproved of Marla's personal history.

Of course, being so young in those days, what do I know about such rumors and scandals? But then again, one might consider me young at the time--I was eight going on nine--but I *had* the adult instincts and keen sense of picking up gossip.

At any rate, along with the end of their short marriage came the end of my short *sidecar* rides in the evening.

I'd like to meet Alex someday. I'd like to have a drink with him and ask him personally what really happened to his marriage with Marla who by the way, I heard now operates a clothing business somewhere in the Middle East, as well as several Facebook accounts with doctored and Face App enhanced or "filtered" profile photos. Quite a vain old woman, I think.

Once, I made friends with a charming lady named Nessy. This was back in 1989, I was twelve at the time and she was perhaps fifteen years older than me. Despite the age difference, we got along fine.

She was renting one of the rooms in the ancestral home of the Lechero clan at the time. The Lecheros were distant relatives who lived not too far.

I find it surprising that I got along well with Nessy the tenant instead of her landlord's daughter, Reema Lechero. The Lechero family, although practically related to the Mateos by blood, was a bit on the "stuck up" side. Their clan feels a certain kind of entitlement within the entire neighborhood which to me is all bull shit. Sure, they acted uppity and hoity toity most of the time, but I didn't pay attention. To me, unless you have a mansion in Beverly Hills or a wing inside Kensington Palace, you will always be a Tondo girl, or boy--*batang Tundo* as we say in Tagalog.

My Grandmother told me stories that back in the day, the Lechero elders would tease my Uncle Manny because he did not have "pad paper"--or writing pad--to write on in class. My grandparents, as they were starting a family back in the early 1950s, did not have a lot of money. Apparently, young Uncle Manny and one of the Lechero kids were classmates. They would tease Uncle Manny with "*Si Manuel walang papel!*" ("Manuel has no writing pad. Aww. Poor guy!")

My Grandmother never forgot that.

Sometime in 1989, when Reema Lechero threw a pail of water at me and my friends, Ana and Nang-Nang, while we were playing outside her house, I quickly ran back home to tell my Grandmother. It was payback time!

My Grandmother, fuming mad, rushed to the Lechero residence, yelled from the outside of Reema's house, and gave Reema a *piece* of her mind. Reema heard a mouthful from my Grandmother. Reema and her mom, Clotilde, never said a word. They couldn't even get out of their house, out of fear, to confront my Grandmother.

Another incident that took place in the late '90s had something to do with one of the Lechero men. My Grandmother told me that Bayot Lechero was so drunk and had become very belligerent that out of the blue, he cussed her out as she passed by the Lusoryo residence; my Grandmother not doing anything at all to provoke him. She just happened to pass by that damn house. My Grandmother felt very disrespected.

I remember my Grandmother telling me during one of our *tete-`a-tete*, "*Tangnang Bayot na yan, minura ko nyan eh!*" ("That son of a bitch cussed me out!"). I wanted to call the Lechero residential landline in Manila outright so I could cuss out Bayot myself, but my Grandmother begged me not to, to avoid any further tensions between our family and theirs. At that point, I was so fed up with arrogant Mabuhay Playground residents that I didn't care anymore if they were relatives or not.

Going back to my friendship with Nessy--Nessy, coming from the central part of the Philippines, was trying her luck in Manila (as with any provincial girl or *probinsyana* would do), looking for work and hopefully, finding success. Unfortunately, it did not happen for her. After staying for a couple of months in Manila, she decided to return to her native province, Oriental Mindoro.

She did, however, leave me her home address which up until now, after thirty years have passed, I still remember by heart. This goes to show that friendships know no time and boundaries. It was also a precursor of things to come personally: I've always cherished the company of people older than me. I appreciate their solid grasp on life and things, and of course, their wisdom.

Once, I had a promiscuous middle aged neighbor in Manila named Vikki who enjoyed "victimizing" working men in the neighborhood: telephone line repair men, electricians, garbage collectors and anyone with two legs and a dick in between. My god! Sometimes, I think of her house as a brothel of some sort; only this time, the "madam" is the one paying the male guests--to fuck her. Oh yes, Poison Ivy said it right, "This is a one woman show."

Vikki falls in the *matrona* category, or middle aged woman. And in the Philippines, when you're a rich *matrona*, men flock around you and flirt with you, and if you fall for their charms, make sure they have easy access to your wallet and other valuable material stuff because that's the only reason why they'll want to be with you.

A sad societal stigma in the Philippines is that when a woman reaches middle age, she is not *that* desirable anymore unless there are other things, mainly monetary and material, that are *to* be desired. Think of *The Roman Spring of Mrs. Stone.*

Vikki, because of her US dollars and US supplied makeup products and beauty creams, managed to look very attractive to the man wolves in the area, thus becoming the neighborhood Sugar Mama.

Vikki, that wild woman who was a self proclaimed dead ringer for Miss Universe 1969 title holder Gloria Diaz, would fuck anyone with two legs and a dick in between. What I liked about her was the fact that she was a genuinely nice woman; generous to her neighbors and with a pleasing personality, no pun intended.

Once, when my Grandmother instructed me to collect Vikki's share for the telephone bill--it was common in the Philippines for neighbors to share one residential landline, also known as *partyline*--I saw a much younger man, shirtless, eating at Vikki's dining table as the latter looked on. The guy was chowing down his food as if he had just gotten back from a marathon.

Vikki was never a bitch (except maybe in the bedroom, with her numerous lovers) to anyone in the neighborhood. She was married to an American at the time who chose to stay in the US but would visit the Philippines twice a year.

The last time I've heard some news about her was perhaps some ten years ago: her husband had divorced her and she was living in poverty. Apparently, the *kano* found out about her infidelities and right there and then had stopped any form of communication and financial support.

A relative of mine ran into her once at Puregold, a grocery store, and she was shocked by Vikki the Voracious Maneater's appearance: gaunt and dressed like a peasant. Gone are the regular trips to the hair salon and the immaculately made up face and the influx of US dollars. It was a classic riches *to* rags story.

If only she saved the money her ex husband would shower her instead of showering her lovers in turn with the poor white man's hard earned money, maybe she would still be living a decent life these days.

Subconsciously, I sometimes see myself in her during her glory days: I have an armada of lovers and am not ashamed of it. But unlike her, I know something about being cautious with my spending habits and carefully saving for my future.

Another important lesson: I intend to save my money in a bank, not put it in my bedroom safe where cunning and cunnilingus loving men could easily get a hold of it after they break *me* wide open.

Once, the mayor of Manila in the mid 1980s--Mel Lopez--came by our house to have a chat with my grandfather. I had the slightest idea what they talked about, but that short meeting really did make a lasting impression: my grandfather was truly one of the coolest guys on earth. Not long after that meeting, he also had an audience with former Philippine president Ferdinand Marcos--in Malacanang Palace--along with my Dad.

Once, I had a sleepover at my cousin Nino's house in Balut, another suburb of Manila. Naturally, I couldn't sleep right away so I decided to wander the hallway on the second floor of their two story home. During my self-initiated tour, I ran across a vast collection of books and encyclopedia sets and an endless array of vintage dolls on display atop dressers and cabinets lined up along the hallway. One particular doll stood out: an astronaut Barbie (most likely from the 1980s). I was so fascinated by it.

Looking back, after almost thirty years, that experience might have helped in igniting my passion for books and for collecting Limited Edition Barbie dolls, not to mention blue nylon jumpsuits.

Once, there was a hit song called "Supersonic" which left quite an impression. Sometime in 1988, "Mabuhay Quadrangle" or "Mabuhay Playground", an area near my grandparents' house in Manila, also the childhood haven of my forebears, had some sort of a dance-a-thon where the DJ played the latest dance pop hits as well some "New Wave" chart toppers like "Bizarre Love Triangle" and "Domino Dancing".

I chose to attend the event wearing a green top and a pair of brown slacks. Although I was barely in my teens, I was ready to party. I was only eleven but was bold enough to show off my dance moves.

When the DJ played Prince's "Kiss", I totally went to town. It's no wonder that for more than thirty years, it's still one of the songs that makes me get up and dance the moment I hear it on the radio, or on my Android phone's playlist.

Funny how my great uncle, Onoy, who lived in the area, would hand me a glass of cold water from time to time because he thought I might need a periodic gulp between my nonstop dancing. I did not take offense. I knew it was a humorous gesture. After all, I was having one of the best times in my young, innocent life. Onoy, or "Kuya Onoy" as I fondly called him, was one of the few people in Mabuhay Playground who understood and respected me. He was my grandfather's younger brother.

When I was about 11 or 12, I placed a bet on the adult gambling game of numbers called *jueteng* and won forty-five pesos. I gave Kuya Onoy some of it so he could buy himself some cigarettes, his favorite *bisyo* or vice. He was genuinely happy about it. In the Philippines, small, kind generous gestures have a big impact on people especially if they're poor or barely making it.

I didn't really need the money at the time. Both my parents and grandparents were giving me money for school expenses and snacks and what not, so I decided to make Kuya Onoy's day a happy one by giving him some cash that one morning in 1988.

Some ten years ago, I made a request to some of my relatives in Manila to gather the dates of births and deaths of my Mateo forebears as part of my documenting my family's history and ancestry. Kuya Onoy was the one who volunteered to personally visit the Manila North Cemetery or Norte, the resting place of my forebears or *ninuno*, to do the job. I was so thankful to him and his wife.

He passed away a few years ago, but I'll never forget his being nice to me and his cheerful attitude and sense of humor. Like my grandfather, he will be in my heart forever.

JJ Fad's "Supersonic" was a major hit back then and I fondly recall dancing to its superb and unique sound. Never have I heard such a fresh sound. It was the advent of hip hop music in the Philippines. I'm proud to have been part of that young generation who first welcomed that fresh new music genre and danced to its super cool beat.

One of the many interesting facts about the neighborhood in Tondo where I grew up is the fact that there is an actual area called Ocean Eleven. Sure, it's missing an "s" at the end of "Ocean", but for someone who spent their childhood years thousands of miles away from America and had not the slightest idea where that name came from until they saw the George Clooney movie remake is simply dumbfounding--and exciting at the same time.

Once, when I was about 13 or 14, in the early 1990s, I did a little "runway" show in the living room of my grandparents' home in Manila. Although we had our own separate bedrooms upstairs, for some reason we all slept on each of the three couches in the living room. It was around nine in the evening and assuming that my grandfather was sound asleep, I put on a chartreuse colored table runner over my head--turning it into a turban-- and did a Linda Evangelista strut. As Murphy's Law would dictate, my grandfather was still awake, peeking through the covers with the classic one eye open. My Grandmother, who was still up at the time and watching me with glee, burst into laughter when she saw how mortified I was upon learning that my grandfather--that super masculine patriarch of the family--caught his grandson doing very feminine things right before his very eyes.

He never said a word and that's why I love my grandparents so much. They've accepted me for who I am and for what my sexual orientation was from early on.

Around the same time, my Grandmother and I, who were making ends meet by cooking breakfast and lunch and selling them to our neighbors, would do an impromptu *cha cha* dance in the living room (to the delight and amusement of my grandfather) to blow off some steam and enjoy ourselves in the process.

What wonderful memories to be cherished for a lifetime!

ODE TO MY GRANDPARENTS

Once, almost twenty years ago, a dear friend of mine and I were chatting over the phone when out of the blue she asked what I was going to have for dinner. My short and simple response was "sardines". Although she was a generally sweet and loving soul--she passed away in 2004 unfortunately--her tone had a subtle hint of prejudice. Sardines in the Philippines, to put it bluntly, has a reputation for being peasant food; a staple for the impoverished.

Imbued in the Filipino psyche since time immemorial is the idea that sardines is the poor man's food.

I did not take offense in the cuisine query that my friend was stirring. My attitude was as easy as mac and cheese: let it slide down your throat and move on.

While growing up in the Philippines, food was abundant in my household. It didn't matter if we were having *lechon* (roast pig, mainly served at birthday parties and other huge gatherings) on a regular day, or a can of sardines or corned beef. Food is food and it's all good.

When you were brought up appreciating whatever's given to you the way my parents and grandparents taught me, you simply didn't care. We were always thankful to God for the blessings, big or small.

Simplicity was key to a happy life. Learn to accept and appreciate what you have. That was how we lived. We weren't filthy rich but we weren't down and out either. We ate three times a day and had decent clothes on our backs and that was enough.

My grandfather, Manolo, was a retired police sergeant in Manila and his pension, along with the occasional monetary assistance from my Dad and uncles who were already living in the US at the time, seemed to tie up our daily expenses. To supplement this, my Grandmother would sell traditional Filipino breakfast in the morning such as *champorado* (chocolate flavored rice porridge), *lugaw* (congee) and the classic *sinangag*, *tuyo* and *itlog* (fried rice, dried fish and fried eggs). Sometimes, if she isn't too tired from all the morning's work, she would cook a couple of dishes to sell during lunchtime. My Grandmother makes the best *kare kare* (stew with thick savory peanut sauce).

Most of the time, I would be manning the stall in front of our house so that my Grandmother could take a break and rest a little bit.

Years later, when I was already living in the US, my Grandmother mentioned a most charming story. She told me that one of our elderly neighbors, Pacia, who used to work as cook for the landowner Gracing Rivera, recalled how she'd observe with amusement the very feminine way I'd fix myself up before I start entertaining customers: a slight stroke on my hair or making sure my T shirt looked neat. It brought a smile to my face.

Some Sunday evenings, my grandparents would take me and my siblings--and some cousins occasionally--to Luneta or what is now Rizal Park, posthumously named after Philippine hero and martyr Jose Rizal, for a picnic. We would all squeeze in my grandparents' "owner type jeep" and drive to the central part of Manila to enjoy the sights and sounds and savor the fresh cool breeze coming from nearby Manila Bay, world famous for the gorgeous view of the "Manila sunset". We'd munch on egg sandwiches my dear Grandmother had prepared earlier. On some occasions, we'd have *Reno* liver spread sandwiches as well.

Ah, the halcyon days of my childhood; so sweet and simple and filled with many happy memories.

ODE TO MY GREAT-GRANDMOTHER

I have been a horse lover for so many years--a lover of horse figurines and equine inspired art and jewelry. Horses, for me, are magnificent, steady creatures, but deep in my subconscious I'm still figuring out why I have such a soft spot for these strong, hard working animals.

February is just around the corner and it is the birth month of my paternal great-grandmother, Leonila, my grandfather's mother. She has been on my mind a lot lately. 2018 would have been her 107th birthday. It wouldn't take me 107 seconds to figure out why I have such an emotional connection with this revered lady.

Like my Mom, my great-grandmother was widowed early. She was only thirty one at the time. Twelve years into her marriage, her *mestizo* husband, Antonio, died from a heart attack in 1942. For the next forty three years of her life, she never remarried but instead devoted her life to the service of her growing family, particularly her grandchildren. She also became a *labandera* (laundress) to earn some money and not totally depend on her eldest son, my grandfather, for financial assistance.

From my farthest and fondest recollections I have of her, she would bring me toys of all kinds. One in particular was a horse figure made of brass (the kind that jeepney drivers would mount on the hood of their vehicles as some form of decoration).

My great-grandmother, that diminutive old lady with a great big heart, had set an example by showing me that the genuine act of giving has no price tag. It's the thought that really counts.

Coincidentally, my other great-grandmother, Teofila, serves as sort of like the missing link to my unexplained interest in collecting tea cup sets from different parts of the world.

It dawned on me not too long ago that in my grandparents' house in Manila, there stood a small table with a collection of miniature tea cups on top. My Grandmother would repeatedly tell me that they belonged to her mother when she was a little girl. This would have been in the 1910's. My Grandmother was so proud of those tea cups and that they had survived for many decades..

Another thing that I would like to add to these "grand" collections has nothing to do with horses or tea cups, but rather with horse hung men in my drawings and sketches. It was grand in the sense that I felt so extremely embarrassed by that *faux pas*.

Sometime in 1991, as my grandfather was going through some personal documents lying across his desk, he ran into some pornographic sketches I made the night before. I had become restless before bedtime and decided to "interpret" my creative juices through drawing--naked men and women, *highlighting* their private parts.

By the time I realized that I had left my sketches on top of my grandfather's desk, it was too late. The next morning, as I headed for the kitchen to get something to eat, there stood my grandfather, holding on to my "art", with a big grin.

Surprisingly, he just took light of it all; yelling out to my Grandmother (with intermittent bursts of laughter): "*Norma, tingnan mo yung drinowing ng apo mo! Mga titi at puke! Ha ha ha!*" ("Norma! Look at what your grandson drew! Penises and vaginas!")

I was so embarrassed I quickly bolted out of the kitchen as fast as Usain Bolt.

One last thing that I would like to share with the younger generations of my family is the fact that while growing up in our ancestral home in Tondo, there was an abundance of unique things, ephemera and novelty stuff that very few Filipino families had: an accordion, a Ford Mustang kiddie toy car made of solid metal as well as a VW Beetle, a musical instrument by *Melodion*, an intricately carved eagle that is made of solid wood and a whip crafted from a stingray's tail that belonged to my Grandmother's father, Emilio. And, of course, being that I came from a clan of police officers, there were all kinds of guns and ammo in the "weapons room" or what we simply called *bodega*. They were part of my grandfather's collection and personal effects. I've seen it all: shotguns, armalites, M16s, grenades, pistols and a carbine. They may be all done and gone, but there they are, all stacked up in my memory.

In June 2013, my Grandmother became a great-great grandmother. She is now in her late eighties, living at home in San Jose with my Uncle Mario. I like telling people how proud I am with the fact that my Grandmother is still around; me being in my mid-forties. It's a rarity, I think. And a rare gift from God.

MY PARENTS' HOUSE

Within the residential compound in Manila where I grew up stood a separate duplex style edifice where my parents and siblings lived. I had a bedroom there that I shared with my brother wherein I would sleep once in a while. Remember, I had my own room in my grandparents' house next door. In essence, my parents' house was *my* family home.

In the mid-'80s, my Dad was witness to its construction from core to roof. A decade later, when a Chinese businessman purchased the land where it stood, he was also witness to its demolition. Although there's hardly a trace of it today, the happy memories I had in that house remain crystal clear.

I clearly remember--and read--some of the dozens of books my Dad had purchased for us children to enjoy and be educated with: Edith Hamilton's *Greek Mythology*, Agatha Christie's *Ten Little Indians*, and LIFE's *Animal Kingdom* series to name a few; not to mention a slew of TIME and People magazines and countless issues of *Reader's Digest*. My parents not only nourished us physically, they also nurtured us mentally.

From this childhood experience came my love and passion for books. Books, books, books! I can never get enough of them. In my vast collection one will find books about the holy grail of jewelry and other jewelry collections as well as long gone Hollywood giants and the who's who in history particularly on British royalty and other European monarchies.

I'd probably give the ancient library in Alexandria a run for its money if someone were to host a contest on who has the most books in their collection.

Also in my parents' home were piles of vinyl records from decades past: The Beatles' *Abbey Road* and Carole King's *Tapestry* to name a few. My Dad was such a music lover and so am I. I think I inherited it from him. He was not a good singer though. My Mom is. I think I got my singing skills from my Mom.

I may not be a 100% confirmed person that holds a four octave vocal range but surely I have an abundant perfect "100" score on my record when it comes to my stint with the karaoke, or what is now called *videoke*.

Bring it on! Laura Branigan's "Gloria" and Roxette's "Dressed For Success" are some of my favorite karaoke numbers.

I credit my Krobel Inn rooms for helping me improve my singing skills. I'd practice there every week, you know.

Those Krobel Inn rooms have thick walls, thus making the acoustics near perfect. The echo is just right and my vocal projection is solid. It's like I'm in my own personal recording studio.

But, of course, it all comes down to whether you possess a good singing voice or not. A good singing voice is inborn. It has to come naturally. You may practice, train and rehearse for years, but if you really don't have *it* then you don't have it! If you don't have *the* voice, go find another hobby.

Whenever I'm in my Krobel Inn room, I always make sure I make the time to do some practice singing, not because I am joining a competition or something, but just because. It's one of my favorite luxuries when I have my "me time".

Singing for me is like sex: it's so therapeutic. I'd go on YouTube and sing along with posts that feature songs by Regine Velasquez such as her 2000 live performance of "What Kind Of Fool I Am" and "Ikaw Ang Lahat Sa Akin".

During these hotel room "mini concerts", I'd leave the door slightly ajar. Once, the crowded and noisy hotel courtyard went on silent mode. I knew the people there were listening and I loved every second of it.

I may not have the American Idol level of singing but by god everytime sing I make sure I give my 110% best!

When doing karaoke at home, I could be doing a love songs and ballads repertoire one moment and be segwaying to the rock category next. My voice could play around with different music genres. I'd be singing Nat King Cole's "L-O-V-E" this moment and jumping to Guns N' Roses' "Since I Don't Have You" next.

Once, back in my freshman year in high school in the Philippines almost thirty years ago, I did an impromptu performance of Minnie Ripperton's "Lovin' You" with all the whistling and such. My classmates were so impressed. One of them attempted to do his own version, but failed miserably. Those were fun times.

Chapter **2**

REFLECTIONS

THE CRYING DAME

Once in a while, I'd just let *go* and go on a crying mode. Oh yes, crying for me is a form of release. It's another form of therapeutic release. Mentally, it clears my mind of sad thoughts and physically, it cleanses my eyes; saves me a bundle of money from purchasing Visine at my neighborhood Walgreens.

I don't know why I'd cry all of a sudden. Maybe because of my deceased loved ones? They are always on my mind. They are always on my mind! There's my Dad and my good friends Tess, David and more recently, Lucy.

But, I also cry for the victims of the Sandy Hook Elementary School and Pulse Night Club massacres, the San Bernardino and Parkland shootings and most recently, the Gilroy Garlic Festival and San Jose VTA shootings. The last two happened not too far from where I live. A very good friend of mine works for the San Jose VTA. I went hysterical that Wednesday morning when he did not answer his phone.

And who could forget 9/11? You are one cold hearted bitch if you don't think about those lost souls and not shed a tear.

There you go! Maybe there are several reasons why I'd cry all of a sudden. I miss my loved ones number one, and second, my heart constantly bleeds for the innocent victims of gun violence and the selfish, intentional and malicious use of guns. I think it's the most evil act; to take precious lives just because you're feeling trigger-happy at the moment. Sad but true, there will be upcoming victims of gun violence and the reckless and irresponsible use of guns. Oh yes, 21st century people, get ready for more! We are in for a bumpy--and deadly--ride.

But, after all the fears and tears, there is hope: That life remains good and that the world, after all the deaths and bloodshed, is still a better place to live in.

BITCHIN' REALITIES

There was a point in my adult life--in my late thirties--when I only had a small fraction of the amount of money that I used to have.

But curiously, my passion for the finer things in life--jewelry in particular--remained. What's a girl inclined towards vanity like me to do? For a time, I contented myself living like a college student on a budget: eating ramen noodles on most meals and frequenting the local Dollar Store for my groceries and other basic necessities.

By growing up not rich and with only the simplest of things, I think it was beneficial and useful for me in my adult years. It made me adapt to change easily without the common depressing--sometimes deadly--consequences that go along with it (which some people find so hard to swallow). A classic example: the Bernie Madoff pyramid scheme victims who eventually committed suicide.

So, the next time some distant relative of mine implies that I look older than my age, I suppose my initial response would be "At least I was successful with my goals in life and I've got the bling to show for it. Mean bitch!"

I faced hardship and hard times head on and it made me one tough bitch that people would not want to mess with.

IT'S FAKEBOOK NOT FACEBOOK!

Never substitute face to face social interaction with social media interaction! Here are a couple of reasons why Facebook just doesn't do it for me.

FACE TO FACE TIME:

I have a pretty good sense and clear overview of the things I want in my world and social media isn't one of them. Facebook is for the socially inept and insecure. It's for people who lack the crucial skills to communicate and interact with others on a more human level. A face to face meeting or encounter, *por favor*!

If you want to show off your Blaniks and Louboutins, why don't you put them on and do a runway catwalk show in front of me at the lobby of the Four Seasons while I take a sip of my negroni? If you want to show off your new Dodge Charger, meet me at the Denny's parking lot after I have my Grand Slam breakfast and show me some donuts. If you want to impress me with your Martha Stewart-esque hosting skills, invite me to your *soiree*! You're the self proclaimed rich bitch from North Carolina, right? Surely you wouldn't mind adding me to your guest list.

IT HAS BECOME A MUSICAL CALLED ANYTHING YOU CAN DO I CAN DO BETTER

So, I say to this certain Mrs. North Carolina, a one time neighbor in Manila, why not establish your own personal department store since you have a penchant for declaring to the great United States of America that you are a rich bitch and you have a vast collection of Manolo Blaniks? That you know and own every major brand from BMW to Panerai. Impress me! Oh, and by the way, do share with us your "work" *experiences* back in Japan before you met Mr. Cuckold.

AND THE OTHER REASONS:

1) I'm a real person and I'm *real*!
2) Facebook can be a haven for traitors, terrorists and trolls!
3) It destroys relationships.
4) It causes depression.
5) It's a spy machine.
6) It's crime friendly.
7) Seriously, I'd rather read books.
8) I prefer meeting a potential friend face to face.
9) All my material possessions and treasures are in my bedroom. I don't need to upload photos of them for anyone. You want to see my bling? You call me and make an appointment.
10) I prefer telling someone who has a beef with me that they're a "nasty, disgusting piece of shit" face to face.

SOCIAL MEDIA SITES THE ROOT OF ALL EVIL? MAYBE.

I really believe that the major reason why some people hate me so much on Facebook is because of the fact that I know how to fully exercise my freedom of speech. I say and post whatever's on my mind without hesitation and with no regard for what trolls and toxic people think. I think I even offended some of its moderators, operators and employees, that's why my account became a constant target; Facebook would prevent me from posting anything for days. Facebook employees are humans, too, remember that. They get jealous and envious, too, and can be mischievous once in a while!

Regardless if they blocked me or not, I just continued posting and stating whatever's on my mind during those times that I was on Facebook.

When you have that kind of power, some jealous people treat you as a threat; you hurt their pride and in retaliation, they will try each and every form of detestable and cowardly act to bring you down.

Back in July 2017, Facebook blocked me from posting anything. Here are my suspects: a cousin, a distant relative and a miserable insecure bitch named Francisca. She used to be friends with a mutual friend until drama and jealousy destroyed their relationship.

I have since unfriended these witches. Never trust anyone online! Plus, I don't want shady characters in my domain. If you're not my friend in real life, then it is very likely that you'll be excluded from my Facebook Friends list.

Funny how one year later, at a family friend's funeral reception, I ran across one of my suspects. She was seated at the table next to mine. Strange how she never said a word to me nor did she ever make eye contact. She avoided me completely!

You can easily identify someone who has crossed you when you cross paths with them. Well, I can!

These people are as guilty as Judas Escariot. They act like vampires and you are the crucifix--they couldn't stand your presence!

That is how that snake acted the entire time.

I don't need Hercule Poirot to solve a mystery for me. Sometimes the answer is right in front of me; or for that particular incident, sitting at the table next to mine.

But, just like Jesus of the Crucifix, I know how to forgive. But that backstabbing bitch is blacklisted for life. For life!

It's nice to return to a normal life--no Facebook, no drama and drama mongers and jealous bitches constantly criticizing you and raising their Morticia Addams eyebrows on you. The latter part of my 2017 has been my own version of *Pax Romana* and I love it!

The blessings and good things are abundant. I'm less stressed (but of course, we all get stressed out. Anyone who disagrees is a big fat liar). Best of all, my sex life has gotten way better and far more exciting.

One poignant irony that came out of my complete rejection of Facebook as part of my daily life is that when I started posting photos and comments representing my interests and opinions, the bad apples came out rolling. It was a defining moment. I subconsciously rooted out the traitors, backstabbers and haters. Funny how Facebook brings out the worst in people--the grudges they secretly hold against you, their anger and envy...without you even asking them about it.

I sometimes wonder if Mark Zuckerberg had something to do with all this chaos and drama. After all, he is the Wizard of Social Media. Did he see it coming and intentionally conceptualize it, with a grin? That or people just happen to have an evil bone in their body. Beats me. Questions, questions!

I wouldn't call it a blessing in disguise, though. I think it's more of me rooting out the evil people disguising themselves as "Friends". My dangerous enemies were literally at my fingertips!

People ask me if I miss the friends I had on Facebook and the answer is no. Why would I? One former friend–Ricardo–a closeted queen with a wife and daughter who lives in a city outside Manila called Caloocan even "hijacked" a handsome friend, Charles G, many years ago. He probably did that so he could jack off to the handsome stud's sexy photos while his wife sleeps in their daughter's bedroom.

It's so hard to trust people on the internet these days.

For the past twenty three years of my living in America, I've met and dealt with a bunch of different people with different characters and personalities; a few I've remained friends with, very few I've *kept* as friends. Those belonging in the "very few" category I value the most. And they're not even my relatives.

In my living in America for over two decades, I realized that friendships must have an open door policy. People change. Attitudes change. You have no control over the people you'll meet and end up having relationships with--whether it's platonic or sexual. You simply have no control. So, when that pivotal moment comes and you realize that this damn friendship you have is not working and not worth saving anymore, do what Rose did to Jack Dawson in *Titanic*: you have to let go!

Pragmatism is key and I consider myself a very pragmatic person. Just like the Empress Frederick of Germany (1840-1901), common sense reigns in my psyche. It's so fucking hard to bullshit someone like me. When I know the friendship is dead, it's over for us. *Hasta la vista*, baby!

COMFORTABLE IN MY COMFORT ZONE

I really don't believe in the phrases "out of the box" and "getting out of your comfort zone". Hey, if you're comfortable and happy with the life you're living right now, then go for it! Life is too short to focus on getting out of the box or out of your comfort zone. Focus on the things that you love and love doing. It may not bring you lots of money and success, but at least you're not killing yourself by overdoing it. Rich or poor, we're all going to die anyway. Take it one day at a time, like the Croatians. By being overly ambitious and presenting yourself as an overachiever too much, you might get to the grave a little faster than you think. Avoid having a heart attack because of too much stress and excitement!

One thing's for sure though, I really enjoy opening small boxes with precious, sparkly pieces inside. Nothing compares to the feeling of opening a small box with a beautiful piece of jewelry inside. It's a testament to my hard work, struggles and survival. It's like telling the naysayers "Hello, bitches. I made it!"

In life, when you work hard, you can *play* hard. What's that tumblr quote again? "Work like a slave, eat like a king." That's me!

GOD AND DIVINE INTERVENTION

"I believe in God the Father Almighty," a certain prayer goes. It is one of the most sacred lines I learned while attending Catholic school in Manila in my younger years.

I truly believe in God and his inexplicable and unsurpassed powers. In fact, my faith is so strong and indestructible that I feel like I have an instant connection with Him; a direct line of some sort. It seems like he always comes to my rescue in times of need.

Once, I passed out while driving home a little intoxicated on the 880 freeway in Fremont, CA. I was in the fast lane and next thing I knew when I opened my eyes, I was on the right most lane already, about to exit the freeway. How did that happen without me getting into a horrible collision with other drivers? The power of God is my answer. He immediately sent his angels down to safely lead my car to the right most lane during those few seconds that my car was drifting from one lane to another while I was totally–totally–unconscious.

God led me out of danger that night.

To this day, I still don't have the words to explain it, but I do have words of gratitude towards the powerful guy up there: Thank you, Heavenly Father!

Back in the summer of 2000, I received a frantic phone call from my good friend, Lucy. Her roommate had gone berserk in the living room and she felt very threatened by him; that he might do her physical harm. She was calling from the house phone. Out of panic, she had misplaced her mobile phone and couldn't find it. I instructed her to go to her room and lock the door and that I will call the police right away. As soon as we hung up, I immediately dialed 9-1-1 and reported the incident to the police. After making the call, I immediately drove to Lucy's place--in the Autumnvale area of San Jose--to check on her. While driving, I kept on reciting all kinds of prayers. I was so worried for my friend. I was hoping that nothing bad happened to her. When I arrived, Lucy had already been escorted by the cops out of the house and her roommate handcuffed in the backseat of the patrol car. I was so relieved and so thankful to God.

Sometime in the fall of 2005, I had to play ambulance driver for a family friend, Shahani, from Fremont, CA. She was about to give birth and she did not have health insurance to pay for the paramedics to transport her to a hospital in Hayward, CA. The pregnancy was out of wedlock. Shahani had no one to turn to for help. Sadly, the people who she was working for--as a daycare provider--did not want to cover the expenses. Shahani, out of desperation, begged me to drive her to the hospital on her due date. Sure enough, when the actual date came, she was about to pop!

In addition to becoming an instant *NASCAR* driver that night, with my Mercedes topping speeds of more than 90mph on the 880 freeway, I probably ran through ten red lights that night just to get her to the hospital in time. Luckily, since it was very late, there were hardly any cars on the road.

As Shahani was screaming from labor pains in the backseat, I was *screaming* out all kinds of prayers to God. "Please help us, Lord! Please guide us!!" were the words that came out of my mouth. I was hysterical. I was probably more hysterical than Shahani. Never have I imagined that I would be put in such a delicate life and death situation. "*Nakakawala nang poise!*" as the common Tagalog expression goes.

All I kept thinking about was getting Shahani to the hospital on time and that she will have a safe delivery. And she did.

Once again, God sent his angels to guide me and my car as Shahani and I made our perilous journey to the hospital.

PEARL POWER

I recently attended the funeral of a beloved family friend from Dixon, CA. She was almost ninety when she passed away. I loved and adored her dearly. She was a great woman. I can't really say the same thing for her daughter, Greta Betchi.

Greta, who lives in nearby Roseville has a penchant for making fun of my looks out of the blue. Maybe she thinks I'm not "passable" enough as a female. Maybe Greta was just being a *bruha*: a total bitch.

Over the years, she has mocked my personal appearance just because. Absolutely no reason! She just felt like doing it, that's all. Now you believe me when I say people just happen to have an evil bone in their body. They may not be aware of it, but there it is! That's just the way it is. The sad thing is, innocent people fall victim to it.

In 2007, at a relative's birthday party where Greta was invited as well, she had the audacity to tell my face that I looked "depressed". Maybe she should have used the word "tired" instead. I was helping out in the day-long preparations for that party and believe me when I say Filipino parties are some of the most elaborate and exhausting. Unless you have Kevyn Aucoin for a makeup artist, most likely you will look tired and haggard. That's just the way it is. I live in the real world. This is me and this is how I look. Greta, on the other hand, lives on a planet called Uranass.

In 2016, when a distant relative posted a picture of him in drag over the internet, Greta, again in her very own obnoxious and offensive ways, commented out of the blue that he *looked* like "Vanessa".

To outright and blatantly compare a masculine man wearing lipstick with someone so feminine like myself is just plain rude, disrespectful and absolutely shady.

Greta was trying my famous Taurus patience, or what's left of it. She was trekking an unknown, dangerous territory called Donfakwidvanessa.

At the dead old lady's funeral reception, Greta, in her third and final attempt to embarrass and humiliate me, backfired. This time I made sure I bit her back in her fat ass, not with my mouth but with my mouth watering pearls instead. Oh yes, Greta, also a jewelry freak, was salivating over my pearls. She couldn't take her eyes off of them!

As a final gesture in honoring that old lady friend of mine, I came out dressed to the nines. I wore my long Italian made trench coat and had my best pearls on, the ones I call my "Coco pearls". They are big!

When Greta approached me and started commenting on my slim figure, insinuating that I might be sick of something or something to that effect, I in return acted as if I never heard a word she said, let alone acknowledge that she was standing next to me. I gracefully made a 180 degree turn--without letting her finish her sentence--and walked away. That, my friend, is how a true lady responds!

Let your jewelry do the talking!

I remember when I was growing up in Manila, a relative of mine confessed that some people in the Mabuhay Playground area are so annoyed by my "chin up" demeanor whenever they'd see me pass by. They easily dismissed it as me being arrogant or haughty, but in reality, that's just me. That's my posture. That's how I walk. That's me! I won't change my ways for anyone just because they are annoyed by it.

Princess Alice of Gloucester (1901-2004), a daughter-in-law of England's King George V, was my inspiration. She always had a straight back well into old age.

I chose to avoid and ignore that Betchi woman throughout the event. Funerals symbolize the end of certain things and that includes letting go of negative and unhappy memories. I've decided to symbolically close that chapter with Greta right there and then. I hope I never see her face again.

REGRETS (I'VE HAD A FEW)

In life, it's either *our* way or the highway. People leave and move; in most cases they die. How I wish I could turn back the hands of time and pull these special people closer to me and tell them "Please stay a while." They did, however, leave me with a trunk full of happy memories. I know I could open it during my moments of melancholy or when I simply feel like reminiscing.

On Mike Easten

I miss you a lot. I wish you never left California. Every time I pass Thornton Avenue I think about you and the fun we'd have. I remember Racks your labrador gawking at us while we're fucking. I miss the one hundred dollar bills on your side table. I fucking miss you a lot!

On Mark Baldwin

I've loved you with all my heart. You should know that. If only I could turn back time I'd show you how I've matured and changed for the better. Now that I don't have you anymore, all I have are the leftover fantasies I have of you; the imagined possibilities of how things would be for us had we kept our relationship going; and how I'd show you how to better appreciate you and please you. But you've moved on and there's nothing I can do but tell the world how much you really mean to me.

On David Sekkell

I wish I made time for you during your visit to California in 2014. God damn these money making ventures that get in the way of the more important stuff: the people that matter. What I would give to see you again, to share happy moments with you and have another quiet walk at Lake Elizabeth Park with you. Sit in my car for hours because of a flight delay? I'd fucking sit there for eternity just to see you and hold you again. I'm so sorry, Dave.

On Chris Flanerty

I wish you didn't do the stupid things you did. That is not the person I know and love. I am praying for you and am hoping that eventually you'd be able to slide yourself out of the sticky situation you are currently in. Stop hooking up with crazy crack whores! They mean trouble for a lifetime!

I still clearly remember one visit you made and how you chose to leave your shoes outside my hotel room because you did not want to stink up the place. Baby, you know I've always completely accepted you for who you are since day one, the way you've accepted me for who I am. It's totally okay, baby. I'd kiss you all over again if given another chance. You were perfect. Just perfect.

On Chris Desanto

You gave me true love's first kiss. You had the sweetest lips. The world simply ought to know. After thirty years, I am setting my feelings free. Memories of you still tickle my senses; the way your playful fingers would tickle my body. Chris, you will always have a special place in my heart. We were living in a hostile environment back then, let alone the Philippines, where homosexual feelings were not tolerated. One thing you should know, I was never ashamed or embarrassed about my feelings for you for one bit. I can still feel the light pat you gave my thighs when we crossed paths back in 1993 after you paid my grandparents a visit. Koneha, the mother of your sons, was slightly ahead of you so you took the opportunity. She did not see it. But I *felt* it. I knew you still cared. You were my first teenage crush. God damn, I was head over heels in love with you! I'll be lying if I say you weren't my first love. I wish you the best. Who knows? Maybe we'll cross paths with each other on my next visit to New York.

On Brian Todd

Your autism never bothered me, but my relationships with other men did. I sometimes felt like I was in the middle of a tug-of-war: should I let you go and just totally give *in* to the other lovers who were about to consume me, and didn't really care about my feelings? And then there was the issue of making a living for myself. Work got in the way and we lost touch. Here I am, twenty years later, wondering where you are. One of the few men who genuinely cared for me and loved me and I let him slip away. Once, you waited for me at a parking lot near my house, hoping I'd show up. I never did. Now, it's the other way around. Everytime you come to mind, I am transfixed. I see myself in an empty room with no windows, staring at a blank space. Maybe this is how you felt when you waited for me in your car for an hour. The only difference for me is, there are tears in my eyes. I have a feeling I may have to wait for a very long time. Brian, where are you? I'm so sorry I let you slip away.

On Joseff Tran

For the dozens of times that you begged me to be your full time girl friend, the same number of times I declined. The allure and attractiveness of money got in the way. I was picking up a bunch of phone calls from the dozens of lotharios and casanovas out there, but not a single one from the dozens you made. Now that I am in my forties and the idea of making tons of money is past me, I wish one day you'll pass by my neighborhood again like you did one time when you were so desperate to see me.

Now, all I need is a friend to share good, happy, quiet times with--with wine or beer--and lots of holiday cheer and joy throughout the year. God damn it, I'm starting to sound like a Hallmark greeting card. Joseph, I miss you. Come back, please. Hold my hand. I could really use a warm hug right now.

Erik, My Beautiful Boy

In early 2002, I met a young guy named Erik through Yahoo Personals. He was a bright, good looking young man of Mexican descent attending UC Riverside. At a time when the fast paced world of the internet was the major form and portal of communication, Erik and I, believe it or not, would still communicate through good old fashioned hand written letters. I guess he wanted to show me his being an authentic and a classic gentleman.

Through the letters he sent me, I got to know Erik better. He had big dreams and he loved his family so much. He wanted to give them a better future, especially his mom and younger sister. He also wanted to set a good example for his younger brother, Daniel.

Hard to believe that at the young age of twenty, Erik had the emotional maturity and mental stability of a man twice his age. He had a clear overview of what he wanted to achieve in life: finish school and become successful, so he could share the blessings with his family.

In the early 2000s, the internet was booming and a degree in Computer Programming was the one college students were aiming for. Erik, at the time, was working towards a degree in Computer Programming at UC Riverside.

In the summer of 2002, Erik and I decided to meet. He invited me to stay at his studio apartment not far from campus.

So, in June 2002, I drove some 500 miles to Riverside and there, Erik and I finally met. We decided to meet at the local diner--a neutral place. I wanted to have a *feel* of Erik first, observe what kind of personality he has, and how he communicates; more importantly, to find out if we have chemistry.

Erik had the most beautiful big brown eyes, full of life and curiosity. I was smitten.

Erik, despite his young age, was most courteous and gentlemanly, something rarely seen from guys his age. He even offered to pay our lunch bill, but myself being aware of his financial situation--a college student with a minimum wage job at McDonalds--I insisted that I take care of the check. I told Erik it was my treat and he was genuinely happy and appreciative about it.

Erik insisted that I stayed at his apartment for the remainder of the day. He had to go to work that afternoon but he consented with me having access to his apartment. I remember watching TV that afternoon and taking a long nap. Sometime in the evening, Erik arrived with food from McDonalds. "Aww, you brought me dinner," I told him. "You didn't have to."

After eating, Erik asked if I wanted to take a dip in the swimming pool within the apartment complex. I obliged. There, he gave me a sweet tender kiss on the lips which eventually led to us making out.

It felt really special, something I've never experienced before. The majority of guys I've dated before meeting Erik were *not* into kissing.

Erik wanted to take his time with me. He wanted to know me first, not know my bedroom capabilities. A sweet innocent kiss was the first step. It felt heavenly. He treated me with respect.

Nothing *else* happened. After the dip in the pool, we headed back to his unit and went to bed. Erik insisted that I slept on his inflatable mattress and that he'd sleep on the couch. We needed rest. We had a big day ahead of us.

The next day, a Saturday, we decided to play some games at the campus arcade and saw *Lilo & Stitch* afterwards. After the movie, we grabbed a bite to eat at a taqueria nearby and drove back to his apartment. I was scheduled to drive back home that evening. Erik did not want me to go on an empty stomach.

Around six in the evening, I was packed and ready to go. Erik walked me to my car and before I had the engine running, tears started running down my face.

"Aww, Bumble Bee (Erik's pet name for me), you're crying," Erik uttered with empathy.

"Because you're so nice to me. Thank you," I told him. My voice cracked as my heart broke.

For some reason, I had a feeling it was the last time I'll see Erik. Maybe he'll stop communicating with me and move on. Maybe he'll fall in love with a real girl and forget about me.

All I know for sure is that in that brief moment of my life I met a wonderful, caring young man who accepted me for who I am--a transgender individual still in the process of discovering herself. Erik was instinctively telling me "It's okay, Vanessa. You'll be fine."

For the remainder of 2002, Erik and I would communicate periodically through Yahoo Messenger just to say "Hello" and chat for a few minutes. In early 2003, I met a much older man and started a serious relationship with him. In March of that year, I flew to the Philippines to accompany my Mom for a two-week vacation. Upon my return to the US later that month, I resumed my relationship with the older gentleman. At that point, Erik and I have lost touch.

Not long before I started gathering material for this book, I ran across Erik's old letters along with the photos he had sent me sixteen years ago. I started to wonder what happened to him after all these years. Several searches on the internet led me to a very sad discovery: Erik, that beautiful young man from Riverside, who treated me so well and showed me such a wonderful time, passed away back in March 2003--the same time that I had been vacationing in the Philippines.

So, after sixteen years, I cried again for Erik; only this time, I wept. The November rain simply had no chance to compete with how flooded my eyes were.

Back in 2002, when Erik and I first started communicating, I could tell he had big dreams and great ambitions. He was well on his way to reaching his goals and having a better future. It was undeniable: the hard work, the discipline (he never smoked or did drugs) and the determination. He was so *excited* for life.

I can only dream of what other wonderful opportunities the world could have offered Erik had he been around today, and how he would've put his achievements to good use for the betterment of his life and the lives of those close to him.

I miss my beautiful brown eyed boy. I think about him often, especially when I'm in Los Angeles. I miss him a lot.

Dream no more to be with the angels, Erik, for you are one of them now. Watch over your mom, brother and little sister.

Chapter 3

THE BARONESS OF FREMONT

BARONESSIMS: Quotes, opinions and one liners reflecting the ever colorful life and creative mind of the self proclaimed Baroness of Fremont, the one and only transsexual Vanessa.

Only I know what's really on my mind and inside my heart--my loves, my fears, my dreams and how I view the world and the people both near and far. Who better interpret and lay them out in the open than myself? Not some quack biographer or rookie journalist who's missing all the important parts and delicious details. When it comes to Vanessa's story, there is only one reliable source: Vanessa. In this part of my book, I am pouring them in!

Sex is the cure.

You are a public figure? Then you *are* public domain. So, if you see your name, don't complain!

You are not a public figure, but you saw your name? Then shut up and don't complain! I"ve been around in this world for more than forty years. And never for one second did I hear from you nor did you make your presence known or felt. I wouldn't want anything to do with you starting today and for the next forty years and beyond! Don't be a hypocrite. Scram!

I criticize and scrutinize people in this book. I make fun of other people. I make fun of my friends, relatives, lovers and acquaintances. I even make fun of myself, for crying out loud! Myself! Are you kidding me? No one is safe! Deal with it!

You are over the age of eighteen? Then you're old enough to read and *absorb* the sexually charged topics and explicit contents included in this book! And don't act surprised or grossed out. I have a feeling you are doing the same thing.

You are under the age of eighteen but you've been in other people's bedrooms more than the Merry Maids employee? Then, you know what I'm talking *about*--the sex and sexcapades mentioned in this book. Don't act surprised or grossed out. You still have a long way to go in life. I predict you'll be doing the same things in the future.

My gift to men is the gift of earth shaking pleasure and complete satisfaction that no other person could give.

My gift to Buster Posey, for all his hard work and hard hits, is the gift of tongue.

Aside from gorgeous bubble butts, nothing excites me more than beautiful, unique jewelry and evocative works of art and paintings.

In this age of sex via iPhones and iPads, I still opt for the real thing: a real man beside me, behind me and on top of me. A man who will push my *buttons*, not me pushing electronic device buttons for sexual kicks.

If you're not getting some kind of a discount on the purchases that you make whether in store or online, then in essence, you're letting yourself get robbed. I'd like to take this opportunity to thank the wonderful sellers, dealers and thrift store managers who gave me a price break on some of my significant and fabulous purchases recently: Beladora of Beverly Hills, Dover Jewelry, Arnold Jewelers, M Barr Antiques, Antiques Colony and Savers.

I know already I'll die happy because I was able to acquire and enjoy the precious pieces I've always wanted to own. No use in dying with lots of money but lacking a sense of satisfaction and fulfillment, right?

Money is meant to be acquired and spent on material things that will bring us joy and excitement.

It's better to be humble than act like a high brow with really nothing to show for it.

Success is not measured by the titles some people put before their names and the abundance of wealth. What's the use of being called a "Doctor" if you can't really bring cure and medical assistance, free of charge, to the people who need it most: the children of third world countries. My advice to Roldita, a former schoolmate in the Philippines who is now a practicing physician, please knock on poor, sick people's doors and offer pro bono assistance rather than doing Tik Tok and taking plenty of selfies...in the Operating Room. Yikes!

So you're a Hilton? How about donating some of your money to the displaced and the desolate in Afghanistan? Maybe coordinate with other countries and the UN to build some sort of a housing community somewhere far from the Taliban strongholds that can shelter the displaced and the homeless? On a more personal note, I'd like to acknowledge those in the medical field who bravely put their own lives and health at risk during the Covid pandemic just to help out others who are in dire need of assistance. You are all heroes in my eyes. Thank you!

Sometimes I think I'm poor despite my material possessions. But then again, just like the Duchess of Windsor in an episode with Diana Vreeland wherein she confides about the Abdication in a trance like state, I'd snap out of it, come back to my senses and wake up to reality. I would then look around my room that is filled with treasures, trinkets and pieces of art and realize I am *not* poor after all.

Now that I am past forty and certain views and opinions have changed, for me, the three greatest pleasures in life are high karat gold jewelry, sexy lovers with great asses and good food and entertainment at Cache Creek Casino. Simply the best!

Jewelry--my fabulous jewelry--are like my lovers: They each have their own special characteristics, they give me so much pleasure and I love having them all over my body.

My haters should spend more time focusing on themselves instead of focusing on my fabulous single life including what I do and who I do in bed. No wonder they look older than their actual age. Not a lot of endorphins being released. Just envy.

A friend of mine recently asked if I got what I wanted for Christmas 2017. My simple yet straightforward response was "Yes! But I don't wait for someone to give me what I want for Christmas, or any time of the year. I am not my cousin Linnie. If I want something, I buy it right away and with my *own* money. I don't need a man to buy me stuff. I *buy* men sometimes, are you kidding me!" My friend was in stitches after hearing that.

I revel in the fact that some transsexuals I come across with in public would make the craziest animalistic noises and act obnoxiously just because I am *out* there with my fabulous clothes and fine jewelry, taking over the world stage. It's called power, my friend. At the Great Mall of the Bay Area back in January 2018, two tacky trannies dressed in streetwalker clothing burst into a hyena like laughter the minute they saw me. I was about to enter the Marshalls department store wearing my blue KLM Martvisser trench coat and white Ferragamo pumps. Always a classy lady in public (because I have such a reputation to protect), I did not dignify their behavior but continued to walk instead with my chin up and queenly demeanor. This separates the treasure from the trash. When you make insecure people act stupid with what you're wearing without saying a single word, that is pure power. "Vanessa Voodoo" maybe? I'm not sure. Whatever. As long as I didn't have to touch the maggots.

It's the plain simple truth: Guys prefer a glossy pair of pink lips, not red, because it makes them think they're fucking a young, fresh, plump juicy vagina.

Winter Warmth: At the Men's Figure Skating competition during the 2018 Winter Olympics in PyeongChang: I've never seen so many male asses sticking out, not since my last visit to Panama Beach when a bunch of cute college guys mooned me during Spring Break.

There's a naughty grin on my face every time I see one of my lovers rush to the bathroom to wash and scrub his body hard after having sex with me. I love his demeanor--one that is being instantly quarantined.

There's a naughty grin on my face every time I hear my lover hack out a loud spit while gargling on Listerine after making out with me.

To my haters on Facebook: All those nasty and negative perceptions you have of me are reflections of your equally nasty and negative mentality and filthy existence.

The following three statements are rebuttals to accusations thrown at me in the past.

I'm not a slut. It's just that a lot of men love me and adore me. That's all.

I'm not a homewrecker. It's just that your husband finds you boring in bed. Actually, *your* kids from your previous relationships are the ones wrecking his life! That's the truth! It's the truth!

I don't steal boyfriends. You just don't know how to suck dick properly. So, he sneaks out late at night and comes to visit me.

Sex is life. If you're not doing it or getting some, you're missing out on life big time. You're not living at all!

Mira Sorvino, move over! There's a new Mighty Aphrodite in town. On December 26, 2017, I made eight men *climax* in the most intense, explosive manner. These are strong, healthy mature men, mind you, and by the time I am done with them, they were all weak in the knees and drained; completely out of strength. One woman versus eight men. How exciting. Are you a Mighty Aphrodite like me?

Chris, my first young love while growing up in Manila, would regularly use a fragrance by Estee Lauder. I can still clearly remember its mesmerizing scent thirty years after I took a whiff of it off his neck. A man's scent, just like an unwashed construction guy's ass once it's in your nose, is just like the title of a Natalie Cole album, unforgettable.

If the love and compassion we receive from others help make us become better human beings, sex on the other hand, is like fuel for the body. For me personally, it improves my mental well being and I become better at performing other physical stuff.

Sugar Coating: It's okay to eat lots of sweet, sugary stuff even when the doctor tells you no. It's okay to cheat a little. Men do it all the time and so can you!

You'll find more mystery men in my bed than in the Hallmark Channel movies on cable TV.

I think the reason why God continues to give me blessings is because I am always thankful for what I receive, big or small. And I give back!

On the FX television series *The People Vs. OJ Simpson:* I watched that show with a passion like a horny cougar mom watching the young, hot jocks at his son's baseball game.

Why bother putting expensive makeup on my face when I know damn well it'll all be gone the minute I do the nasty in the bedroom? I just put on stuff from the Dollar Store. Cheap makeup for cheap sex. Makes sense!

I don't need to use a Christian Dior foundation on my face. I need some serious Christian intervention rather--especially a splash of holy water--for all the sinful acts I commit in the bedroom.

Sometimes the best way to prevent a big disappointment is to think small of people who you initially thought would make a big difference in someone else's life and would be truthful and understanding towards you. Words are useless. Actions are priceless.

Butthole Surfer: "Oh my God! I've become Anakin Skywalker! I've gone to the dark side."

No to Facebook fuck ups and yes to face to face meeting and conversations!

Mojo Motto: It's not with who you're going to do it with but rather what nasty, kinky things you plan to do that gets me going and inspired.

I'm a visual person: While looking at nude photos and dick pics on my phone that my lovers send me from time to time, if they make me cum then it must be true love. There is no other way to explain it.

Another interesting side note about my past and present lovers: each one of them has a brother. No sister or sisters. Just one sibling: a brother.

Advice I would give the quarreling sons of Aling Ne had I still been living in Manila (in Tagalog): *"Sa mga anak ni Aling Ne, wag nang mag suntukan, mag sandukan na lang ng tinda nyong ulam! Isang order nga ng kanin at dinuguan. Pakibilisan!* ("Stop punching each other and start serving food!")

Sexy Sinestro: *The Green Lantern* definitely got my mind going green the minute Sinestro came to the scene. British alpha actor Mark Strong is such a daddy! I could see him sitting on top of me while wearing that tight body suit, calling me every dirty name in the book.

One time I thought I startled a couple of hotel employees--Chuck and Dionne--when I walked in the lobby one early Wednesday morning to get my coffee. There were hardly any other people around. They were probably messing around with each other.

Once, in Manila when I was very young, maybe 6 or 7, a good looking friend of my cousin came by our house not to play with my cousin but *play* with me rather. Rich tried to put his uncut dick in my mouth. Minutes later, another friend, Reggie, showed up as well. He then laid on top of me as if he wanted to make out with me, wrapping his arms around my head, his face so close to mine. What is up with these pre teen males trying to have their way with me? Maybe even back then I had such strong sex appeal; that or I was a sex magnet already. Who knows? All I know is a man is born with two brains: one in his head, the other in his dick. They each have a mind of their own!

Personal views and opinions and strong convictions: This is what I know and what I believe in. Now, unless God and his son Jesus came down from the heavens and personally tell you and me that neither of us is right, then you can not tell me that my beliefs are wrong! Bitch!

Twenty two years later, I can still feel my Dad's hand giving me a gentle pat on the head, asking me if I was still mad at him. Sometime in 1996, we had some sort of a misunderstanding and I refused to speak to him for a couple of days. On the third day, he walked into my room with an olive branch and family peace had been restored. What I would give to see him again, tell him "It's okay, Dad. I ain't mad at you", give him a hug and tell him I love him so much. My dear friends and readers, put all your family differences aside. Let go of the petty issues. Life is too short.

Minor setbacks could never hold me back from moving forward with my major plans.

I have more horse hung Arabian characters in my hotel room than in the book *Arabian Nights.*

In late 2014, I ran into my sexy "daddy" friend Bob at a local Filipino restaurant. We briefly said "Hi", chatted a little bit and bid each other good-bye. A week later, he was chasing me on the hotel corridors, running after me during our Daddy-catch-me-and-fuck-me role play scene. He couldn't wait to get me in bed.

My friend, Rudy, who was well aware of the fact that I frequent that Filipino restaurant, once told me that he had an affair with the wife of the owner. He probably mentioned *me* to her previously, that's why strangely, the woman would all of a sudden disappear into the kitchen everytime she sees me walk in. I'd advise her not to be intimidated or scared by my presence. Her secret *liaison* with Rudy is *safe* with me.

Fifteen years ago, I ran into this cute Hispanic sales rep offering free samples and promoting some beauty products along Downtown Mountain View. We briefly chatted and exchanged information. Later that evening, he was offering me his beautiful fit naked body inside his BMW, convincing me that he's got a lot *more* to offer than a bottle of beauty cream and some marketing scheme.

I sometimes fancy myself as a Nintendo X Box: Every guy wants to play with me.

Oh, come on! Lower those eyebrows. Otherwise you'd be looking like drag queen Divine after reading this chapter. Your mean looking eyebrows way past your forehead. Stuck. It's ugly! You'll look like a demon. You wouldn't want that, would you?

Once, in 2005, my other "daddy" friend, Gene Hagen, bought a used coffee table at a local thrift store and carved a hole in the middle, latrine style. I requested the whole thing and he happily obliged. He wanted to make his naughty girl pleased and satisfied.

Quotes from a song that I dedicate to my former lover Chris Flanerty: "And I'll remember as the years go by, till the day I die, you and I. And we were lovers."

Song quote ("Always On My Mind" by Pet Shop Boys) dedicated to my other true love, Mark Baldwin: "You are always on my mind. You are always on my mind."

I don't miss people too easily. I just miss those who really mattered to me, those who helped me get through my struggles and tough times and stayed with me until I found peace and success.

Some writers from this popular women's magazine must be sluts from a very young age, with their no holds barred sex advice and articles and other disgusting bedroom suggestions. That or they're simply Xaviera Hollander wannabes. Nowadays, they're encouraging their readers to venture on once taboo acts like licking a guy's ass and other nasty stuff. I'm guessing that's part of the MeToo motto: "Be proud and glad while tossing a guy's salad!" *Bon appetit*, bitches!

A *not* too funny section from another popular women's magazine reeks with hypocrisy and stupidity. It's full of shady back alley sexcapade shares, seedy hook up episodes and awful anecdotes about some promiscuous women and the stupid shit they get themselves into--mainly lascivious acts with strangers and pervs--and then rant about it. No wonder the Trump administration didn't take them seriously.

The Hatridge Family: The likely reason why I've decided to permanently ditch certain families that I used to hobnob with a lot--the Askals and Chenromubs in particular--is the fact that you can never be good in their eyes; but they expect you to fall down on your knees and be in awe of them. A bunch of selfish, self centered hypocrites! To them, you're some kind of a threat, a competition, especially if they see that you are well dressed and have better jewelry on. I simply cannot be in that toxic environment anymore. I particularly loathe the patriarch of the latter family I mentioned. Once, in 2012, at the wedding of his step granddaughter wherein I wore a bright yellow Calvin Klein dress and a vintage fur stole, the old Jewish SOB walked to my table only to make a snarky remark to the effect of 'Is that a raccoon?' (referring to my mink stole). Now, I've been taught long ago by my parents that if you have nothing nice to say, keep your mouth shut. Obviously, the old Jewish SOB had the opposite kind of upbringing. So tacky and acting like a bitch to others all the time! These are the last things you'd expect from guys in the military who are retired. Normally, they'd talk about their pussy conquests in the East during their younger days and not be a total cunt in old age! His step daughter, who is also a jewelry lover, is another nut case. At parties, she would be the first one to approach me, not to compliment my Cartier or Bvlgari, but rather brag that she plans to buy a new set of jewelry in the future. Well, bitch, why not buy it first then talk about it later? This is a very typical Filipino mentality: the classic "anything you can do I can do better" charade. I refuse to be in that kind of environment. It's a death trap. I'd rather join the Keatons or the Jenners. At least, I could borrow some of Caitlyn's dresses. We're both tall women.

A message to those who have always shown indifference towards me: To you I am nothing, I am worthless, I'm a threat and a competition. That's why we're not friends and we will never be! You're a mean person! GTH!

Regrets hold you back. Disassociating them from your train of thought helps you move on in life.

A message to self when starting a new project: Go on full speed with your plans. Focus on reaching your goals. Thinking about what others will say just holds you back. Finish your project first and read the comments and criticisms later!

You gotta do what you gotta do. You gotta roll with the punches, but remember to stay focused and do your best. Brock Lesnar, a classic example. No matter how much beating he got from Shane Carwin, he still came out winning!

Life is not a piece of cake. It will never be. Just like any kind of cake, you'll need to work hard for it if you want it to be perfect.

Always look on the bright side. If something didn't turn out the way you wanted it, turn that negative experience into something positive. We are all given a second chance. Try to make things right this time.

A Sexy Production: Sometimes I look at sex as some kind of a Broadway production: There's a setting, there's a hair and makeup department; a plot is hatched, the performances are executed and finally, there is a happy--often loud and boisterous--ending.

So unforgettable: Foothill College, 1996. My music professor asked one of his students from the other period--a gorgeous white guy--to play a Chopin piece on the piano. The young man hit the ivory keys with such passion and intensity that one of his fingers bled.

A lasting impression: Del Charro Apartments in Mountain View, CA, 1994. A black or dark green pick up truck with a "Blind Melon" sticker at the back.

Rush's "Limelight" and one of the Australian duo The Divinyls' songs have similar bass riffs.

Sometimes I like comparing myself to Disney's Princess Ariel, also known as The Little Mermaid: I have a treasure trove, my hair is long, I can sing and I have a big strong daddy--an older lover that is-- who's half naked most of the time.

On putting makeup on and getting dressed as a transsexual woman: It's like Diana Vreeland putting up an exhibition at the Metropolitan Museum of Art. It takes a lot of work and, of course, it takes a genius!

A movie so moving: *Billy Elliot*, a tearjerker. Some scenes remind me of the bond and friendships I made while growing up; moving to greener pastures to reach my dreams and how my father learned to accept me and my happiness.

Don't get mad: Why I try so hard not to let my nieces and nephews see me get angry: Because it will leave a lasting negative impression!

No relationship with a relative: Why do you try so fucking hard to impress me and get my attention through social media, and when you realized you were non existent to me you took a step further low and made false accusations and filed malicious reports--that are all lies--on Facebook against me? You are one sick, miserable, old, worn out bitch and I'll let karma do its thing on you!

Favorite movie at the moment: *Valmont*. An instant classic! So sexy and stylish. And, of course, the costumes!

Another favorite movie at the moment: *Goodbye Again*. A May-December love affair themed classic starring Ingrid Begman and Yves Montand. I hardly noticed the infidelities and dalliances going on, but was mesmerized rather by the dresses, gowns and jewelry. Plus, the matronly mother of Anthony Perkins--actress Jessie Royce Landis--is a dead ringer for my good friend, Irma. How could anyone miss that movie? One scene reminded me of the time when my ex boyfriend, Jon Drissom, broke up with me, telling me he won't be able to see me anymore. I drove home that night in my Mercedes crying buckets. He did, however, write me a five thousand dollar check to help me move on; a "separation pay" of some sort. I used the money to buy myself a very beautiful diamond ring and a nice big gold bracelet from the 1940s.

There are only three important things that a man likes to hear: that you love his cock, that he looks good and he's exceptional in bed.

There is an actual neighborhood near my ancestral home in Manila called "Ocean Eleven". Most likely, the pioneers in that area named it after the classic Sinatra film. They obviously left an "s". I simply find this very interesting. Sinatra is truly an international icon.

Why certain things in my room that others might find worthless or ordinary are actually irreplaceable and priceless, for me: Because they were given to me by people who at one point in my life meant so much to me. They may be gone or I simply don't see them anymore but the happy, fond memories I have of them live on. One particular piece is the Hot Wheels toy car set my good friend David had sent me many Christmases ago. He knew I was a Hot Wheels collector.

I once used an Irving Penn work--a still life--as an inspiration for my Photography class project back in my senior year in high school. I got an A for it.

Where the boys are: If I were to join the military I'd ask to be stationed at Fort Dix for basic training. That place sounds like a lot of fun.

Why Mariah Carey's "I Still Believe" is special, despite it being a remake: It was the song that was playing on the radio when my ex lover, Mark Baldwin, started making out with me as he stood outside the driver side of my car. I was parked outside his Belmont, CA home, oblivious to my surroundings. Only Mark mattered to me that very moment. Young love or just pure lust? I don't care anymore. It was a very sexy experience.

People are so curious about my sex life ("Who fucks you, Vanessa?" and "What kind of sex do you have?" are some of the questions I get from the curious crowd). I guess that's one of the stigmas that comes with being a sexy, single and fabulous woman. People are so obsessed with what you do and who you do in the bedroom. I make no bones about it (although I'd like to make whoopee with super hot porn star Ryan Bones one of these days). To me, if they want to know whose boner it is that I play with or put in my mouth they'll need to hire a private detective or even the FBI. I'll give those bitches a run for their money. I've said this before and I'll say it again: I am the 21st century version of Mrs. Alice Keppel- -the Queen of the Discreet. I plan to take my deepest and dirtiest sex secrets to the depths of my grave.

When you're a sexy, single and fabulous woman, everybody wants to know about your business--particularly your sex life. And when they can't find dirt on your wall, they'll try their very best to paint a nasty image of you on their Facebook wall using their filthy minds and dirty fingers. No wonder I've unfriended and blocked a bunch of these low life maggots and haters recently. There you go. Problem solved!

One important advice to Facebook users: Don't let Facebook manipulate your relationships with your friends and family. There is malice behind that "Like" button, and when you choose *not* to click on it. One famous political commentator once said that "Facebook is pitting people against one another." I believe that. 21st century people, be very cautious when conducting your Facebook business. Don't forget that you have real friends and relatives *outside* Facebook. In the end, they are still the ones who will come to your rescue in times of need. Not Mark Zuckerberg!

Mother Time: When I was in my twenties, I was the "baby girl" to most of my lovers who, at the time, were in their forties and fifties. Now that I am in my forties, my young lovers, Andy and Jay, both call me "mama". I, in turn, simply call each of them "baby" with genuine affection. Interesting turn of events in the ever colorful and ever changing life of transsexual mama Vanessa.

The worst kind of "No" is, in my case, when I have to turn down a lover's request for time and attention just because another lover is already with me. One night in spring 2016, I had to literally kick my Turkish lover, Gino, out of my hotel room simply because my LWS (Lover with Seniority), Steve, was already waiting in the parking lot of my hotel. It felt like I was holding one lover who's hanging on the edge of a cliff with one hand and I'm holding on to the other lover with my other hand, reminiscent of *The Good Son,* a movie back in the early '90s starring Elijah Wood and Macaulay Culkin. I had to let Gino go. Oh, it was unbearable. I've never felt so distraught and so guilt ridden. Lesson learned: Know your priorities. Never set up multiple dates at the same time unless both men know each other and are okay with each other's company.

As of 2017, the roster of my favorite actors and athletes has expanded. New additions are: Taron Egerton, Henry Cavill, Luke Evans, Chris Pratt, Timothee Chalamet, Matt Bomer, Tye Sheridan, Charlie Hunnam, Niall Matter, Andrew Walker, Brennan Elliott, Vince Guadagnino, Cristiano Ronaldo, James Rodriguez, Fernando Torres, Mike Trout, Keiran Klermeier, Buster Posey, Brett Lawrie, Matt Chapman, JJ Watt, Kris Bryant, Giancarlo Stanton, Bryce Harper, Anthony Rizzo, Anthony Recker, Danny Amendola, Justin Verlander, Tim Tebow, Ryan Switzer, Carson Wentz, Jared Goff, Christian McCaffrey, Jason Witten, Baker Mayfield, Nick Bosa, Payton Pardee, Logan Couture, Joe Pavelski, Tommy Kahnle, Adam Peaty, Jake Lamb, Devon Allen, Luka Doncic, Tyler Herro, Grayson Allen, Collin Gillespie, Matt Anderson, Italian volleyball superstar Filippo Lanza, WWF star Cesaro, San Francisco 49ers head coach Kyle Shanahan, Kike Hernandez and the majority of the Dodgers, Patrick Mahomes and the men of the Saracens rugby team. In the world of basketball, Stephen Curry and Klay Thompson can both *shoot* it in me at the same time! I love me some threesome with the Splash Brothers! I mean, just by the name "Splash", I have a feeling I'll get drenched!

The key to achieving peace of mind is to expect nothing but the worst from people you thought you could count on. A small tinge of pessimism is crucial to keeping things balanced and working in your favor. You know what makes a car run, right? It's not just the engine, it's also the battery. In a car battery, there is a positive side but there's also a negative. Sometimes we need a little bit of negativity in our perception of others to help us go through life with less stress and disappointment. I always go by the saying "If you want something done you have to do it yourself!" In the end, it's only you who really knows what's best for you, not others.

No one's perfect. I am not perfect. Just like everyone else, I have some physical flaws. But still, I make no big deal about it. "It is what it is," I tell myself. Likewise, I do not judge people by the way they look. When I'm with the person I truly adore regardless of his or her appearance, I make him or her feel like the most beautiful person in the world. I don't care if you're the Hunchback of Notre Dame or the Elephant Man. I think that's one of my powerful traits--I can make a Cabbage Patch doll feel as if she's a Limited Edition Holiday Barbie; Mr. Potato Head feel as if he's Ken.

Bitch Perfect: Once, at my favorite thrift store, Savers, a rude Asian woman was going through some clothes in the vintage aisle as if she was hurricane Katrina--unstoppable and ready to make landfall. Only in this particular situation, she was ready to make landfall on my face, with her reckless moving and pushing of clothes. Little did she know that I too was a different kind of storm—one that packs a more powerful punch. When I "returned the favor", I pushed all the clothes that she had been fantasizing of slamming on my face in one firm, steady move. I call it my "tsunami move". (I've done the same thing many years ago to a Russian bitch in one of the stores at the Gilroy Outlets). I also gave that obnoxious Asian woman the famous "Vanessa death stare": my steely gaze fixed at her for a good five seconds. She was motionless for a little bit and when she came back to her senses, she quietly turned around and walked away. Obviously, the old bitch hasn't learned anything from Confucius' teachings about patience and giving. I have a feeling she's been menacing peace loving people since the Ming Dynasty. Well, I had to "educate" her myself: In America, you give people their personal space. I had to remind Madame Chiang Kai *Shrek* that we were not in a crowded Beijing wet market.

Vanessa the Fashionista: It's what you feel like wearing at the moment that matters, not what the industry is telling you to wear at the moment.

Which one is it?: Baby Ronnie, should we Facetime or Sit on my Face Time?

More on Baby Ronnie: "Baby you got me all burning up like California wildfires."

On paying retail prices: I can't believe the sky high mark ups some home shopping networks put on the prices of the jewelry they sell. It's almost criminal! There's this particular shopping network whose name rhymes with "wine" that serves as a third party seller for a high end jewelry company based in Beverly Hills who'd put a mark up close to 100% on the prices of their diamond rings set in 14k gold. Ridiculous! I'd advise shoppers to use reputable online vendors like Ruby Lane or Etsy if they really want to know the true meaning of the phrase "more bang for your buck"; in this case, it should be "more bling for your buck." Back in 2014, I purchased a one carat diamond ring set in 14k white gold with F color stones and weighing a hefty 14 grams for only $800. $800! You can't even buy a one carat diamond ring in sterling silver for that price anymore; if you happen to come across one most likely it has commercial quality diamonds, not those high quality ones like De Beers or Helzberg. The catch was--and it's good one--the online seller had a 30% discount going on in her inventory. I took advantage. It was good timing. Well, you have to do your homework as well. Browse reputable online jewelry websites and look for discounts and promos. If it's your lucky day, you're most likely to snag a good piece of jewelry for a much lower price. Plus, if it's a private seller or a "small business" shop, you are most likely to get a better piece of jewelry. There is a 90% chance that it is an estate piece. I love estate jewelry! Purchasing jewelry from home shopping networks is risky. It is highly likely that you will pay not only for the mark up itself but also mark up from the original seller himself. The gold content is light, too. Commercial jewelry, unlike vintage, estate pieces, have lesser gold content in them. Jewelry, particularly diamond jewelry, that came from an estate has better quality diamonds. They're probably made during the Edwardian or Art Deco period–the golden age of diamond jewelry manufacturing. Plus, if the home shopping network host has that haughty, diva-esque, *Real Housewives* streak, most likely part of what you pay for your jewelry also goes to her hair and makeup, botox filler, etc. I hate that. "Candee", one of these *Real Housewives* wannabes, with a fake Hampton-esque twang is a classic example. I immediately change the channel when she and this other botox broad, Heather, pops up on my TV screen.

I recently started a snuff box collection. I'm attracted to those with Oriental and Italian designs; some made of alabaster, some with a Mother-Of-Pearl inlay. I think in the back of my mind I just want my special pieces of jewelry--the jade and cameos and gold coins in particular--properly organized so that it'll be easier for me to find them when the time comes that I have no use for them and have to bequeath them to my loved ones.

Treasure Found: The real treasures in life are not the ones you bring out from the grave like those of King Tut's or Queen Shubad's, but rather the ones you *take* with you: The wonderful, happy feelings and precious memories that left an impression while you were alive.

Dane Dehan reminds me of those *uber hot* Bel Ami models from the '90s: so innocent looking and hung like a horse.

Don't call me Nos-trans-damus, but I predict that if ever Floyd Mayweather Jr. were to write an autobiography ten or twenty years from now, he'll definitely include the fact that Manny Pacquiao is one of the hardest hitters he's ever encountered in his entire boxing career; maybe the *one* with the hardest punch. On the other hand, Pacqiuao should reconsider his stance on gay marriage and his being against it. Manny, this is the 21st century and you have 4 kids. What if one of them turns out to be gay and decides to marry his or her partner? It might turn out to be the hardest punch you'll ever receive. How will you handle It?

No Diplomas Required: In life, it's not the college diplomas and certificates that you hang on your wall that matter but rather the kindness and compassion that you show to others that create a lasting impression.

Fancy This: The older I get the more I gravitate towards rich fabrics with ornate and fabulous prints. For my caftan collection, the exotic beauty of Marrakech is my ultimate inspiration.

The jock is on me: Who could forget these bad ass alpha males and college jocks from California who showed me the true meaning--in the bedroom--of the term "contact sport"? Varsity football player Johnny from Moraga, the gorgeous bodybuilder Ryan Higgs of Hollister, former high school wrestler Dylan Oldenberg of Hayward, football jock John Adobe of the Tasman area in Sunnyvale and my BOTD (Bae of the Day) Andy, another former wrestling champ, also from Sunnyvale. Unforgettable bodies that gave me unforgettable body *punishment*! I love it.

Luxury within reach: The gift of luxury is the best gift you can give yourself. It wouldn't hurt to have a glass of scotch on your left hand where a 34 carat amethyst cocktail ring is in full display on one of your fingers while clicking the Add to Cart button on Louis Vuitton's website using your right index finger with a five carat Burmese ruby ring on it.

Mind over Matter: Sometimes my body is telling me "Stop!" but my heart and mind keep saying "Go, go, go!"

Classy Lady: When I walk into a public building--the DMV, the State Capitol or even Safeway--people gawk at me as if I'm a Grand Duchess or something; impressed by my demeanor and fascinated by my sense of style and fabulous jewelry. On two separate occasions, the business owners even kissed my hand out of the blue. But, I am no blue blood, I am simply Vanessa, Baroness of Fremont.

Who's Your Daddy?: On single moms looking for a man to be a "father figure" to their kids from previous relationships: Good luck! It is highly likely that the man you'll end up taking home would just want to play the "Who's your daddy?" bedroom game rather than wanting to play the daddy role to your little devils. Sad but true. Sad for you! Keep in mind, it's not his. New boyfriends are only after a single mom's body, not the *baggage* that goes with it. I clearly remember one controversial comedian's material: *"Rock-a bye baby on the tree top, Your mother's a whore, I ain't your pop!"*.

Hater Disclaimer: Don't call me a hater! I read a lot, that's why I know a lot! So now you want to blame books and magazines and newspapers? The media? Google? Go ahead! Knock yourselves out, bitches!

Stop the comparisons! Stop comparing me with others. Everybody's unique in their own way. Each person has a unique skill. I possess many skills! I'm sure you know it by *now*. I am a unique individual. Just like a Piaget watch, I am one-of-a-kind. Aside from the ability to sing, dance, write, draw, design, create, please and satisfy, I also possess that fabled sixth sense: the ability to sense hate without the other person saying a word. It's in the body language, baby!

Dungeons and Drag Queens: I once explored the dark and devious dens of The Power Exchange in San Francisco back in 2002. That place is teeming with delightful debauchery! I actually did a *performance* there. I gained many instant followers, literally, that night. That said, I think I'm the original menstagram star. I've gained quite a following. All men.

Shower me with your love: Sometimes while taking a shower, beautiful and bittersweet memories fly by my mind. When I wake up to my senses--thanks to the warm water--I just continue to focus on the day's agenda. I tell myself "Life has to go on, Vanessa." But I never forget to thank the people who have showered me with their unconditional love. They are always on my mind.

It's the Truth: When you look good, some people feel bad about it. When I walk into a room, I notice how the faces of some of the people would turn grim all of a sudden--as if a giant crane fell on them. Why? Why not smile and be happy for your neighbor? Take for example, Clint, an androgynous looking employee at the thrift store that I frequent. Physically, he is what I refer to as a "not quite": a young gay man on the brink of gender transfornation. But what I really think he needs is to transform his bitter attitude towards me first and foremost. Every time I walk in the store dressed to the nines and cross paths with Clint dressed depressed--with his long unkempt greasy hair and untidy looks--I'd catch him giving me either the side eye or the evil eye. Such a negative person! But as the "sassy but classy" little diva that I am, I choose to turn negative experiences into something positive once and for all. So, not too long ago, I made a suggestion via the store's online survey system, letting them know about Clint's bizarre ways and what management in turn could suggest to the former to help improve not just his looks, but also his entire outlook on life in general. Come on now, Clint! You're working at a clothing store, not in the sewer lines! Off with that stink face!

B.C. bs: Once, there was a life rule set by some figure from the B.C. era that goes "Invest in people, not on material things." I say "Nay!". What's wrong with investing in fine vintage and antique jewelry? Hey, if I prefer precious sparkly pieces over obnoxious, snarky people that is, like Bobby Brown once sang, my prerogative.

Text me Not: Never make an issue if your most sincere text messages and emails aren't replied to or acknowledged. The most important thing is you were able to say what you wanted and were able to express your feelings to that special person. I just assume she is just busy, or just being cranky at the moment. Maybe it's that time of the month--to be a bitch. That's all.

Say it to my Face: If you have something important to say to someone you really care about, do it right away because you'll never know if that person is going to be around tomorrow. Life is precious but it is also fragile. Today we're alive, making love or playing with our sons and nephews with their toy trucks and Legos, and the next day we are in a coma due to a stroke or we're on life support with major injuries, got run over by an eighteen wheeler truck. A few years ago, an uncle of mine was dying of cancer, but he could still hear and speak. He was convalescing in the Philippines. I made a couple of phone calls to thank him for all the help he's given me and my family when we first arrived in the US many years ago. I also wanted to let him know that I love him. Not long after that, he passed on.

A Major Contribution: One of the greatest contributions I brought to mankind--the men in particular--is a sense of ecstasy and excitement in their most private and intimate moments; something that is often lacking the minute they enter the proverbial white picket fence: his home, with his family. On my side of the world, they find sheer and intense pleasure, the kind that makes their eyes roll at the back of their heads. In my bedroom, they are treated like a king for once; not a bread and butter husband with a boring wife; not a take-me-to-the-park daddy of a spoiled, needy child; and not the buy-me-a-pregnancy test kit-late-at-night boyfriend of an annoying and insecure girlfriend (whose baby turns out not his after all in the end). When my lovers are with me--and it doesn't matter if they are single, married, divorced or involved--I make them leave their cares away, take them to heaven with my sweet passionate kisses and treat their body like a temple--worship, worship and worship! Move over Christopher Columbus! I've got new discoveries and explorations to make...in the bedroom.

A Fashion Statement: Before, I dress and do things to please and impress people who now I know didn't give the slightest fuck. Now, I do things and dress solely for me and my own pleasure. Fuck the rest! They can all kiss my Azzedine Alaia dress!

Mother Dear: When I am no longer in this world, never let anyone tell you "*Sayang sya*" or "*Bakit sya nagka ganon*". Your response should be "Vanessa lived a wonderful, exciting and happy life. Shut the fuck up."

My social and sexual schedules are as eclectic as my jewelry collection: One Saturday afternoon you'd find me at City Hall hobnobbing with the mayor and other city leaders and the following Monday I'm shacked up in a motel, hanky panky-ing with hot construction workers and handsome, sexy strangers.

A Moment Like This (November 25, 2017): It was a good day. I saw a handsome guy working at a cafe in Downtown Menlo Park whose good looks and big hazel eyes reminded me of my Turkish lover, Gino. He had me thinking about him for the rest of the day. James Blunt, this is the perfect time to sing me your signature song!

Cum Again: When a guy you are intimate with has nothing on his mind but how to please you right and make you cum hard and good, he is a keeper! So happy to have sexy daddies Neal and Bob and the gorgeous Rusty Pogi in my life!

Rare Collection: Once, back in the late 1990s, my family and I had owned almost every make of vintage Vollkswagens. I had a gold 1975 Super Beetle Fuel Injection in pristine condition, but my favorite was the Karmann Ghia. It had an immaculate paint job--in plum--and it was so much fun to drive. Not to mention a head turner.

The Royal Wedding of Prince Harry and Meghan Markle: My favorite footage was that of David Beckham looking for his seat. How I wish I was there as an extra chair! And what about the Duke of Edinburgh's honest thoughts on the bride (who is also a divorcee`)? Some naughty minds were quick to interpret it with (in reference to the Duke's alleged racist views in the past): "Oh good god no! That means my great grandkids will be black!" What about the Queen? This one should be easy: "She is not Elizabeth I. We don't think she's a virgin."

General Admission: Admit it! Most redneck country songs are all about drinkin' beer and whiskey and gettin' some pussy. Welcome to Kentucky!

Yes, Papi!: I still haven't forgotten how Yahoo Personals member Alex Papichullo destroyed *mi culo* back in 2001 with his enormous *pinga*. Oh, what pain and suffering! And how damn good it felt!

There is no doubt that male porn stars these days are hotter and sexier. They have bigger dicks, too, and better haircuts. Sometimes, I feel like asking these guys: "Are you fucking some bitch or murdering that cunt with your monster size dick?".

Uncle Sam Wants You...to work!: Some people should quit bitchin' and complaining about how they're poor and miserable. Hey, guys! I didn't wait for Uncle Sam to make things work for me. I *made* things work out for me by working hard and doing all kinds of things just to make a buck. Stop being lazy, get your butts off the couch and go find a job!

Not Happy: When it comes to entertaining, I'm not one to lay out a mile long table runner with fancy candles and napkin holders and other nonsense. Bitch, I'm not Happy Ongpaco! Arch nemesis of Filipino actress Aiko Melendez. Oh, I love the bitch fight that took place between these two spoiled brats back in the day! It was big news in the Philippines. Drunk and belligerent Happy allegedly called Aiko "fat" and a has-been. Aiko, in turn, allegedly punched the drunk bitch in the face. Since most of my guests are men anyway, I keep my menu list simple yet satisfying: chips, dips, chicken wings and ice cold beer.

Unforgettable, that's what you are: One afternoon in the summer of 2013, my lover, Chris Flanerty, invited me to his place in San Jose. He used to live at a residence near Berryessa Road. After an hour or so of "afternoon delight", it was time for me to go. On my way out, I took one last glance at my tall and handsome lover and immediately James Blunt's "You're Beautiful" came to mind. The song's lyrics couldn't have been more relevant. Have you ever seen a guy in his most beautiful and virile state? Chris was *it*. I'll never forget his glow; his smooth alabaster white complexion with a hint of rosy. He was wearing his favorite blue 76ers jersey. Chris has the Irish good looks of Ryan Reynolds and Mark McGrath combined and the demeanor of former Golden State Warriors David Lee. When it comes to physical qualities, Chris has the sex appeal and cock size of my latest favorite smut stud, Kristof Cale; not to mention having a very smooth butt crack. You can probably imagine why I am so head over heels in love with that man. I've said this before and I'll say it again, Chris is probably the most beautiful man that came out of San Jose. A 21st century version of Montgomery Clift!

Christmas in July: In this day and age when mass shootings and the threat of world annihilation via nuclear war are imminent, I don't wait for December to come so I can buy myself a nice Christmas present. I buy stuff the minute I get the urge! A good and wise friend of mine once told me "Don't wait for tomorrow to do the things you want because that day might never come." Life is truly unpredictable.

Don't be Cute: Some movies from the '80s are fun and cute, no doubt. I just can't stand some corny ones wherein a Navy pilot is at a bar, a little drunk and singing to a broad that he wants to bang afterwards and marry later on. Fast forward to 2018: I'd like to ask Tom Cruise "Why aren't you singing to me now, now that you and that naval base bitch are no longer together?"

Cross (in) My Heart: Whenever I cross paths with a mean looking woman at the store who's giving me the evil eye, I take my cross pendant necklace out of my purse and put it on right away. It's my way of telling the wicked witch of the East Calaveras Blvd. Savers store "Bitch, stay away from me! You're bad luck!"

Touch me in the morning...and evening: Big thanks to my masseurs over the years for straightening my not so *straight* back: Joseph and Robert from San Jose, CA and Jim, Tom and Big Jon from the East Bay.

One wish to Genie: A Time Machine. I'd like to travel back to the 1970s and observe the daily lives of my paternal great grandparents, on my Grandmother's side. They died just a few months from each other back in 1977, the year of my birth.

One Wish to Gene: Daddy Gene, let's hook up again for all time's sake and use that latrine style coffee table that you had custom made for me. Such a turn on!

Beautiful India: What really attracts me to Indian style and culture are the food, the vibrant colors and rich fabrics, the fabulous gold jewelry and some of their men. For fifteen long years, I had an intimate relationship with a handsome and hung young Indian American guy. Oh, the wonders he had done to my body!

Three reasons why I couldn't resist watching *The Lord of the Rings: The Fellowship of the Ring* every time it's on: First, when it came out in the early 2000s, that was also the time when I came out as a full time transgender woman. Second, it was around the time when I enrolled at the Adult Ed Program in Sunnyvale, CA where I met some interesting characters: the "Bundok ng Tralala" woman (a Filipino woman who would talk about all kinds of stuff but would characteristically end her blabbing with "bundok ng tralala", a mountain region in the Philippines). The other characters were a soon to be mother in-law-daughter-in-law duo, both Filipinos, who'd sit behind me all the time and would chat nonstop about all kinds of nonsense stuff and be reprimanded over and over by our teacher,

Mrs. Bye. I tell you what, I was so happy to get out of that class around noon and would head to nearby Vallco Fashion Park, a mall, to get some refreshments and do some walking. Coincidentally, there was an Optometry in that mall where the "Bundok ng Tralala" woman worked as a receptionist. I'd catch a glimpse of her once in a while. Interestingly enough, the Optometry where she worked sits right next to a store that sells mythical figures like dragons and wizards, constantly reminding me of and making me ever more fascinated with *The Lord of the Rings.* Lastly, the movie is simply iconic. If you grew up in that era or at least paid attention to pop culture and the blockbuster movies that came out, you cannot miss it!

Once, I visited a black inmate at the Redwood City Jail, listened to him talk about his wild sexual fantasies and watched him masturbate. It was my Truman Capote moment.

Spoiled Brat: Let the older gentleman spoil you with gifts and money if he wishes because it only happens once in a lifetime. Once you become old and wrinkly, rest assured that no gentleman would even dare spend a penny on you.

Mixed Feelings: Sometimes, I feel like a whore in need of a desperate score especially when my text messages and email to men are ignored. Sometimes, I feel like the Michelle Pfeiffer character from *The Age of Innocence*, Countess Ellen Olenska--I choose not to meet any man at all, shut the front door, close down my window and call it a day.

Shower Scene: Perhaps one of the sexiest comments I heard from a man was "Wash those men off of your body." This one time lover of mine who now lives in Washington state knew I was a promiscuous woman and wanted to make sure my body was fresh and clean before his visit.

I'd like to ask Kim from this housewives series on TV "How often does your ex football player husband sit on your face?" Her lips look like a dilapidated red couch.

Unless San Francisco 49ers quarterback Jimmy G abstains from hooking up with filthy whores from Downtown Los Angeles then maybe, maybe, there'll be some hope left for the legendary football team for the 2018 season. Jimmy baby, there's a lot of good and *clean* women out there. Why hang out with filth? Hooking up with whores brings bad scores!

I really believe that San Francisco 49ers quarterback Jimmy G's misfortunes on the field are caused by bad vibes and bad karma brought by the Los Angeles streetwalker he was seen dining out with recently. You try to *score* with garbage and the actual scores stink! Jimmy be good next season, please.

It Used to be Mark's Playground: My one time lover, Mark Baldwin, made a confession once: that he had thought of dirty things about me. What man would not? He compared my body to a playground. "Everything needs a ride," he said.

Rub a dub dub: What a sexy scene it is to be taking a nice, warm relaxing bubble bath in the locker room of the Saracens football rugby team with each of their big, hunky players lathering me up and touching me here and there. So soothing and calming!

Let's Go See My Movies (Imaginary): *The AIDS of Innocence* (Tragedy befalls a popular prostitute from Punxsutawney named Innocence. No matter how many twenty dollar bills you have in your purse, money can't buy you freedom from the devastating disease); *The Fat and the Furious* (A young man's struggles with extreme obesity and how he brought down a popular fast food chain, not by his enormous body, but by filing a hefty lawsuit in the millions. Will he spend the payout on a lifetime membership at 24 Hour Fitness and treadmill equipment or spend it on more burgers, fries and milkshakes? No one knows as of yet. McDonny's Burgers doesn't open until 6 am); and finally, *Who's Eating Gilbert's Gape?* (Pimps, pimples and pedophiles plague this pretty white boy from suburbia who moonlights as a street hustler at night in the mean streets of Philadelphia. Will he spend his earnings on Neutrogena and Nintendo or save it for his college tuition? Well, it all depends on how much his pimp gives him for his cut).

On Martha's cooking show: She is not the most graceful cuisine queen. She prepares and cooks meals like an unhappy and disgruntled kitchen staff at a homeless shelter cafeteria, dropping and banging pots and utensils like a lunatic. Her attitude: She could care less. "Die, you bums!", she screams out.

A penis for your thoughts: The first thing that comes to mind every time I see a hot guy with a nice bulge is "Oh, shit. Fuck me!"

I've said this before and I'll say it again, I have an issue with women from other countries who use their vaginas as an entry point, literally, to get in the United States. They got it easy and it's an insult to those hardworking, educated individuals with college degrees who went through the proper visa application process and are waiting to hear from the US Embassy... for years. Those women with questionable characters must be sent back to their country of origin and be made to apply--not reapply–by themselves, without their American boyfriends or spouses standing next to them at the embassy. They must be ordered to go through the same long, legal and tedious process that other regular US visa applicants go through. Let's see if they really qualify to set foot and live in the US. "An eye for an eye," the old saying goes. Oh, I could scratch out the eyes of these cheating jezebels!

Hallmark greeting cards better not copy these lines I've come up with for my own greeting cards line; unless they want a big, fat lawsuit from me. 1) "Happy Holidays! Let's fuck!" 2) "It's your Birthday! I want to Fuck you." 3) "Merry Christmas, baby! Fuck me!" and 4) "Happy Birthday, Daddy! Let me suck you!"

A threesome with handsome Hallmark Channel actors Sean Faris and Andrew Walker? Bring it on!

On *Dirty John*: If only these horny hags would put their red flags up first instead of their legs, I suppose the likelihood of ending up with a psycho would be zero to none. But, that's the problem. These middle aged man eaters and cavorting cougars can't help themselves from preying on the freshest meat in the dating market.

On male gymnasts: Nikita Nagornyy makes me so horny and I just want to be Sam Mikulak's pommel horse.

Listen to me, young man!: "You need to put away your X Box now and start playing with my *box*."

Another Vanessa original: LYBO (Let your bitch out!)

My Life in America: Things didn't just work out for me overnight by spreading my legs like that bitch from North Carolina who landed in the US by landing on her back first for a desperate cuckold. I made things work for me by using my brains instead of my vajayjay and secondly, by hard work and perseverance. I am a strong, independent woman!

There is only one valid reason why some people would react negatively or be affected, in a sense, by some of the things that I write especially if it pertains to a certain individual: it must be true then! You are, in essence, announcing yourself as the guilty party! I've said this before and I'll say it again: I speak the truth! If you read something in this book and you think it's you and you fret because you couldn't contain yourself and your anger, then you are the guilty party! That's your motherfucking problem! To the reactionary party out there: First of all, don't be a hypocrite and second, you cannot bullshit me! Nobody can, no one has! No one can tell me that they're angry about what I wrote just because. Nope! In my book called "Life", it doesn't work that way. The only reason why you're fuming mad right now is because of the simple and obvious fact that you *think* you are the person I am talking about. Therefore, you are guilty, bitch! I spoke the truth. The truth came out. It affects you.

Too bad! Deal with it! Otherwise, if you think it's not you, shut the fuck up and continue spreading your wobbly legs for your cuckold husband! End of discussion.

History repeats itself: Sometimes, I feel like I am literally the country of the Philippines back in the 19th century: First, the Spanish--in my case, the Mexicans--ravaged me then it was the Americans' (white boys) turn. As soon as *el senor* dismounts me, *el gringo* takes over. *Ay, dio mio*!

Human Nature: I might be sorry sometimes when I act like a nasty bitch--once in a while--in public, but absolutely not when I'm in the bedroom! It's the spice of life!

Don't you forget about me: Strangely, my late paternal grandfather would frequently appear in my dreams during the months of November and April, the months of his birth and death, respectively. I think it's his way of telling me not to forget about him and to say a little prayer for him.

No matter how bad things might look sometimes, I put some red Chanel lipstick on, spritz some Versace perfume and face life head on because once it's over, it's over!

Another lesson in life: What's absolutely great or special to you is absolutely worthless like garbage to others, so just *do* you! March on with your head and middle finger held up high and don't look back.

James Bond 007 For Your Eyes Only flick trick: In the real world, when a helicopter malfunctions in mid air, you'll likely crash and burn. In James Bond's world, you get to override the system within a few seconds and survive a fiery crash. That's why I only watch the opening credits in that movie because Sheena Easton, one of my favorite singers, sang the theme song.

Tried and True: You move and act like a queen and everyone around you will treat you like one.

You're so full of Bong shit: I have a fucking issue with the Filipino adage "*Basta wala kang natatapakang tao*" ("As long as you're not stepping on anyone or putting someone down…"). A B movie actor and wannabe comedian named Bong N has a penchant for uttering these lines when being interviewed. It's almost as if he's warning others who are becoming successful in their own field--and reaping the benefits--to not get too excited about it or be jubilant. Hey Bong, I didn't tell you to venture in my territory first and foremost, so you stay in your little corner and continue doing your corny jokes and boring movies and I'll continue doing what makes me happy and unapologetically proud, okay, motherfucker? Oh, and by the way, I think you need to see Vicky Belo right away and get a heavier dose of glutathione.

The (fake) whiteness of your complexion is quickly diminishing. You Filipino "celebrities" in the Philippines are so desperate to have a very light complexion which I find sad. It's a terrible sign of insecurity and not being able to love and accept yourselves for who you are and what you really look *like*.

Whiteout: Sad to see some Filipinos unable to accept their true, god-given, natural skin tone, so they had to desperately come up with money to pay for the skin whitening drug glutathione; to the point that they'd skip a meal or two. Some would even borrow money from other people or pawn their appliances and jewelry. Pathetic!

Discipline is all about knowing your limits and when to exercise caution and practice discretion.

Bold Gold: For some strange reason, every time I wear my big and bold gold jewelry, I feel a special kind of pick me up. I walk a little taller and my self confidence level skyrockets to a new high. Maybe it's that fabled "power of gold" effect on people.

Better than Clorox? Strange how bad dreams and nightmares act as cleansing agents for the mind. I feel a ton of toxic thoughts and worries have been removed as soon as I wake up.

There's no place like home...especially when you're with a very good lover: When you've experienced the things you want and made your fantasies turn into reality, you really don't need to go anywhere. Travelers and other so-called globetrotters are in some way lost souls still searching for some sense of fulfillment and satisfaction in other places. I stay where my whole being is happy completely. I'll watch my DVD collection of *Rick Steves' Europe* if I want to have a glimpse of the Eiffel Tower in Paris or the Colosseum in Rome.

Just Do It: Write while you can, sing while you can and dance while you can because when it's over, it's over.

In late February 2018, I witnessed Father Time work his magic in front of my very eyes. In my hotel room that day came three men from three different age groups: Young Andy who is 30, Daddy Andy who is 60 and Grandaddy Morris who's as old as Jessica Tandy.

What's your secret?: Secrets to long life as shared by a home shopping network customer caller and the Prime Minister of Malaysia, both in their late 80s: Keep working and don't eat too much.

Euphoria (December 2016, my hotel room in Fremont): After taking care of seven men who visited me that day, I bathed, cleansed my body with fragrant oils and luxe soap, rose from the jacuzzi like Charlize Theron in *Snow White and the Huntsman*, put on my expensive

18 and 22 karat gold jewelry, laid on my queen size bed and had my young lover, Justin, give me a most relaxing full body massage. Move over, Belinda! This is the real *heaven* on earth!

Relationship Real Talk: If it's over, it's over! Don't make it any more complicated by thinking it over (if you did the right thing or not); rather contemplate on the possibilities with the positive people around you. You have a full life ahead of you. Create new memories! In the meantime, you sit back, have a glass of wine, smoke a joint or two and just reminisce about the good old days.

More Relationship Real Talk: If I'm really at my wit's end and breaking point, I will reach out to a trusted friend or relative. I will try at least twice. If I sense that you're not responding, I will stop. I'll have to let you go. It doesn't matter if we've known each other for two years or two decades. You *have* to go! I will then turn my attention to others. I will reach out to those who'll tell me "I'll be with you on this journey, Vanessa." Real friends will respond and make time regardless how busy they are. Remember that.

That's why it's called a "Public Restroom": Whether or not I should or shouldn't use the women's restroom is none of the public's concern. There's a reason why a "public restroom" is named as such. It's for the public! It's for everyone! Man, woman, girl, boy, straight, gay or trans! If you need to *go*, then go! Women's restroom or men's! Your poop and pee shouldn't be made to decide which restroom--men's or women's--to use! As long as there's a toilet seat available, use it! Curiously, I've been using the women's restroom for a long time now without any problem. Likewise, I've used the men's restroom a couple of times in the past. Once, at a Jack in the Box fast food restaurant in Southern California, I had no choice but to use the men's restroom because the women's restroom was occupied at the moment and I couldn't hold my pee any longer. A Caucasian male was inside. He never said a word. I did have a problem about this thing some twenty years ago when I tried to use the men's restroom inside the USPS facility in San Jose, CA while I was working there. It was during my period of transition from male to female. A big burly man yelled at me and told me I was going in the *wrong* restroom. Ironic, isn't it? Straight (or straight acting) male Republicans try to harrass and humiliate transgender people and attack their basic human rights but in the real world--not inside their fancy offices at the Capitol-- real straight macho men were preventing me from going in the men's restroom, telling me to go to the women's restroom instead. People and politicians who think transsexuals and transvestites use the women's restroom to perform lewd and malicious acts on children are the ones who should be accused of malice in the first place. How did they come up with such nasty ideas? Where did it come from? From their equally nasty, dirty minds, where else! The Republican Party cradles some of the biggest perverts in the country. I wonder what Larry Craig is up to these days. Same thing with Matt Gaetz. I'd like to ask him about his favorite hobbies and recreational activities these days. Going back to my public restroom sentiment, do they (Republicans) have any proof or evidence that my main intention in using the women's restroom is to harass young children? It's a pure machination of the dirty, malicious Republican mind. That's the plain and simple explanation. These are serious accusations. Sooner or later, someone might take them to court if they do not refrain. Most of these Republican politicians have a degree in Law, but they always seem to come up with the most stupid and insanely ridiculous argument. It's baseless! And lacking evidence! Children who go in public restrooms are accompanied by a parent or an adult ninety nine percent of the time. I know this because I use the public restroom all the time! I see them there! And the major reason why transsexuals and transvestites use the women's restroom is for protection from assault, insults, harrassment and bullying from regular, straight men who are not too fond or accepting of their kind. I'm not saying transsexuals like me are free from attacks and harassment from biological women. At the USPS facility in San Jose, CA where I worked twenty years ago, I encountered a mean and bigoted Filipina employee who hurled insults at me. I reported her actions to my supervisor, a nice white middle aged gentleman, and was reprimanded and issued a warning. On top of that is the major issue stemming from the fact that a Filipino supervisor had warned and prevented me from using the women's restroom. Can you imagine the hell I went through in that place? But, because I knew myself and where I stood, plus the fact that I fight for what's fair and right all the time, not to mention my defiant nature when the going gets tough, I fought back and emerged victorious. To put an end to this bullshit once and for all, I requested an audience with my white supervisor, laid out my concerns and sentiments and reported the harassment I was experiencing from a few Filipinos. Eventually, I was given full permission to use any of the women's restrooms in that building. More importantly, the harassment and insults stopped. Thank you, Mr. White Supervisor, and thank god for gender neutral public restrooms! So, my message to these malicious, unhinged and crazy Republicans living in their own world called Planet Hate: Do not attack my basic human right to use the public restroom of my choice because maybe in the future, one of your children or grandchildren will decide to live as a transgender individual and he or she will no doubt go through the same hell. Karma is a bitch like Vanessa that you wouldn't want to mess with. Remember that. So, try to be a little tolerant, will ya? You don't have to be nice to me, but don't be an asshole!

Thank you, Sir!: Big thanks to the white gentleman in a white pick up truck from Gustine, CA who led me to the main highway after I got lost in a remote area off Interstate 5 back in 2004. This was before GPS became available. When I realized I was driving in unfamiliar territory, I pulled to the side of the road and waited for a car to pass by. It was around 3 in the morning. I was driving home from Los Angeles and somehow missed my turn. I asked myself "Who could be up at 3 in the morning?" It was a gamble. It was my first time being in Gustine. Luckily for me, a Good Samaritan came to my rescue. After a couple of minutes of waiting, I saw two headlights headed in my direction. I immediately gave a signal using my SUV's high beam lights, alerting the incoming vehicle. The pick up truck stopped in front of me and as soon as the Caucasian male rolled down his window I yelled out "Sir, I'm lost! Do you know how to get to 5?" "Follow me," was the driver's short response. I trailed behind him and after a few minutes I came back to civilization. The guy continued on and I never saw him again. I wish I had the chance to thank him face to face. Who knows? Maybe he was actually an angel. Nowadays, people wouldn't even give you a second of their time especially if you're a complete stranger; let alone a transgender individual. To this day, I scratch my head sometimes and ask–with a smile– "Where the hell did you find the guts to do that, Vanessa?" You can only find that in a Quentin Tarantino movie script!

Marjorie Taylor Greene following a Parkland High School shooting survivor and harassing him is creepy and malicious, almost perverse. Yikes! What's up with these older broads having a hard on on young guys? Attention FBI: Here's another crazy bitch in the Capitol!

On my Playlist: "Automatic", "Physical", "Maneater", "Kiss", "The Greatest Love of All", "When I Think of You", "I'm Still Standing", "Always Something There to Remind Me", "The Search Is Over", "One Thing Leads to Another", "Hands to Heaven", "Rock the Casbah", "You Might Think" and (believe it or not) "We're Not Gonna Take It". The last song is the perfect anthem to the LGBTQ cause, I think. I don't think I'll be getting make up tips from Dee Snyder though.

I really believe some rock stars write songs and sing about their pussy conquests in their younger days (i.e."Glory Days" by Bruce Springsteen and "Summer of '69" by Bryan Adams).

"Enough of the Hadids, Jenners and Kardashians," I read on tumblr not too long ago. Good point. Why are some people obsessed with them anyway? What have these self serving botox whores and sex video characters contributed to society that might help improve the lives of regular, minimum wage earning folks? None! Their lips and asses keep getting fat, but the poor and hungry kids in America and around the world remain skinny! Maybe my opinion about them will change after 10 years. Let's see if these social media vampires will do something good to humanity by helping the poor and the needy.

Scroll Down: I'd scroll down on your negative attitude towards me as fast as I scroll dick pics on tumblr.

Slow Down: Don't rush life. Take a deep breath, *live* and enjoy the moment.

So True: If I didn't believe in myself, who would?

Advice to some people in the Philippines: Know your history and respect those in the LGBTQ community for they are your friends, relatives, cashiers, food servers, hairdressers, market vendors, carinderia owners and basically anyone who makes your life easier! Without them your world will stop spinning. So, don't hate! Appreciate!

No Witherspoon fan here: Her chosen roles are so un-MeToo--always playing the Barbie-esque, feline character in a tug-of-war of men fighting like dogs. Can you come up with something better next time, please?

Game of Trans: I never got to follow episodes of the HBO series *Game of Thrones*. People tell me I'm in the one percent of those who do not watch it and ask me why. My short and simple response: "Bitch, I'm so fucking busy scheming and plotting my own games in Fremont every Tuesday I don't have time to watch that show anymore!"

Just an observation: Filipinos in the Philippines need to learn to say "Thank you" more often, especially when receiving help and other kind gestures. Don't just stand there and stare or leave without saying a word! They also need to applaud when attending awards ceremonies and other recognition events. Lack of gratitude and showing no appreciation is plain rude. If you're not going to move at all and become a statue in your seat, you might as well stay home or stand beside the Jose Rizal monument in Luneta. Frozen for all eternity!

Zyrtec, anyone?: I'm allergic to peanuts, pollen and the word "promise".

Pain Relief, anyone?: You don't know what physical pain truly is unless you're *in* my body. You just don't. But, I try my very best--everyday--to survive and push through.

A Quote: "Don't feel guilty. It's called life."--FitQuest spokesperson on HSN

Sometimes in life you really don't need to explain *anything* to anyone. Just act like the US Government on the controversy surrounding Area 51 in Nevada: no explanations!

Mother Eartha: From now on, I'll do what the great Eartha Kitt once sang about: proceed with caution. People who you initially thought stood there by your side, "showing" support were actually *casing* you--observing your every move and in the end, betraying you. Be very careful who you welcome into your life. Demons can take an angel's disguise, too.

I thank the Lopez family–Judie in particular–from Castro Valley, CA for treating me with respect and for being a friend.

Leave him alone: I wonder why some people hate Mr. Rogers so much. Why don't these motherfuckers just shut up and focus on being good parents to their kids instead? Please stop spreading vile and vicious rumors about America's Favorite Stay-at-Home Dad! Leave him alone!

Another Favorite Quote: "Soar! Fly higher like an eagle! Outrun the crows and other birds that irritate you, like chickens and turkeys."--Joel Osteen

One of the priceless gifts a strong, independent woman like me with infinite sexual capabilities could receive is a man in his most natural form--still in bed naked, unshaven, pungent and musty, and oozing with limitless libido, ready to overpower me and make revel in fits of sexual ecstasy and pleasure with no abandon.

Quote of the Decade (2000s), from my ex lover Mark Baldwin: "I'll plant my ass on your face."

My Lucky Charms: The Jewelry Exchange TV ad, a *Good Housekeeping* magazine with a smiling Trisha Yearwood on the cover and my daily morning chant "Thank you, Lord, thank you, Dad, thank you, Lola Rita."

After meeting sex god Master Larry: I'm a bitch, I'm bothered and I'm bewildered.

Video Killed the Pornhub Star: I never got in the business of recording my sex acts and posting them online only to be seen, scrutinized and criticized by millions of viewers. Why? Because I have common sense and a reputation to protect. Those wannabe porn stars are toast! Are you kidding me? They are done! Their families are done, especially their kids. Their character? Revolting. Their reputation? Repulsive. Their existence? Disgusting. Respect from their neighbors and other people who know them? Most likely zero to none. Sure, men might like them, but I don't. Sure, they might act like they don't care, but in reality people who know their *business* look at them as if they're rats from the Bubonic Plague. It's the truth! It's the truth! I don't care if you argue and disagree with me until you shrink like a deflated balloon. It's the truth! Just ask the church lady next door. Just ask the gentleman father of four who's also a church pastor. Can you imagine your son or daughter going to school every day only to be mocked and teased by other students just because they've seen you eating ass and cum, drinking piss and doing other nasty acts on the internet? I don't know where they get the nerve to even leave the house for one minute. Sure, they can do what they want–get anal gangbanged by 15 men even–but don't do it in my neighborhood! I wouldn't want you in my neighborhood in the first place! I'd probably hire the National Guard to physically remove my suspicious acting neighbor from her residence if I find out she's sucking a bunch of cocks and exposing her loose pussy regularly on OnlyFans and Pornhub. Bitch has got to go! Bitch has got to go! I don't want children in my neighborhood growing up with rotting fish like that nearby. The only poison I'm okay with is Bret Michaels. Period. I'd probably use a megaphone while yelling out "Dump that trash in the San Fernando Valley!" repeatedly as the National Guard hauls her skanky ass away.

That's your problem, not mine: Back in 1999, during the first few stages of my transition from male to female, some people would sneer at me and give me a dirty look because of my androgynous appearance. I'd go like "What the fuck is *your* problem?" I was the one who's weirded out by them! I was the one who was baffled by their actions! That's how powerfully resilient I was even back then. Stones will hurt me, not stares.

May babies? How about May daddies? Happy Birthday to my daddy friends Neal, Keoni, Kenny, Jeff, Chris and Richard.

Cheers to that! I like my wine just like how I like my men--white and over 50 years old. Aged to perfection!

Peace at last: I found peace and happiness when I detached myself from the bitches and became attached to the *bears*--the big, strong sexy guys in my life.

Round trip to Reno: Fifteen years ago, I made a back and forth trip from the Bay Area to Reno, Nevada when my guest from the East Coast, Steve Rind, visited and expressed his desire to see the gambling town that same night. He was in town for business and was scheduled to start work the next morning, so it was important that we came back before dawn. So, around 5pm that Monday evening we headed to Reno, got there around 9pm, hung out at the Silver Legacy hotel lounge for some cocktails and live music and drove back to the Bay Area just a little after midnight. We had a great time. Despite the eight hours of my driving in one night and being so tired, we still managed to get intimate. By 7 in the morning that Tuesday, we got up; Steve got ready for work and I went home. Martha Stewart, eat your heart out! Now I know the true meaning of being the perfect host.

Another important life lesson: Resilience, perseverance and detachment are three pointers that I follow when it comes to moving on and moving to higher ground in life. They're also perfect for thwarting negative energy from some people.

Mascara is a must: Back in the fall of 2001, as I was picking up my sisters from school, I called 911 on a deranged individual who was violently banging on my driver side window just because she wanted me to move my car further ahead so she in turn could squeeze in her car within the legal yellow line. Problem was, there was a big white van parked in front of me so there was *no* way I could've moved further ahead. Her behavior that afternoon was reckless and her temper was totally out of control. I made her pay the consequences. I called 911 on her and within a couple of minutes a swarm of police cars had converged in the school parking lot. When the handsome police officer took my statement, I told him "I was putting mascara on and all of a sudden this crazy woman started banging on my window, screaming at me, telling me to move my car forward. Officer, she was so scary and my sisters were traumatized." The old miserable hag looked like a witch who just got off her broom on Halloween night, dressed in black, with long gray messy hair. I mean, she was U-U-G-G-L-Y! The cops found her hiding in the office and were issued a citation. When the officer asked me if I had a message for her I told him to warn her never to approach me and my SUV again or else I might punch her in the mouth this time.

Must be shocking to my ESL teacher in high school, Lydia P, when she read my journal about one of my favorite bands, The Divinyls, and their hit song "I Touch Myself". In the journal, we were asked to write a brief description of why. In it, I wrote "In the song's music video, Christina Amphlett's sexuality is electrifying. I like her voice and I love the beating of the drums."

Rotten Girls vs. *The Golden Girls*: Funny how guest actresses from *Murder, She Wrote* would likewise appear on certain episodes of *The Golden Girls* and act like pure evil bitches. For example, Blanche's sister (Barbara Babcock), Rose's daughter (Christina Belford) and the meddlesome daughter (Molly Hagen) of Miles, Rose's boyfriend.

Some relatives of mine will never know that in my solace I really pray for them and their well being sincerely despite them hating me and being indifferent towards me.

Just like an immigration officer at the airport, I can deny entry to anyone by whim or will; deny entry to my life and social circle, that is.

Important advice from the late Philippine president Corazon "Cory" Aquino: Never forget the power of prayers.

The new sex gods on the internet for me are Cristian Lopez, Nath Wyld, Kristof Cale and Sam Drew. These guys get me all hot and wet like Julian Edelman's jock after an intense game. I love Ryan Walker's big bubble butt, too.

I love it when Gem Shopping Network host and auctioneer "Mike" does his auctioneer garble and starts to sound like the Looney Tunes cartoon character Porky Pig. Who knew that Auctions can be humorous, too; not always a serious, high brow affair.

Christmas 2019 Wish List: A ring from Cartier and Sam Mendes' used underwear.

Overheard (TK Noodle House, September 2019): Mexican guy in the home construction business: "I live with this lady and she's very bossy." Indian woman (real estate agent): "Oh, no, no, no, no! Don't let her do that to you." Vanessa (seated at the next table, trying her very best not to burst into laughter, telling herself): "She's not a lady. She's a bitch."

Bittersweet memories: Either you cry about it or just smile and reminisce. I'm done crying!

It's the truth!: Men and their fickle mindedness. One minute they're all over you like you're the fuck of the century. The next day they spit you out like a chewed piece of gum.

A Revelation: Remember Ryan Phillipe"s facial expression of instant euphoria the first time stepped on the dance floor in *54*? That's how I feel every time I dance at Cache Creek Casino's Club 88.

Double Talk: I've said this before and I'll say it again, I really believe the reason why some people--mostly relatives--hate me so much is because deep in their minds they *know* I'm having the best sex ever and that I can turn any kind of fantasy into reality. In the sage words of Sophia Petrillo, "Jealousy is a very ugly thing."

One important advice to the younger generation: Respect your elders.

Pioneer trans-Woman: Looking back from twenty years ago, when I fought--and won--for my basic human right to use the women's restroom while working at the USPS Facility in San Jose, CA as a full time transgender woman, in essence I became a pioneer of the LGBTQ rights movement.

Q&A: Vanessa, what do you do when you're not in Fremont? Shopping, scheming and sleeping.

High School Ass-chievements: I was never in the Honor Roll but Honey Lynn was... always in the Ho-in Roll. I heard she liked doing anal all the time with a bunch of guys.

Love it!: Thirty years after it was first played on the radio, Tiffany's "It's the Lover (Not the Love)" is still one of the most beautiful love songs of all time in my opinion.

I once dated a handsome bodybuilder from San Mateo, CA named Paul. He had a medical condition known as dwarfism. I never cared one bit about what people thought. I met him a couple of times and he was an amazing person--kind, ambitious, positive-thinking and so full of life. He was a beautiful person inside and out. He'd come visit me in my hotel in Fremont. I remember referring to the clicking and clacking of his knee braces and custom made shoes as a signal of his arrival. You could hear the damn things from miles away!

Takes my breath away: Breathe's "Hands to Heaven" playing on the radio while making out with Christian, a distant relative, back in 1989. What an amazing feeling.

What a comment! From Mother Lynne, a friend and mother figure from the late '90s: "You are a lady of leisure."

Overheard: "Impeach the son of a bitch!"

Overheard by Lucy: Her roommate, Bebe Hope, moaning loudly one night: "Ah! Ah! Ah!". Lucy assumed the Middle Eastern boyfriend was either putting it in her hard and deep or he was eating her pussy. *"Vaness, ang lakas ng ungol ni Bebe Hope, tang ina! Baka kinakain nung lalake yung puke nya."* ("I could hear Bebe Hope's loud moaning. I think her boyfriend was eating her pussy.") She cracks me up. Filipinos have a unique, funny way when it comes to articulation and telling stories.

A Vanessa original: WGBOM (Who's Gonna Bitch On Me?)

Norman Rockwell definitely knows the importance of focusing on men's thighs and their backside surprise.

Good advice to bad store employees: Cut down on the attitude and focus more on servitude. Your rudeness will not get you anywhere but the manager's office.

I credit tumblr, *W* magazine and *The Golden Girls* reruns for keeping me sane in this mad, mad world we live in.

My daily life guides: Fortune Cookie messages, Channel 943 Soundscapes and common sense.

A Warning to a relative who unfriended me on Facebook a few years ago: Bitch, don't mistake my art for porn and stop reporting people with unique, artistic talents to Facebook authorities! You are infringing on my First Amendment rights. It's sad that you don't have *any* kind of imagination.

That's life!: Sometimes I get so fucked up, fed up and fueled up.

Sex and the Rich Single Woman: So, as I get older my fucking style becomes classier? Is that how it works nowadays? I enjoy getting fucked while wearing my furs, pearls and diamonds; in a king size bed and showering my lovers with nice gifts afterwards.

Richard Marx hit the mark: "When you're trying to make a living, there's no such thing as pride."

Dakota Johnson to me is a fad, an anomaly; a Hollywood passerby. Her famous dad, Don Johnson, however, forever remains on my DILF list.

Keeping it real: Let's face it. Unless you regularly watch some variety shows on TV in the Philippines like *ASAP Natin To* or you happen to be an expat and your next door neighbor happens to have some Spanish or foreign blood in him, the faces you'll encounter there are so-so. So, every time the masses see a *mestizo* (half caste), like Enrique Gil or James Reid, they immediately fall on their knees like the Three Kings from the Nativity scene and bestow on the lucky light skinned lothario hero worship. It's th*e* truth! Watch and observe and you'll see what I'm talking about. The cheers and screams become deafening as soon as the *mestizo* celebrities come out on stage. No wonder they're so head over heels in love with Korean boy band pop sensation BTS and other Korean *telenovela* actors, with their light complexion and chiseled features.

Fear Factor: I can only imagine the constant fear the people (staff, students, custodians, cafeteria employees, etc.) in Baron Trump's school have. Either they kiss his half Ukrainian half American ass or they kiss the school goodbye.

Think of Laura: Laura Branigan, the late singer with a one in a million voice, to me is still the best female vocalist ever to walk the face of the earth. It gives me goosebumps when I listen to her songs. The power and range in her voice is out of this world.

Drama Queen: The only drama I'm totally fine with is the one found in my jewelry collection. Have you seen my statement necklaces?

From Dino: "Skinny Vanessa, you must be loved by many."

Assurance Policy: I prefer an assurance over an apology. By demanding some form of an assurance from someone who has done you wrong, you are putting them in check. It's like me telling him or her "I'm watching your every move now, bitch. You better not make a boo boo next time!" An apology is basically lip service these days.

A defining moment (January 2, 2020): At some point, I simply had to release the stress and feelings of pain and misery, and dance, dance, dance, as tears were falling down my face.

Yes, I was dancing *while* crying, but they were tears of therapeutic release. My cousin had just died the previous month and his passing made me feel so depressed. I just lost someone who I looked up to as my big brother all my life. I simply *had* to dance while in my hotel room, and let go of the pain; while the music was in full blast. It was very liberating.

Take it from the expert: My good friend, Stewart, a car enthusiast, once told me "You don't wait for that one morning in the winter when your car won't start. Replace the battery right away!"

Unfriended? Don't blame the person who unfriended you. Blame yourself! Unless, of course, that person is a total jerk.

Moving On: You cry one moment, then you wipe your tears away and finally, you get up because you realize you have things to do and a life to live. You move on.

Vanessa on Vanessa (Why do some Mabuhay Playground people hate you?): Well, I really don't know. I really don't know. It's mind boggling. I've never done anything wrong to these people. For the life of me, I have not a single clue why these people treat me this way. Maybe because of the color of my skin? Most of the Mateos in that part of town had light complexion and *mestizo* features. Maybe it's my being gay? Or maybe they sensed that I was a force to be reckoned with from early on. I mean, I spoke my mind. I was very close to my Grandmother (who most of them loathe, from the rumors that I heard when I was growing up. I also observed it when I was a teenager. People in Mabuhay Playground did not like my Grandmother! I know it, they know it!) The only people in Mabuhay who were nice to me and treated me with respect were my grandfather's younger brother, Onoy, and his first cousin, Azon. The wife of my grandfather's cousin, Juliet--may she rest in peace--was nice to me, too. April and Rannie, hairdressers in the area, were nice to me, too. They are siblings and both of them are gay. April would cut my hair for free. I've said this before and I'll say it again, there is a stigma on gays and people with dark complexion in the Philippines. Filipinos are some of the worst when it comes to being prejudiced on almost every living thing on earth. My god! They act like they are the main authorities when it comes to beauty and what *is* beautiful and what is not! Some people would sell their mothers for a dose of the skin whitening drug glutathione! That's how ridiculous and vain some people are in the Philippines. I really thank my Dad for bringing us, his family, to the US. Life for me in this beautiful country has been peaceful in general, and most important of all, my freedoms are not attacked and violated.

As a follow up on the previous statements, I really think those Mabuhay Playground people knew I *got* to Christian. You know, we had done things intimately. Chris was one of the very few "hotties", if you will, in that area. So, jealousy, perhaps? I know one girl at the time who was so annoyed by the fact. She's an old broad now. You'll hear N-O-N-E from me about this thing anymore.

A Second Opinion: I've been told by two different men (who, by the way, did not know each other) that I have a "one track mind."

Good Reviews: In a span of one week, three men have praised my bedroom skills; commenting that the experience they had with me was "incredible" and "amazing."

Christmas and the Spirit of Giving: Someone asked me what kinds of gifts I like giving people on Christmas. Well, anything but department store freebies, especially empty makeup bags and pouches. That is just terrible. I learned my lesson very well. Many years ago, a one time friend of mine would give me empty makeup bags from department stores as a Christmas present. It was so sad. So, for good karma, I give friends and loved ones stuff that they can *actually* use and consume (i.e. food, money, perfume or jewelry).

The Tupac Impact: Once, a black employee at a Goodwill that I frequent approached me to thank me for wearing a sweatshirt with Tupac Shakur's image.

Colorful Memories: Here are some color combinations that have stuck in my mind since childhood. 1) A *Mamina* tank top (white and teal) 2) A fashion catalog from the US brought by a relative when she visited the Philippines in 1984 that featured clothes by Esprit (white, blue green and pastel pink) 3) A rainbow reflection on a puddle that revealed multi color striations (purples, greens, pinks) 4) A plastic rhinoceros toy in chartreuse green that I purchased from a store on Maria Guizon Street 5) A Colgate toothpaste in mint green and 6) Christmas decors in vibrant shades (purple, blue, green, red, gold, silver) at a general merchandise store not far from my house called Torresian.

Show me your art: If you're aspiring to become an artist, don't try too hard to be the next Picasso or Monet. Just be yourself.

Be original! Use nature and your surroundings as an inspiration. You can even use past experiences and memories as an inspiration. The world around you is your canvas! After all, art has to be fluid, not an imitation of another one's work.

Peace be with you: Let go of your fears, worries and other people's criticisms and soon you will experience peace and bliss.

An Optimist: If it doesn't happen for me today, I'll make it happen tomorrow!

A tumblr quote: "Haters gonna heat." There's a grammatical error, no doubt, but it makes a good point. Personally, I just let them incinerate from the intensity of their envy and hatred towards me.

An Aspiring Architect: Foundations are critical to all structures.

An Aspiring Actress: Practice these two important things in front of the mirror: versatility in your facial expression and flexibility of your facial muscles.

"Mahomes!": What I blurt out from out of nowhere every time I see a good looking young mulatto guy with an athletic body and a cute bubble butt, wearing a pair of red Nikes and tight black compression pants. I imagine that ass has the right amount of stank.

Valentine's Day 2020 gift to self: The gift of gold. 24 karat gold, that is. Diamonds are so overrated and not a lot of people receive solid 24 karat gold as a gift these days.

Pity please: I once asked my good friend, Imogen, about the two women who used to be friends with me with whom she maintains communication: "Did they for once ask you how am I doing or if I'm going through tough times?" I don't think so. All these bitches cared about was themselves and their crappy relationships with the losers they've hooked up with.

Vanessa Paradis was Johnny Depp's ex, now let me introduce you to Vanessa Parodies: *Heath's Ledger* (about a male escort and stripper and the raunchy stories found in his diary after he was found dead in his Santa Monica Blvd. hotel room from an apparent suicide). He was a coke snorting casanova, no doubt. *My Best Friend's Whining* (about a divorced woman who has a revolving door of boyfriends coming in and out of her messed up life, and constantly bothering and harassing a successful single female friend, looking for a sympathetic ear to bitch to).

Another valuable lesson in life: I just laugh, let go and *live*.

Another High School memory: Cutie Kevin P asking me if I had a quarter in me. I did and I gave it to him. Even back in high school, people thought I'm a rich bitch. Fast forward to 2019: Happy to see him as a handsome and successful family man working for the US Military.

Touched by a goddess: My lover, Martin, telling me "You have the hands of a goddess." (February 25, 2020)

Bold Statement: Do you know why men can't resist me? Because I'm so fuckin' good in bed!

You Ought to be Committed: Some people ask me why I'm not in a committed relationship. Well actually, I've been asked many times by dozens of men over the years to be in a serious, exclusive relationship with them. I just find it a tough situation to be in. I know myself very well. I am prone to falling for more than just one man at the same time. I am *that* romantic. So, in the interest of not hurting the feelings of one man or more, I've decided to remain single for now.

A lesson in Photography: A picture must always tell a story. Otherwise it's a useless piece of shit.

Not another Taylor song: Bitch you try to sound like a Taylor Swift song all the time-- you pretend you're still a virgin when you've already gone through the entire varsity football team.

Hamburger vs, Humble Bragging: I'd rather peruse the latest Burger King coupon ad than view your Facebook video posts showing off your mini liquor collection and how your family is "living comfortably" in your small house in Manila while sheltering in place during the Covid pandemic, with your kids' dirty feet on top of the coffee table where your food and liquor are conveniently placed. What a healthy and sanitary situation!

A lesson in History: Study certain events of the past in order for you to have a forecast of the future, and possibly avoid past mistakes from happening again.

Giving you the best that I got: I give what I give. Take it or leave it.

The New Kid in T-own: Ten years ago, I fell for Tim Tebow. Now, I'm into Tyler Herro.

High School Memories (and I'm not talking about that old porno movie starring Annette Haven): Some freshmen and sophomore kids in my high school would periodically ask for change or $1 bills during my senior year. Even back then people thought I'm a rich bitch.

A Filipino fact: The problem with most Filipinos is the fact that they have no interest in learning about important, historical events in other countries as well as the other cultures that exist.

Advice to media companies in the Philippines: Why not feature educational shows about other countries and cultures? Too much telenovela is not good for the *cabeza*.

Sanders out of the 2020 Presidential Race: Bye, bye Bernie!

From Kuato *(Total Recall, 1990):* "Open your mind. Open your mind."

From Veruschka *(Diana Vreeland: The Eye Has To Travel):* "Don't be boring." Iconic!

From the wisdom of Joel Osteen: "Don't carry other people's garbage. You can't keep it from coming but you can keep it from *coming* to you!"

More Filipino facts: It's funny how some Filipino women I'd cross paths with would gawk at me and give me the shocked and surprised look as if I came from another planet. But what's funnier is the way I'd give them the look that says, "Yes, bitch! I exist and the world is my stage!"

You are in denial: Some women in my social and family circles act like they're not paying attention to my sense of style, my jewelry and the way I take over the goddamn room, but in reality they are already taking notes and contemplating on copying me from head to toe. It's the truth!

Copy That!: Back in the day, when I used to operate a Facebook account full time, a lot of women "friends" would all of a sudden be wearing similar clothing--fabulous outfits I had on from my previous posts--and emulating my sense of style. Some even bought Mercedeses, too, as their vehicle of choice. I just tell myself with a smile, "Yes, bitch. You've seen my post."

A Career in design: You've got to have a mothership size of an imagination--fully loaded with ideas--in order to succeed and get noticed. I'm not talking about Motel 6 interiors here. Don't get me wrong, I love my Motel 6 rooms. I stay there sometimes.

I Say A Little Prayer For Me: It takes centuries for some people to come up with the things that they should be thankful for. With me, it's completely the opposite. The minute I open my eyes in the morning, all I see are the beautiful things surrounding me and *that* alone is worthy of being thankful. Next, I thank God for the very fact that I am still alive and breathing and for the blessings that might come my way.

A Testimony on Faith, Hope and Perseverance: I remember a time when I almost had nothing to go by, but hope helped me to continue, faith made me believe that something good will happen and perseverance pushed me to rally to the finish line. And by the end of the day, I realize I've accomplished something: I reached my goal. Make success an everyday goal!

Put some lipstick on!: Sometime in the summer of 2019, while visiting my Grandmother, the old lady commented on my cousin's girlfriend's lips--why were they too red and why did she feel the need to put lipstick on in the first place; considering the fact that she's just home anyway. Morinne just smiled and quietly walked away. A few months after that curious incident, my cousin was dead. In hindsight, I applaud Morinne for doing what she feels like because to have lipstick on and look pretty for your man *all* the time is a beautiful thing. Most women don't even realize it, but it's a must do in a relationship. There is absolutely no point in having lipstick on if your husband or boyfriend is six feet under already. Wear red lipstick every fucking day of your life!

Point to Ponder: You can never be called a secure, confident person unless you're able to self deprecate and not care about it one bit.

The Final Word: In the end, it is my ultimate decision to leave the questionable people behind; those who live and breathe drama; those who are harbingers of negativity and whose existence is pure toxic.

Then and Now: Ancient Greece's basics were food, cloth and oil. Vanessa's basics these days are food, men and money.

A Head Scratcher: Getting drunk and doing illegal drugs instead of trying to assess the situation and come up with a solution baffles me big time.

Not a Weekend Warrior: Sometimes, all you need on a Friday night are chips, dips, ice cold beer and a really bad zombie movie.

Let's Talk About Love: Love has no rules and restrictions.

Let's do business!: Unforgettable business proposals from these nice guys: Greg Allan, partly responsible for the reconstruction of a major bridge in the Bay Area; Davey Brown, friend and business partner of Jaime Augusto Zobel de Ayala, business tycoon from the Philippines; photographer John Naldy and *The Wave* publisher, Chris Rhoads.

Not the shy type: I may act shy and ladylike in public, but I can be a loud, nasty aggressive bitch in the bedroom. If I feel like it.

Silent Grief: Unlike other people on Facebook who would outright "broadcast" and publicize their so-called mourning over the death of my cousin Marvin, I choose to grieve in silence, reflect and pray. They don't know Marvin's story. They think they know the real Marvin, but they don't. They just know the gregarious, loud and outgoing Marvin, but not the broken and flawed Marvin. So, I say to those people in Mabuhay Playground, "Shut the fuck up! Mind your own fucking business!"

Movie pick up line of the decade (1960s): "You're quite a girl, Pussy." (*Goldfinger*, 1964)

Blue Angels, Daredevils of the Sky!: Now, we're not talking about Pussy Galore's *Flying Circus* here. That bitch is just a character in a movie. This is the real thing! These are real pilots! They're the gods of the San Francisco skies. I've dated US Navy airmen and all I can say is bitches get your pie holes ready because these men are gonna turn them upside down! Oh yes! Experience that 2,500 mph thrust--pure Mach1 excitement!

Sentimental Jewelry: When all the men in your life are gone or have moved on, is there anything left? Yes! In my case, it's the happy memories, the very intimate moments and the jewelry. That's why I make it a point to always--always--spend the money my lovers give me on beautiful fine jewelry.

Real Talk: Sometimes being a total bitch with big balls is the only way for a transgender individual to get noticed and get her message across. Every day is a form of survival for me.

An aria so grand: I find myself in tears every time I listen to "Nessun Dorma" from Puccini's *Turandot*. I don't know why and I don't care. I'm only human. Chryssie Hynde was right.

Alarm bells ringing: Some Facebook posts and comments from supporters of the current Philippine president have become so alarming and at times, very scary. They are encouraging vigilantism and immediate acts of violence towards people accused of committing even the pettiest of crimes without due process. The most worrisome part is, those "alleged" crimes are unproven and could not be backed up with any solid evidence. It's almost a form of entrapment. I hope fair, non-partisan politicians, lawmakers and even law enforcement agents do something about it as soon as possible. Please protect the innocent!

Achtung Baby: Guys, stay away from the bad pussy. Your mother warned you about it a long time ago. Now, mama Vanessa is reminding you about it. You know what I'm talking about. The kind of pussy who's got a lot of *baggage* with her. Soon that *baggage* will be at your doorway, waiting to be carried inside...and ready to make your carefree, happy bachelor life a living hell. Eventually, she drains your bank account and spit you out like chewed gum and moves on with another man. Be smart, guys. Be very smart.

Did you drink too much Hate-o-rade? So, you don't like what I wrote and don't agree with my views and opinions? Borrow Thor's hammer and feel free to hit your head with it so you can wake up to reality! What were you expecting when you bought this book? Fairy tales and other make-believe fantasy crap? No way! This is me. This is my life and this is *real* life!

A *totally* universal question: How do we know we are the only ones in the universe?

Questions, questions: Question everything! ("But why?")

That's what friends are for: Whether or not we were together for a long time or just long enough to share a bottle of wine, you've made my life good and exciting in some way, and I'll never forget you. You are my friend and rest assured that every time I hear songs by Skid Row, I remember you! Thank you, Bobby, Joverni, Marie, Neptune, Majo, Kathy, Amy, Myra, Raquel, Lulette, Nestor, Itzel, Sally, Raymond, Didith, Anna, Rochelle, Donna,

Alona, Bongbong, Eric Bacla, Charito, the Garcia Family, the Cooper Family, Marvic, Azon, Joniz, Mylene, Milbert, Lannie, Jenny Tatang, Chi Chi, Julia, Lucy, Angie, Nunally, Joleen, Rosie, Tess, Mother Lynne, Milla, Pootie, Grace T, Robert, William, Kevin, Danley, Johnny G, Erik, David, Mani, Brett, Frank, Frankie, Russell, Brian, Nick, Brian Todd, Mike, David K, Don G, Don H, Don S, Stewart, Mark B, Mark R, Mark T, Mark Womvat, Mark Roko, Mark Digger, Marty, Chris, Chris F, Chris R, Ronnie, Carl R, Carl (Norcal Eddie), Daddy Michael, Daddy Mike, Daddy Andre, Daddy Andy, Daddy Art, Daddy Bob, Daddy Carl, Daddy Gene, Daddy Jim, Jeff Steel, Daddy, Daddy Neal, Daddy Roy, Daddy Scott, Daddy Richard, Daddy Dave, Daddy Dan Tall, Daddy Dan R, Daddy Dennis, Daddy Joe, Daddy Keoni, Daddy Jon, Daddy Nick Michaels, Daddy Ron, Daddy Wayne, Dan Fotto, Jeff Virginian, Doug Alan, Pat L, Papa John Leonty, Uncle Jeff, Uncle Ken, Uncle Frank, Dave S, Lee Calv, Walter, Kevin Cawley, Kevin Hilton, Kevin E, John Cawein, Nick Nobrige, Erico Dolo, Jaime Avals, Jamie K, Trevor, Aaron, Mac, Jared, Nasser, Morris, Morris K, Derrick N, Brendan, John Howard, Keith, Loren, Bill, Paul, Ben, Matt, Wade, Adrian, Ali, Avi, Stephen, Eric Brazilian, Scott Integra, Scotty James, Steven Lazerda, Will Cuebas, Marc Rickets, Dave Silverdragon, Dave Monterey, Brian Rodeo, Lance Wending, Tony B, Tony L, Merl, Glen, Greg Han, Greg S, Jason, Sal, Geoff, George, Steve R, Steve A, Mike E, Mike A, James V, Brian Zeethree, Mike Pacificchamp, Mike S, Mike Aztec, Mike Airpersia, Mike H, Mike Croley, Ron J, Jose A, Jose L, Jose J, Alfonso, Alan, Alex, Alvaro, Aaron Lutherav, Chris Ryan, Bashir, Julio, Art H, Art Sunol, Aaron, Bruce, Miguel, Shaheen, Ethan, Ravi, Rusty, Rick T, Brent A, Luke Carmichael, Jon Michael C, Nate, Gleb, Gino, Bryce Castel, Georgie, Dino, Adrian Serno, Jon Concord, Randy M, Randy P, Randy Atrium, Ryan, Lee S, Lee Willow Glen, Daniel, Dale, Dani, Yuji, Dylan O, Jeffrey Boway, Jeff Wizen, John Italian, Neil Fremont, Andrew Aussie, Angel Santa Cruz, Dennis Papa Bear, Master Pete, Master Larry, Michael S, Max Simoni, Pete Workoutca, Richard E, Robert San Pablo, Officer Alex, Officer Nick, Officer Anthony, Officer Rob M, Rob Ver, Rob Photographer, Nick San Jose, Neil P, Vince Cang, Vince Hostetter, Vinny E, Zach Williams, Zach R, Jay, Jamie, DJ, Baby Jay, Jon J, JJ, JC, JD, JP, German daddies Werner Baumahn, Markus Webber and Heinz Aurer and last but not least, the man who introduced me to the music of Skid Row, John Sherty. Cheers!

Play Tom Barabas' *Lovers in the Moonlight* and *Dolphin Dream* at my funeral.

Don't do it: Don't ask me the stupid question "Where do you see yourself in 5 years?" because right now I'm only thinking of where I will be in a couple of days, bitch!

People--especially Filipinos--have a penchant for asking me if I have a boyfriend. To them, having a long term, romantic relationship with someone is like part of the Ten Commandments: you will go to hell if you don't do it! I mean, that's one of the ridiculous things I ever heard. I tell these bitches "Do I really need one?" Seriously, I prefer a boy toy rather than a boyfriend. No issues. No arguments. No drama! Just fun, fun, fun.

Pathetic Politics: The biggest liars, hypocrites and deceivers are those who capitalize on important issues and discussions such as LGBTQ rights and Immigration reform and politicizing them for their own personal gain but not doing a single thing about it after winning the election and taking office.

Dream On: When I was a young child, I had a crazy dream about me missing a flight to somewhere with my Uncle Tony standing by my side, looking up at the sky pointing towards a vintage 1950s passenger airplane and telling me "There's our plane. We missed it." Now that I'm in my forties, every detail from that dream remains crystal clear in my mind.

Planet Neptune: It's true, children live in their own world sometimes. I had a passion for drawing graves, coffins, and dead people at one point in my young life and my friend, Neptune, had a penchant for drawing hens, birds and chickens laying eggs all over the place; with the caption written by me that says "Lay your eggs here! Lay your eggs there!"

A business establishment basic: EAEWO (Eyes and Ears Wide Open)

Don't be a motherfucker to Mother Nature: But why would I travel to some place warm during winter and do the same thing in the summer and go somewhere cold? Aren't you supposed to live, breathe and appreciate each season for what it is? It's like giving Mother Nature the middle finger.

Jean Claude Glute God: There's always a few scenes here and there in a Jean Claude van Damme movie that features his beautiful *derriere*. Gays, let me hear it! *Universal Soldier* is a universal favorite!

Amen to that!: Celebrate the day just because you woke up alive!

Why I love the movie *Joker*: The deep rooted pain and *the* dancing.

My simple beauty regimen: I wash my face with cold water--a favorite routine of Catherine the Great--and with Neutrogena, the best facial cleanser on earth.

A new sense of luxury: Luxury is not all about driving a Bentley or spending the weekend in Bora Bora; it can also be a state of mind. Comfort, convenience and the freedom to do outlandish things just because are other forms of luxury.

The plain and simple truth: If I didn't migrate to the US and got stuck in the Philippines instead my thinking would probably be limited, I'd be a rambling cynic, and I'll probably die young from the enormous amount of stress caused by the outright discrimination on gays and trans people and the endless bullying from jerks and other close minded individuals; not to mention the oppressive heat and the bugs. The government--senators and congressmen-- really need to step things up and establish and enforce laws that will protect the rights, safety and security of the LGBTQ community there. No ifs and buts! No bullshit excuses!

More truths: It would be very difficult for me to live in a country like the Philippines where gays, lesbians and trans people are considered second class citizens; where living as a member of the LGBTQ community is in itself a daily struggle. God Bless America!

Sign of the Times (My marching slogan): WE DON'T NEED ANOTHER HITLER!

Questions, questions!: Pleasing a man as a form of art? Absolutely!

My plots and ideas when it comes to nasty, kinky sex scenes would make *Fifty Shades of Grey* look like an amateur children's book.

Real-ationship Talk: Why it is hard, *so* hard, for me to be in a serious committed relationship with someone: I don't want him to feel betrayed and I don't want to hurt his feelings. I *love* men so much and vice versa. Even if I had myself cloned ten or fifteen times, there are not enough men in the world who can please and satisfy me completely. On average, I talk to ten men every day.

Fashion Police: In some fashion ad campaigns, Dior in particular, black models are always the center of attention; always the racial group where white models are seen gawking most of the time. I am curious to find out why. Questions, questions!

Popular quote from the '90s: "Get a life!"

More Real-ationship Talk: When that moment comes when you realize you can be totally *yourself* with someone--pimples, warts, bad breath, body odor included--and he doesn't care one bit, then that's the moment you'll find out you've found the *one*.

Fundemic 2021 (Vanessa to a Daddy): "Another thing that stuck out last Wednesday aside from your sexy bubble butt was when you said this whole Covid pandemic thing was created by the government."

Sad Reality (From *made* to maid): This acquaintance of mine, a nice Filipino lady who used to work as front desk receptionist at the hotel that I'd visit once in a while now works as a chambermaid, washing cum stained sheets and scrubbing toilets. What a classic irony. Before, she would be dressed elegantly, covered in fine jewelry, made up and not a strand of hair out of place. She would order the maids around with an authoritative tone. Now, she's one of them. It's a classic lesson in life: today you're on top, tomorrow you're under the hotel bed pulling out used Q tips and condoms. But, my respect for her hasn't changed a bit. Every November--the month of her birthday, I'd give her a present. She is so appreciative and the smile on her face is genuine. What's that old saying again? "Enjoy the view while you're on top."

Ramblin' about Rambo: There's only one Rambo just like there's only one Chucky. Can you imagine Elmo acting like Chucky or Big Bird acting like Chucky? Weird! Can you imagine Tom Hanks *or* Forrest Gump taking the role of Rambo? I don't think so. Sly Stallone's just perfect for the role.

Take a Hint: Unlike some people, I don't do the "You should do this, do that" kind of advice. I just tell them how *I* would do it myself. It's really up to them if they'll take my advice. I don't impose on people. It's rude!

Reptilian Resilience: You gotta have the skin of an alligator to be me. Seriously! So, if mean people try to take a bite out of me I make sure they lose a tooth or some of their teeth. I won't go down without a fight. It's a tough and terrible world we live in right now. People are like procrastinating time bombs. Plus, if it's really your worst day, some people are literally walking time bombs. That's why the minute I step out of my house I put my game face on. I smile, I'm polite, I'm ladylike, but I never, ever let my guard down. Hello people, this is the 21st century! That's how life is!

We all have our secret battles. We all do.

Hello, my name is Karma: "You may not face the consequences of your evil actions today, but you'll have your turn soon. Wait for my visit."

The one love song that I really love: Air Supply's "The One That You Love". It's the very first love song that really left an impression on a very young Vanessa. I mean, the melody, the emotion and *that* voice!

Driving Lessons: Driving on the San Francisco Bay Bridge on a windy day? You gotta hold on really tight to the wheel like Jerry Rice holding on to the ball for a touchdown.

New villains in America: That governor from Texas named Greg and that black wannabe comedian named Dave (Robin Williams is the one true comedian!). Attacking trans rights and bashing gays and trans people with homophobic slurs won't do your legacy any good. If you've got any.

The town fool: October 22, 2021: As I was pulling out of the Safeway parking lot in my town's shopping center, a middle-aged transient was being obnoxious and yelling obscenities. He had a shopping cart next to him full of junk and other nasty stuff. I just ignored him. I told myself "I'm sleeping in my warm, comfortable bed tonight and you'll be sleeping with the rats. Asshole!"

Trans on Transients (The mellow, respectful ones): I make sure I hand these fellow Americans a couple of bucks whenever I run into them. I always tell myself "If you could spend thousands of dollars on jewelry and other stuff, surely you could spare a dollar or two on these individuals." Unlike other people–some celebrities included–I don't look the other way when I see a mellow, harmless looking homeless person.

Are you really *a* pro or just happen to be Pro Prostitution? Which one is it?: It's one thing to express support for legalizing the world's oldest profession, but it's another to rave about it like what this woman did during a Lisa Ling CNN interview. Girl, it's one thing to express an opinion, it's another to scream your lungs out about it. That makes you *the* biggest slut in the world! No ifs and buts--you are the biggest slut! Bar none. You are the mothership of whoring! You are an entire galaxy of harlotry!

Pump up the volume: "Let's get loud!" J Lo once sang. I say let's get loud and nasty! I like taking things to a different level.

I wonder if she can really *handle* big Alex and his enormous hot rod. I'd like to ask him someday.

I'm Coming Out? Not!: I didn't need to "come out" to anyone. Ever! Not even my parents! Growing up, I think my family was well aware that I was gay. That was it. I played with girls. I played with my sisters' Barbie dolls. I was effeminate from early on. Always nice and clean and fresh, with a dab of Johnson's Baby Powder on my face. I had crushes on boys. What more "coming out" do you want to see? One afternoon in late 1999, I just fuckin' came out of the house wearing a dress. And the rest is history. Well, I did drive to the 7 Eleven near my house that day to get me a hotdog sandwich and some ice cold beer. It was a good day. Really good.

Trash on the Jersey Shore an author?: Who knew that the trash that ended up on the shores of New Jersey could write a book? I didn't even think that that trash is capable of writing one simple sentence using correct grammar. From what I heard, these are the only words she utters on a daily basis: "suck", "fuck" and "dick". She must be licking her ghost writer from head to toe as a form of 'Thank You'. People who bought her book got snookered, no doubt. I have a feeling it's full of garbage.

Iconic photograph (My paternal grandmother, December 1975): A photograph of her standing outside the police station in Manila shortly after filing formal charges against her ex daughter in-law and the latter's sisters. A violent encounter had taken place earlier.

A Time Capsule (November 2001, Sunnyvale, CA): Me paying Julia a visit. I wanted to check on her and my newborn nephew and have a short chat. She had just given birth the previous month. She is my cousin Marvin's baby mama. At the time of my visit, Marvin was in the living room, tinkering with his work tools. Julia, who was a restaurant worker at the time, was serving me dinner. It was a nice visit. Julia and I got along well. It was nice to see her again--albeit under sad circumstances--at Marvin's funeral back in January 2020. We hugged each other and talked for a few minutes. Although she and Marvin had not been together for more than a decade, Julia was there to support her son with Marvin, Junior. Amazing how time flies. Amazing how the warm, friendly feelings remain.

Say it like you mean it: I'm not one to mince words. I say what's on my mind. I say what others *are* thinking but are too afraid to say it because of various reasons--fear of retaliation, embarrassment and basically, weakness. I like telling these people "I know you're thinking it but you're just too scared to say it."

A Grand Reunion: A reunion with all the guys I've met, hooked up with or had encounters with from 1999 up to the present? I'll need to rent Levi's Stadium, home of the San Francisco 49ers, in Santa Clara, CA.

Just another face in the crowd: I know I am a *nobody*. I'm just another face in the crowd. But why is it that whenever I enter a room I turn heads? It's called presence, my dear: my height, my style, the way I move and the curiosity that I generate.

There's a reason why an indie film company in Los Angeles offered to buy the rights to my second book, *SCANDALOUS!*, and a major publishing company wanting to republish my first book, *Naughty and Nice*. They must've seen something very unique and exciting… in my work, or in me in general. I don't know. Maybe I'm wrong. All I know is, I write from the heart and I put down in writing exactly what I am thinking and feel like saying.

My 7 Eleven basics: Hot dogs, beer, condoms and breath mints. Thanks to Vishnu, my favorite cashier, for helping me!

I Want You Back: I wanted DJ so bad. He was just perfect. The face, the body, the tattoos. That ass! But this whole Covid pandemic thing fucked it up.

Here's Hoping: I hope Filipinos would one day uplift each other instead of competing with each other and constantly criticizing one another and finding fault in others. I also hope that some of them would one day learn not to bash gay people and transgender individuals just for what they are and how they look. And please stop making fun of and mocking people with disabilities!

Fate or Serendipity: Shortly after pulling out Christian's photo from a photo album in the attic, I learned--through Facebook--that his mother had passed. It was like she was telling me "Don't forget me and my son." I did say a little prayer for her.

You are overdoing it!: By overdoing a ballad or love song, with all the *birit* ("sustained high notes", but to me it's nothing but good old screaming) a singer does, she is taking away the true "feeling" of a song and distracts the listener from figuring out the song's intended message. Sometimes a song is best sung in a simple, subdued manner. Mariah Carey did it back in 2002 during a tribute performance honoring Stevie Wonder and his music. I love it. I get to *feel* the song much better that way and am able to connect.

When Will I See You Again?: David Manalang (1992-2021), my dear godson, may you rest in peace. *Ninang* loves you!

Don't Bet Your Life On It: My friend Jim's 3 rules on gambling: Have fun, win some money and "never lose your ass" (don't be an addict).

Building an empire state of mind: You should know that every great empire is forged in blood, steel and conquest.

I've heard it before: Rosa (Ross Milpitas, March 2021): *"Darling, ang ganda ng mga kamay mo. Walang pileges."* ("Your hands are beautiful. They are flawless!"). Urdi (Fremont, September 2021): "You have beautiful hands."

Never heard this before, but thank you: Martin (Fremont, March 2021): "You're a legend!"

There is only one "special moment" and that's when you finally choose to live your life the way you want and make things happen the way you want them to.

Have A Nice Day!: My typical day: Mornings must include some eggs and bacon, then some afternoon nap-a-thon and in the evening, *The Golden Girls* reruns marathon.

Dare-y Queen: Lower your eyebrows on me because of the shocking and provocative things you read in this book. You know it, I know it, you've also done it. Who knows? Maybe you're doing it more than I do. You're just too scared and embarrassed to admit it. But it's okay, I respect it. I don't judge. All I ask is that you keep an open mind as you turn the pages.

To my nineteen year-old boy toy: "You want a new X Box and new Nikes? Pull down your pants."

Sweet dreams: One important question I'll ask the SleepTrain Mattress employee the next time I purchase a brand new bedroom set: "Does the headboard come with a built in airbag?"

Vanessa's Greatest *Eats*: There's just too many of them. I'll have to start with Volume 1, and 2, and so on.

To my lover, Martin, sometime in 2020: "You're so *hungsome*."

The NFL Season: These are raw man times: the sweat, the stink, the stank. I love it!

Not so old yeller: Who could forget that one July afternoon five years ago when my lesbian neighbors heard a mouthful from me after the outsider (not from my neighborhood) girlfriend made a snarky remark as she drove by as I was washing my car. Christie, the lesbian who lived three houses down personally apologized after the incident. She apologized on behalf of the smart mouth girlfriend. After that incident, whenever the girlfriend sees me outside my house, she would turn around and use the adjacent street rather to get to the main road, Arizona. They have since moved out of the neighborhood. Looking back, the whole thing just makes me smile especially when I recall one of the crazy lines I repeatedly yelled out: "You fuckin' whore! Don't contaminate my street, bitch!"

A name change: San Francisco to San Feces-co? Mayor London Breed, is there a widespread human waste problem on the sidewalks of San Francisco? Oh, shit!

My lover Ethan's grace and beauty: A source of peace and calm for me. And that monster size dick! I'll die happy.

A woman with high standards: Just like my cocktail rings, my men must have a nice *undergallery*.

Outcall Massage: It's like *Basic Instinct*, you know? Lots of reckless driving, lots of men and lots of naked bodies.

"And if you don't know, now you know." (*Juice*, Notorious B.I.G)

Cabo Fever: My lover, Ronnie, suggested we vacation in Cabo San Lucas so we can do nothing but drink beer and margaritas and have sex day and night. "Mama, I'll fuck you and make you cum all the time."

Another High School Memory (1995): Mrs. Zelle tells me I should become a writer because she thinks I write "better than whites." I don't know about that. I am no Twain or Hemingway. I'm just Vanessa, straight out of Tondo. But, I write with what's in my heart. I really appreciate the support and encouragement some of my teachers and classmates gave me.

Dancing Queens (Manila Garden Hayward, CA 2003): Me and my aunt, Amven, dancing the night away until it was just the two of us left on the dancefloor. The hostess had to literally--albeit politely--escort us out of the dancefloor so she could resume her karaoke performances. Bitch did not want to be outdone!

Iconic movie grin scene (*Bram Stoker's Dracula*, 1992): Gary Oldman giving Keanu Reeves a devilish grin after he fed his harem a newborn baby.

Forgiven but not forgotten: One of my close relations talking shit behind our backs (me, my Mom and siblings) after my Dad passed away. Reminds me of Scar from *The Lion King*. It was a dirty, hurtful move. I have forgiven him since, but I don't think I'll be able to forget that episode.

Like father, like son?: A relative had denied my cousin's burial in the cemetery plot that's been given (paid for and named) to my Grandmother. It was such a cruel act. My Grandmother raised that cousin of mine from a very young age and they also lived in the same house in San Jose, CA. When my cousin passed away in 2019, my Grandmother decided to let the cemetery plot be used for his remains. The son of the relative who bought the plot for my Grandmother refused to hand out the document indicating that my Grandmother is indeed the rightful, legal owner of that plot. Without that document, the cemetery officials were not able to give permission for burial. Curiously, the father of this relative had wronged me and my family not long after my Dad passed away. Back in 1999, when he visited the Philippines, he did some kind of "smear campaign" on our relatives, spreading all kinds of malicious rumors and lies about me, my Mom and siblings. Now, twenty years later, the son is committing similar hurtful, offensive acts. Is this another "Like father, like son" case? I don't have the answer; only God does. And Karma.

I'm such a bed girl.

How appropriate: "Night and day, I must live for pleasure alone." (Violetta from *La Traviata*)

Ouch: Gays in the Philippines, I think, are the most sexually repressed and frustrated group of people. Why? The homophobia and the discrimation are still rampant despite the fact that we're already in the 21st century. Plus, in a country where gays are expected to spend and bestow money on straight men, not all of them can pay. The Philippines is still one of the poorest countries in the world. I guess one can call it 'No pay, no play' policy?

Personally, it will be very difficult for me to live in a country with such backwards mentality. Good luck on your rights being respected, let alone recognized. In the meantime, please let me *live*. For now, I'll lounge in my living room with a glass of wine and watch *I Want To Live!* Love Susan Hayward!

So Funny (Uncle Frank, Fall 2021): "Not that guy on crank." (Referring to another lover who joined us for a threesome a couple of years ago when I asked him recently if he wanted to have another *menage-`a-trois* with the same person)

So you like announcing to the world you are beautiful? I have relatives like that, I know some people like that. I used to see people like that. My Mom has friends on Facebook like that! When these self proclaimed "beautiful" people have really nothing to go for in life except brag about their light complexion–thanks to the whitening drug glutathione–and perceived *mestiza* looks, then I really don't have anything to do with them but treat them the very way they look at themselves: superficial. To me, they are just fleeting nobodies; annoying narcissists wrapped in total insecurity that in order for them to feel good about themselves they have to announce to the entire world that they are "beautiful"; not even bother asking other people's opinion. I'd probably give these people the two second elevator look and look the other way. The most pathetic and unacceptable people for me are those who like proclaiming and broadcasting to the world that they are beautiful and pretty, without even asking the opinion of another. Let me and the rest of the world decide, okay, bitch? The only person I absolutely and ultimately consider beautiful, without question, is Liz Taylor. That's it. Liz takes the cake! Just look at her face. I mean, she could attend the Oscars in her pajamas and with no makeup on and photographers would still swarm around her. It is also worth mentioning this gorgeous black HSN model with exotic Nubian features and the most glowing dark skin. KRON 4 weather reporter Mabrisa Rodriguez is another favorite. I love Mabrisa! Especially when she lost some weight. In the male category, my one time lover, Ethan D, brings home the First Place trophy. Tall, dark and handsome, with a dick as long as the Golden Gate Bridge, I mean, Ethan just destroys the competition (the way his dick has destroyed any ass or pussy that it encountered in the past). He is just a masterpiece of the male specimen! I am speechless.

A New Age (The Covid Era): I'm so glad I made the time and effort--and took every opportunity--to go out, go dancing, go to parties and festivals, go on vacation, go see blockbuster movies in theaters, go eat at the best restaurants and go experience anything that I find fun and exciting before March 2020--when the lockdown began. It was a dark period in modern history. It's one of the most fucked up times in modern times, I think. But, I have no regrets. I got to do fun, regular, normal things before this "pandemic" period, before this ridiculous "put your face mask on" era began. Sad. I'm happy that I regularly follow my good friend Jeff's advice: "Do what you love doing today because you don't know what will happen tomorrow."

How I got through writing this book: Lots of coffee, plenty of naps and the idea that I'll die a very happy and satisfied woman once I get it published.

Going Commando: I once channeled my inner Sharon Stone on a gentleman friend not too long ago when I met up with him at a posh hotel in the Peninsula. It was a balmy Monday evening, so I put on a short tight white Calvin Klein dress, my diamond stud earrings and slipped on a pair of white pumps and off I sped along Highway 101 in my Mercedes. No panties.

Once in my friend's hotel room, one can only imagine how excited he became when I did a quick leg cross while sitting on the executive chair, smoking a cigarette, looking like an every inch of a sophisticated maneater.

April 30, 2019 Waste *Man*-agement: One guy wants to drink my pee, another wants to eat my poop.

It's a jungle in here: Lover Wade after doing the *deed* with V: "You are an animal!"

Roadside Assistance: I'll never forget these fellow Americans who provided immediate assistance after my car stalled on a dark and flooded Highway 37 in Sonoma County back in December 1997. There was a heavy downpour that night. One gentleman offered to call the towing company and CHP and another lent me his mobile phone so I could call my parents and let them know I am okay. A police officer also stopped to check on me and to let me know that help was on the way. Thank you very much!

Dirt Digger: Is it still possible for people to demand a post mortem beheading like what the British did to Oliver Cromwell? Do you think the (deceased) perpetrators of The Lavender Scare–and anyone who might have gotten away with serious crimes against colored people and members of the LGBTQ community back in the day–should suffer the same consequences? Questions, questions!

Embraceable You: Embrace your inner pervert. After all, who will?

Those who really don't have anything meaningful to do but look in the mirror and babble about how "beautiful" they are doomed to repeat the same ridiculous things over and over again. These are exactly the types of people that I tend to stay away from; as well as people who have a penchant for borrowing money and not paying me back…and acting as if they don't owe you anything.

Clueless: I don't know why I do the things I *do*. Most likely it's for pleasure, money and survival.

Betrayed (Not the Tom Berenger movie): I was so naive and trusting. All I cared about was keeping the friendships going strong and maintaining good relationships with others. I had no idea that people were second guessing me behind my back and having ill thoughts about me. Especially that old Jewish SOB from Hayward. But it's all over now. I've moved on. I moved my memory of him to the incinerator.

Overall performance by you, not the FedEx guy: You gotta deliver because people are expecting. They're always waiting for the good stuff!

Yes, please: You gotta match your words with actions.

If only they had cell phones back then: There wouldn't be that many fatalities in the Titanic disaster and Kurt Russell wouldn't have to go through that kind of trouble in *Breakdown*. Also, Romeo and Juliet's relationship won't end in tragedy.

One has to really try their very best and must come up with a very strong argument, Johnny Cochran style, if they want to change my views and opinions on certain things. Otherwise, shut the fuck up.

Forged in Fire metaphor: Who's got the better, harder, stronger, long lasting dick.

From Lovers to Loving Family Men: Carl, Georgie, Gino, Jamie, John, Mark and Ronnie. Love the dad bod!

Dumb and Dumber: WTF is all this hoopla about Britney and her Daddy? Bitch is old--let her and her millions deal with it! These stupid fans, followers and fanatics still wanting to babysit a multi millionaire grown up bitch is a total headscratcher.

Andy, oh baby: I remember telling my gorgeous young lover if I was his wife I'd *please* him and make him happy every day.

A New Discovery: At 43, I discovered the true meaning of rhythm and fluidity: Let things take their course in a normal fashion. Don't rush it. Just tread on it. Don't over analyze. Don't over react. Don't overdo it. Just go with the natural flow.

My 6th Sense (I See Dreadful People): I always knew I had a sixth sense from early on. I always seem to catch other people's sneaky moves, gestures, eye movement and facial expression, especially if it has something to do with *me*. I can also sense people's emotional vulnerability and susceptibility: an imminent outburst of anger or a tear that is about to drop. I could feel their pain and frustration sometimes. Not too long ago, on two separate occasions, two of my Mom's good friends had tears in their eyes as they spoke about their loved ones. I think they felt my sincerity, my listening ear and my open heart. I like that. They knew I was empathizing with them. All I ever asked them was "How is your so and so doing." And a floodgate of confessions and drama had been unleashed. Damn! I should moonlight as a psychiatrist, too.

On being a tranny out in public in the 21st century: You have to be one tough bitch to survive. I may look all classy and feminine and ladylike on the outside when I *am* outside-- running errands, buying groceries, picking up some hotdogs, beer and condoms at 7 Eleven and what not, but believe me, I'm also in Ghengis Khan mode. There is that warrior attitude in me all the time; like a cop who's armed and ready for a Black Lives Matter protester who might come from out of nowhere.

Little Red Corvette: Almost twenty years ago, I still haven't forgotten about this hot young guy at Tower Records Mountain View who briefly chatted with me and told me I looked good. I was wearing a tight red top with a Playboy logo in the middle and denim cut offs. Later on while driving along El Camino Real on my way home, I was surprised to see him drive next to me, in his early 2000s red Corvette; he waved, smiled and sped off. It's one of those moments that just makes you feel really good; that makes you say "Wow! This is amazing!"

Prisoners of Love-making: The nice thing about making love with men who just got released from prison is you don't have to *do* anything. Just lay on your back or on your stomach and let your bad boy do the work! Hello Brett, Michael, Frankie and Sam! You boys better be good now!

Courtroom Behavior: The shorter your fuse, the longer your sentence becomes.

Patience Only: Impatience impedes progress.

Quotable Vanessa: Instead of living with regrets, I strive to improve the present.

From *Excalibur*, 1981: "You are what you've never known. You lust for what you cannot have."

The world is my stage and here are a couple of roles I had to play...in private: A cat...on a leash, complete with a milk bowl (2004) and a dominatrix, complete with a leather whip and bamboo stick, punishing my little sissy bitch Jimmie (2021). Lots of fun!

Smash and Grab robbers? If I were the store owners I'd hire snipers. These criminals are just pure evil. They are a clear threat to the lives and livelihood of hard working people and a danger to society in general. 21st century barbarians! Governor Newsom, what can you do? Should we deploy the National Guard?

I Support the Police 100%: Never ever defund the police! Never!

Make it Rain: I'll never forget that one time in 1986 when my Grandmother summoned me to the master's bedroom only to show me a thick stack--thick as a telephone directory--of brand new, crisp 100 peso bills. Grandma Norma (holding on to her thick stash of money with a smile): "*Mark, o.*" My immediate reaction was "*Wow, ang daming pera ng lola ko!*" ("Wow! My grandmother is rich!")

Bag Lady (Louis Vuitton store San Jose, CA, 2005): Me purchasing a handbag and paying for it in cash, with my Grandmother looking on. Grandmother (smiling with pride): "*Daming pera ng apo ko, o!*" ("My grandchild's loaded!")

A message to Jeffrey Epstein's alleged "victims": Why now? What the hell were you bitches doing in his house in the first place? Weren't you supposed to be in school?

Dave who? When I see that ugly ass black "stand up comedian" named Dave, I don't see a comedian. I see a crack dealer wearing Fubu. He's no Richard Pryor or Eddie Murphy!

That's Not Funny!: When the "comedy" career of people like this black guy named Dave is turning sour, they mock innocent and unsuspecting people like those from the LGBTQ Community and use them as material for their so-called "jokes." That's called desperation. This motherfucker's "comedy" career is going down the drain. Fo sho!

JFK Assasination Conspiracy Theory? Absolutely! Have you seen Oliver Stone's latest documentary (*JFK Revisited: Through the Looking Glass*)?

Why I love watching *Antiques Roadshow*: Sexy DILF appraisers Matthew Quinn and Brian Witherell. Makes my Monday nights not so boring after all.

Scott, Free?: The Scott Peterson verdict must be overturned immediately! Based on the new *A&E* channel documentary, the prosecution most likely pressured the jurors to convict, not to mention the tampering and mishandling of evidence. Plus, there's really no solid proof or evidence that SP actually committed the crime; not even a legit witness to vouch for the prosecution's case. It's become a media circus and a classic case of "guilty until proven innocent." It's a 21st century witch hunt! The media should also stop interviewing blabbermouth Nancy Grace. That bitch's purpose in this world is to crucify SP! The world doesn't need another TV freak like her! Also, the judge in SP's resentencing hearing must be disbarred. Let's not condemn an innocent person if we really don't have solid evidence or a strong case against him or her. It's an outrageous miscarriage of justice!

Whoever came up with the idea to use a singer with a low, breathy and creepy voice on some commercial jingles on TV must be maimed! And please stop doing remakes of my favorite '80s songs using singers with a similar voice. It's like listening to a coke snorting, drunk teenage jailbait mumbling all kinds of nonsense while zigzagging in the middle of the street late at night after getting dropped off by some stranger she just hooked up with. It's just wrong. It's annoying! Stop!

His story: All men are created equal…except in dick size.

What's your story, morning glory?: Don't believe everything you see on TV. Remember, there is *a* script to be read and the actors are, well, just acting. People sometimes have these weird perceptions and fantasies that handsome TV commercial actors are no different in person than how they present themselves on the tube. I wouldn't really know…unless I spend some private time with them and become intimate. Only then will I be able to confirm how they *really* are as regular human beings, not the wholesome, Aleve-popping daddy characters or sexy boyfriends shopping for a new Sealy mattress or a brand new pair of Skechers that they were paid to represent.

What are you talking about?: Covid-related depression? Not me! Why? Because there are so many things to do in life, so many things to explore, discover and learn from. There are only two reasons why people would become depressed, sad or suicidal in these "lockdown" times: they don't read enough and don't have a lot of imagination! That's it! If you're not willing to learn and have an open mind, literally, by absorbing new facts, ideas and information, then there is a possibility that life will shut its door on your face. Also, if you're not artistically inclined or have no artistic talents at all in the first place, then you are depression bound for sure. Drawing, sketching and painting are so therapeutic you'd be surprised how effective they are when it comes to curing depression. I dance a lot, too. Dancing is so good for the body…and soul. So, put down your iPhone and shake your booty all the way to the library!

A True Survivor: Fuck the "pandemic"! Two years into this so-called Covid pandemic times, and not one vaccine shot, I am alive and kicking. A true survivor. And I even managed to write a book! I credit Vitamin C, caution, cleanliness and common sense for my survival. That's it! I should write a pamphlet or some sort of a guide book about this whole thing.

A Johnny Mathis life rule I follow: Don't get too excited (on things), but don't get dejected at the same time.

No cancellations here: Cancel culture club members? Eat rat shit! They're just basically trolls. And cowards.

Zero Shame: Embarrassed by or ashamed of the things I've done? Of course, not! Are you crazy? That's life! That's how it worked for me! I lived *through* it. Now *you* live with it!

And if you can't accept or tolerate my views, actions and opinions, go to hell or go fuck yourself with a rusty metal bar!

THINGS THAT MAKE ME GO "HMMM... BITCH I DON'T BELIEVE YOU!"

Back in 2016, I saw a documentary about Colombian drug lord Pablo Escobar. In it, his former sister in-law was being interviewed by two good looking American investigative reporters. Funny how the middle aged woman was dressed super sleazy as if she was going to a shady nightclub during her meeting with the two gorgeous *gringos*. I think she was more interested in showing her *box* rather than leading the young American guys to the dead drug lord's safety deposit box.

Not too long ago, this fairly unknown and mediocre character, with the initials LT, who accused Sen. Al Franken of sexual harrassment (which she alleged took place some ten years ago), made national headlines when she made the rounds on various morning talk shows on TV. It also resulted in Franken's immediate resignation.

Well, I join the 350 million Americans in asking the obvious question: Why now? Coincidentally, she is good friends with Republican Party boy toy Sean Hannity and one of Trump's sons. This raises a red flag. Hey LT, your agenda as well as your character are questionable. Go see a psychiatrist immediately! There's something wrong with you. I think you have a condition called bullshitritis. I mean, if you were really bothered and affected by the alleged act, why didn't you immediately report the incident to the authorities back then? Why come out now, in an election year, where the father of your friend is running for president and so is Al Franken? What's your true agenda? You're such a shady character that media outlets should completely shun you and focus rather on more important things like equal pay for women in the workplace and people who make a difference, like Malala Yousafzai and Greta Thunberg. They have good intentions and a good heart. You're completely the opposite!

MY MEMORABLE DRIVES

Long before James Corden's "Carpool Karaoke" was launched, I've been doing my own car jams, but I always leave the singing to the professionals--my favorite artists. Here are some of the songs, old and new, that hit a chord in me and take me to a higher high every time I listen to them while driving. Absolutely no headphones!

1) Chaka Khan's "Papillon": It played as I was cruising along 19th Avenue in San Francisco on my way home from Daddy Gene's place near Geary and Clement back in 2004. The song's lyrics "slow goodbyes" ring with such significance. We always seem to have a hard time saying goodbye to each other after a night of fun. I'm always powerless to get up and leave his bed.

2) The Church's "Under the Milky Way": It played as I was driving my young lover, Pete, to San Francisco back in August 2000. We had just come from a hotel along Dempsey Road in Milpitas and hardly said a word to each other. I suppose there was hardly any energy left in us after two hours of lovemaking.

3) Back in the summer of 2000, I dated a big guy from Cupertino, CA named Mike Tattero. Once, after we had early dinner at Miyake Sushi, we decided to go for a spin on Hwy 17 near Santa Cruz in his pimped out Ford Mustang. What impressed me more was the car's sound system. Smash Mouth's "All Star" and Madonna's "Like A Virgin" were some of the songs that he played. Suffice to say that after that ride, with the deafening sound in his car, my ears were not so *virgin* anymore. Thank God my ear drums were not destroyed...and thank you, Miyake, for the yummy sashimi!

4) Highway 101 will always have a special place in my heart. I call it "The Road to Riches". Ask me why and I'd prefer to keep mum about it. I do, however, would like to share about a couple of memorable drives I made along Hwy 101 and the great songs that were playing on my radio during those trips. "Head Over Heels" by The Go-Go's played on my way home after having lunch with my friend from Gilroy, Randy M, back in 2006. My car at the time, a 1991 Mercedes 300CE, had amp speakers in the trunk. I cranked up the volume and it was the coolest thing. It sounded as if Belinda Carliste and the girls were having a mini concert in my car. Such an awesome sound! A couple of years later, in 2008, I found myself driving

on 101 again--this time near Morgan Hill, CA--with Coldplay's ""Viva La Vida" playing on the radio. My good friend, Dave, was on speaker phone. It was around midnight and there were hardly any other cars on the road. I definitely felt like the queen of the road; having been able to relate to the song's lyrics that go "I used to rule the world." On a more personal note, I definitely felt like I was royalty around that time because I had tons of money. Dave wasn't doing bad either. He had a regular job and seemed happy and content with his situation. What more could you ask for? Maybe some curly fries and ice cold Pepsi from Jack in the Box. I was basking in *the* moment.

5) In April 2019, my Mom and I drove to Northern California for a huge wine festival. It is, to date, the best trip I had for 2019. Nothing can compare to the Camelot-like views in that part of Amador County. Don Henley's "The End of the Innocence" was the perfect song for that stretch of my trip. I just wish the beauty I saw and the peace and calm I felt would never end.

Appropriately, here are a couple of CDs that left a lasting impression: Heart's *Brigade*, because Ann Wilson's powerful vocals would give Steven Tyler and Mariah Carey a run for their money; and The Divinyls' self-titled album which I consider my "sexual awakening CD". Don't get me wrong, I'm still a huge Mariah Carey fan. Mariah might have lost some of her vocal prowess unlike Regine Velasquez--they are of the same age--but she remains my favorite diva of all time.

Chapter 4

RECOLLECTIONS

THE NINETIES

In the mid-1990s, when my family and I were living in an apartment complex in Mountain View, CA, I chanced upon my thirtysomething next door neighbor with Ralph Lauren catalog model good looks walking back and forth in the kitchen in his birthday suit. He was tall with a tanned and toned body and shaved low hangers that looked like a couple of oranges stuck together, ripe and ready for the sucking. He just completely captivated me. The entire thing was in essence, my very first live peep show.

On a few separate occasions, I caught him sunbathing in his backyard naked; his heavenly body totally exposed under the sun's glory.

Whenever I'd drive by that street where I used to live, I would steal a quick glance at my former hunky neighbor's home, wondering if he still lives there. Maybe, maybe not. At any rate, it would be nice to knock at his door one day and say "Hi" and ask him if he needs a bj. Hey, it's never too late to offer a sexy neighbor a very nice gesture. I've got plenty of beef jerkies to offer.

THE LATE '90S

Through hard work and determination, my parents were able to purchase a house in Milpitas, CA in the spring of 1997. Around the same time, I had just started working for the pharmaceutical company Walgreens. From my decent paycheck, I was able to help contribute with the mortgage payment and was able to buy me some cool stuff like a cell phone, a nice pair of sneakers and a couple of Swatch watches.

Oh, I love Swatch! Back in the Philippines beginning in the mid-1980s, if you had a Swatch watch, you were considered cool. Back in 1997, from my first paycheck from Walgreens, I managed to buy myself a nice Swatch wristwatch from the Swatch store at the Valley Fair Mall in San Jose.

When I got hired by the phone company in the summer of 1997, things had gotten better for me, financially. I worked my ass off. I took every opportunity to make extra money--working overtime, working on holidays and working at different Pacific Bell offices. I was only twenty and making good money. My parents--especially my Dad--were so proud of me.

When he passed away all of a sudden in December 1998 after a short battle with cancer, I was devastated. I went through a period of depression, but I realized not long after that I had to push through and move on. I had four younger siblings to look after while my Mom was working two jobs.

For the next couple of years, I did my share of family duties--taking the kids to school, picking them up, feeding them, taking them to their doctor and dentist appointments, the whole nine yards. I even managed to go back to school part time and was able to take a part time job as well at the clothing store Ross. I realized I had more fun working at Ross. I love clothes, jewelry and accessories!

The store manager and supervisors love me! I was doing such a great job.

So, things weren't so bad after all for me in the last few years of the 20th century.

GUCCI MAMA

In the summer of 1997, eight years before becoming my Baby Ronnie's "Nasty Mama", I was first and foremost, a fabulous Gucci Mama. I was already working for the phone company and my paycheck had afforded me to purchase nicer things and first on my list was a fabulous pair of Gucci sunglasses. One afternoon in the summer of 1997, I went to a store called Sunglass Hut located at The Great Mall of Milpitas and got what I wished for. I love my Gucci sunglasses! I felt like a celebrity every time I wore it. The Gucci logo alone got a lot of attention. I remember wearing those shades over my head at work and how one of my

Filipino coworkers--who was also a label whore--would get so excited whenever she'd see them on me. I have since handed those Gucci sunglasses to a dear aunt in Australia as a gift.

OLD FRIENDS

It is also worth noting that I met my friends Angelina and Lucifera in the late '90s, and boy how we had the time of our lives: the clubbing, the parties and the late night visits to Denny's. Thirty-something Angelina and I were chronic mallrats like Shannon Doherty. We were all over the place! Our favorite hang outs were the Great Mall of the Bay Area, Valley Fair Mall and Sunnyvale Town Center, all within Santa Clara County.

Just like any sentimental Asian girl you'd find these days, I am a die hard Hello Kitty fan. My favorite Sanrio store was located inside the Sunnyvale Town Center. I wanted to have everything in that store! They were so cute! But, I didn't have a lot of cash back then. The good thing was, stores back then would still accept personal checks. I was so crazy for their stuffed animals and stationery. I've got to have My Melody!

After shopping, we'd stop by In-N-Out Burger for a bite to eat. I can still clearly remember how Angelina cussed out a worker there--face to face--who was giving her an attitude. Thank god, we weren't kicked out of the place.

Occasionally, we'd go dancing at some local club or pub and have some cocktails and lots of good time.

Lucifera was a totally different story. I met her at Walgreens back in early 1997 when we were both employed by the pharmaceutical company. The beginning of my friendship with Lucifera--or Lucy--coincided with that of my friendship with Angelina. The two didn't really become friends albeit civil with one another.

Lucifera could've been my mother when it comes to our age difference. Although she was only twenty years older than me, she *actually* looked forty years older. People mistook her for my grandmother. I suppose her years of being a chain smoker had taken its toll. Despite the age gap, our interests weren't that much different. We both like clubbing and dancing--and Denny's. The cast of *FRIENDS* had Central Perk, Lucy and I had Denny's near Central Avenue in Santa Clara, CA.

It was at Denny's where one morning in the summer of 1997, Lucifera handed me the toll free number of Pacific Bell's Career/Employment Department. I called and applied by phone, got a call back for an interview and was hired on the spot. It was a momentous day in my young life. Aged 20, I was hired by a major company. My parents couldn't have been more proud.

I never looked back at Walgreens after getting hired by Pacific Bell, except that one last time when I came back to return my work uniform. Gary Zastro, one of the mean managers and a total jerk in general, was there. I personally handed him my work vest, with a smirk. It was like telling him, "Here, motherfucker. Shove it in your ass!"

Gary Zastro was just trouble for Mr. Josef, the store manager, from the get go. Half of the crew quit because of him. He was just a total asshole. I witnessed how one by one, people started leaving or not showing up for work anymore. Lucy even filed a complaint of harassment against him. He was the reason why Lucy quit her job at Walgreens.

How I wish the three handsome former managers stayed: Mr. Konnicht, Mr. Cuzera and Mr. San Miguel. They were all very nice to me.

Many years later, Gary and I would meet again, not at Walgreens, but on the internet. He became one of the many men who responded to my Personals ad on Craigslist. He was looking to hook up with transvestites, drag queens and transsexuals. Look at what the cat dragged in! A Gay-ry Zastro! I just completely ignored the cocksucking son of a bitch.

What I really miss about Walgreens are the people I formed bonds and made friendships with: lesbian Tina, big nice Samoan tomboy Jenny, sweet lady Sema, motherly Sheila and of course, my good friends Angelina and Lucifera. Another Filipina, the very conservative and goody two shoes Bernie, or "Sister Bernie" as I called her, became a friend, too.

Sister Bernie had forfeited the idea of marriage or even having a boyfriend because she said her spinster aunt (whom she was living with and looking after) wanted the same kind of solitary life for her. How sad.

I definitely had more fun with Angelina and Lucifera.

If Angelina and I were mallrats, Lucifera and I were dancing queens. Oh yes, Granny Lucy loved shaking her booty! We would regularly hit the clubs in Downtown Mountain View and Downtown Palo Alto. Some of our favorites were Molly Magees and Q Cafe.

Tower Records along San Antonio Road would have a live band once in a while on Friday and Saturday nights and we'd go there, too.

Although I don't see these high strung women with type A personalities anymore-- Angelina have moved on, Lucifera have passed on--they will never be forgotten and it's just appropriate that I include my fun experiences with them in my memoir.

At the dawn of the new millennium, a new me has emerged.

THE YEARS 2000 AND 2001

Y2K? Why worry? Becoming a transsexual is totally free. Just go on with it. I did. The beautiful Swapnil of Fremont was the first to show me appreciation and give me pleasure. He was only 19 but was "well skilled" in the pleasure department. Janet Jackson once sang about it, but my lover Swapnil--or Mike as he preferred to be called-- knew about the pleasure principle from way back when. Oh, the wonders he had done to my *aching* body! We *did* it anywhere and everywhere! The wild hookups also took place in a remote spot of the Niles Canyon area in Fremont, the back parking lot of a church also in the same city, and most common place of all, the backseat of a car.

Mike had the biggest and most beautiful cock, only to be "dethroned" by the handsome Ethan D ten years later. Once in my mouth, it pacified me. For a moment, I forgot about my problems and my stress was gone.

In hindsight, I should really write a revised edition of *The Kama Sutra* after all the kinky and freaky sex Mike and I had.

He would also invite other men to join us in our bedroom fun. Mike loved seeing me "multitask" in the bedroom and was so turned on by the fact that he was sharing me with other men; me giving those men the same pleasure and satisfaction.

Mike was the person responsible for my first meeting with my future "baby boy", Ronnie. We all engaged in a threesome back in the summer of 2005 and the rest is kinky history.

2000 was definitely meant for the books. It was the year of the Summer Olympics in Sydney. Coincidentally, my handsome lover Vince--who is now an attorney in Orange County--and I were ourselves involved in some kind of "floor exercises" in his apartment unit in San Jose, CA. I myself deserve a gold medal for the awesome performance I gave him that one afternoon. Oh, what a summer to remember!

There were subsequent meetings with my handsome friend over the next couple of years.

Sixteen years ago, Vince in an email he had sent, wrote that I gave him what turned out to be the "best blow job" he had ever received. It made me giggle. And I wanted to tell him 'Really? Then why *did* you marry her?'.

On a more serious note, an uncle of mine was dying of cancer around the same time that Vince and I met and I couldn't help but feel sorry for his three young sons, all under the age of ten. It was just awful.

In late December of the same year, as part of my farewell party for the last few remaining days of 2000, I met a handsome Latin guy in Milpitas for what was to be my last fuck of the year. I forgot his name but I'll never forget what we did that evening: had dinner at IHOP, let him hop in my SUV and let him *hop* on me to give me a good humping.

Thanks 2000! It was a lot of fun. Welcome 2001!

I literally welcomed 2001 with a *bang*. The first stud to give me a dose of dick was this James Dean-esque twenty year-old beauty from Fremont, CA named Brian. I met him online through Yahoo Personals. In early January, we decided to meet at the Good Nite Inn in Fremont. We drove in his vintage black 1980s Camaro and there I became his ho. No complaints here. Well, there was one. I wish he didn't come too quickly. But when horny young men are with a super sexy and kinky tranny like me, what would one expect? A very fast and furious *explosion*. Paul Walker, are you watching from way up there, baby?

Prior to meeting Brian that night, I met a younger stud whose name also starts with a B. Brew was a fresh high school graduate and wanted to start fresh when it comes to his sex life. He told me he had just broken up with his girlfriend because apparently, the latter was not ready for intercourse. I guess she was saving herself for the right man. Good for her, and for me as well. I was looking for a "right now" man! Brew wanted to get lucky and I wanted some fresh booty. I guess the stars were aligned perfectly for both of us that night. It wouldn't take long before I was literally seeing stars while Brew was slamming his young eighteen year old body on me, grinding his smooth fat cock inside my needy twenty something pussy. My SUV's windows were all fogged up after my sexcapade with Brew. I then dropped him off near his house and never saw him again after that encounter.

It is also worth noting that the previous year, I met another fresh out of high school stud by the name of Ross. What is up with these high school grads wanting to hook up with a slightly older woman? Instead of entering college they'd prefer to *enter* me.

In May 2001, I reunited with my Latin lover, Jose of Petaluma, at the Golden Gate Bridge. It was a much daring encounter being that we did the deed in the day time. In the previous year, we did it near the Marin Headlands in the evening and in an isolated spot. This time, he parked his Honda Civic in a busy parking lot, but luckily for us that day, because it was during the workweek, there weren't too many cars and people around. Jose's pretty face and cute dimples and the lines "Damn, girl! You suck dick like a champ!" were all that I could remember in that encounter and that was enough. This one's for the books as well.

In the early part of summer 2001, I briefly went back to working at Walgreens. I did, however, quit after a few weeks due to bad work hours and strangely, good hookups of a sexual nature.

I remember one hot August night, I met up with a handsome daddy in his late forties, Mike Warren. We did the nasty in his lifted white pick up truck that night. I can still remember the musty aroma coming from his nice hairy married ass--reeking with pure masculinity.

Ladies, if you want your men to remain faithful to you, learn to please and appreciate that hard working butt! Literally.

I was scheduled to work the graveyard shift that night at Walgreens but ended up oversleeping. The sex I had with Mike earlier that night knocked me out completely. Eventually, I had to quit work. I knew it wasn't going to work out.

Subsequent sex hookups and other raunchy rendezvous at night with an array of lovers and complete strangers prevented me from focusing on work. Sadly, I had to quit my job at Walgreens selling OTC goodies and candies because of my addiction to man candy.

Hey, men love eating pussy and I happen to love cock! "To each his own," the old saying goes.

By September 2001, I met a new lover with the most loveable behind, Mark Baldwin, through Yahoo Personals.

On September 7, four days before the terrorist attacks, Mark and I met at the Days Inn on Lafayette and El Camino Real in Santa Clara, CA. He was the most beautiful thing--a vision. He wore a pair of dark blue Adidas track pants and nothing more. He got me hooked that night. We were passionate lovers until March 2005.

Why my relationship with Mark, although purely sexual, lasted for many years is because of the fact that he helped unleash my wildest fantasies and we both made them happen freely--almost symbiotic--without any restraint or inhibition, without any rules or promises; only the promise to be good lovers to each other. When your lover is that good and that encouraging, chances are he'll be in your mind and in your pussy for a long time.

Once in a while, I'd cruise along that fabled El Camino Real and would have a glimpse of the spot where the Days Inn hotel used to stand. Fleeting images of Mark in his dark blue Addas track pants in contrast to his smooth alabaster white complexion would appear in my mind, triggering an instant smile on my face, almost wicked, but nonetheless sincere. Why? I made Mark orgasm four times that night! I was *devouring* him for a good six hours nonstop. I drove home a little after five in the morning the next day with my lips smiling... and dripping with Mark's lovejuice.

"Girl, you drained me. He he he (pre emoticon era)..." Mark wrote in an email he sent me the following week.

Our late night rendezvous and other sexy hook ups would continue for another four years. They were some of the best years of my sex life. I was in my mid twenties--my prime--and was full of zest and spunk, no pun intended. We did *it* everywhere--hotels all over the Bay Area, in his bedroom and bathroom, in shopping center parking lots, even in front of his house in Belmont, CA. They are *not* the kinds of stories he'd want to tell his son if the latter asks "'What did you like doing when you were young, Dad?"

In the fall of 2001, I was venturing to different counties of the Bay Area and on a visit to Martinez, CA--in Contra Costa County--I met and hooked up with a big and tall handsome twenty two year-old guy named Charles. He had the looks and appeal of a football linebacker. He was "hidde51" on Yahoo Messenger. He resembled one-time NFL aspirant William Bleakley. Despite his large, intimidating frame, he was a gentle giant. I love that. And he was a gentleman in bed, too: Ladies cum first!

We made love in an empty building by an industrial area near the Concord-Martinez border and it was special. He made sure he didn't crush my body as he laid on top of me, periodically asking me "Am I too heavy for you?". I suppose it didn't matter to me anymore. I was getting the most unique and intense kind of pleasure. I told myself "Damn! If I'm gonna die this way with this motherfucker's big ass smothering me, so be it! I'll die a happy bitch!"

ONCE UPON A TIME IN OAKLAND

In Oakland back in December 2001, I hung out with a bunch of cute young black guys in their late teens and early 20s. I met the leader of the pact at a gas station in San Jose a few days prior when he approached me and asked if he could get my number. I was single, sexy and seeking, so I told myself "Why not". A few days later, we decided to meet somewhere along International Boulevard. I picked him up and as soon as he hopped in he asked if we could pick up his friends, too. "Girl, can we pick up my niggas?", he asked. I agreed and after a few minutes my SUV was full of cute black guys chatting, rambling and laughing. It was actually fun because I found it amusing listening to the stuff they were talking about: music, rappers, shoes, girls and booze. Other guys would ask me what kind of work I do, and what kind of stuff I like to do. I remember answering "You're too young for that." The boys would just laugh.

At one point, we had to make a stop at a liquor store because the leader of the pact wanted to get some Hennessy. They shared the bottle and offered me some but I politely declined, advising the boys "Guys, remember, don't drink and drive." "Yes, miss," one of them responded.

After a few more minutes of cruising they asked to be dropped off at the same spot where I picked up the leader of the pact. They all thanked me, hopped out and I never saw them again.

In San Jose, CA in early 2002, I hung out with AOL member Mystic Ganja or Frankie as he was known in the South Bay. He was a twentysomething good looking guy of mixed race who liked smoking pot. I mean, he *loved* smoking pot. It was his life. I don't even think he had a day job. Maybe that was his *life*--pot. I don't know and I never asked. All I know is that whenever we'd chat online he'd talk about pot, or weed, or whatever you call it.

He'd hop in my SUV alone, sometimes with his buddy, to smoke a joint or two, listen to music, and chat for a little bit before heading on our separate ways. No sex. Just talking and smoking. Sometimes, that's all I really needed--someone I can talk to, with just about anything. Even nonsense. It was relaxing for me in some way. That or just listening to another person talk and babble.

I'm a good listener, you know? Talk to me. Tell me anything. Open up! I'm here to listen and I won't interrupt you or judge you. I'll just listen. That is one of my greatest traits. That's also one of the major reasons why I am so attractive to so many people. In me they see that rare quality.

Whenever I hear Taylor Dayne's ""I'll Be Your Shelter" on the radio, those unique experiences would come to mind and strangely, would put a smile on my face. At some point, my Toyota SUV had served as some kind of a shelter---a Tuff Shed on four wheels--for a few misfits out there in the real world. In the interest of helping and understanding others—to be in their shoes—particularly total strangers, albeit strange and somehow risky, I believe I've done my part for the sake of humanity.

Unlike my favorite wrestling superstar, Rowdy Roddy Piper, I know how to keep my big mouth shut, too, and just listen to another. Just listen. Sometimes, that's all some people need--someone who will listen. It's a rare gift.

In Fremont, CA in the mid-2000s, I'd entertain this middle aged gentleman, Randy, who'd get a back rub from me from time to time. He worked for a *wonderful* bread company. He also liked frequenting the thrift store that I'd go to. Once in a while, we'd run into each other and would discreetly say "Hi" and go on with our business.

By 2010, our private meetings have ended, but I'd still run into him at Savers once in a while. The only difference this time was, he'd completely ignore me or look the other way as if he never knew me, or that I didn't exist. But, the intimate things we did--some considered kinky--still *exist* in my mind and they are not going anywhere soon.

I can still clearly recall how he'd have an instant orgasm just by me tying him up like a pig--*luau* style--using my nylon stockings and talking dirty to him while playing with his penis. He gets off that way--by being bossed around in bed and dominated, treated like a pathetic helpless little sissy. He loved getting bitch slapped, too, telling me "Mistress Vanessa, I want more please!" while moaning like a whore high on meth.

Every time I'd pass by the women's section at Savers and have a glimpse of the stockings being sold, I can't help but think what Randy *thinks* every time he sees those things that I used to tie him up with.

GAY RING LEADER

In Campbell, CA back in 2008, an acquaintance, Michael, who occasionally plays the guitar for Carlos Santana, would share funny and fascinating stories about his gigs and the different people--celebrities included--he'd rub elbows with after the show. He once told me about his encounter with some cast members of the blockbuster film *The Lord of the Rings: The Fellowship of the Ring* and how he found out that some of them were gay.

"Vanessa, they're gay! I saw them at the bar and they were flirting with other guys," Michael revealed.

Now, I really don't care about their chosen sexual orientation. It's none of my business first and foremost. This is a free country. You can be who you want to be--a homo Hobbit or gay Gandalf or whatever. It's just amusing to hear such stories about who's sucking who once in a while.

THE THANK YOUS

In my book of life, being thankful and showing appreciation for the everyday blessings and every kind gesture is a must. A short but sincere "Thank You" is actually key to opening doors and windows for new opportunities. No two words could have a more powerful impact and a lasting impression to those in the receiving end.

First and foremost, I thank David, my good friend from Idaho, for his kindness and generosity. He may be gone now but the impact of his kindness is forever etched in my mind.

David and I met online back in 2005. We'd chat on the phone and send emails for a period of time until the opportunity came for him to visit California. It finally happened in February 2006. We had a great time.

For the next nine years we remained good friends and he'd send me sweet little packages of cookies, Hot Wheels toy cars and other gifts. He knew I was so into Hot Wheels!

But more than that, David was an angel sent from above. There was not a single mean bone in him. He liked helping others whenever he could and he loved his grandmother dearly, staying with her and looking after her till the end of her life.

David was my personal confidante. In him, I was able to share my most bothersome problems, worries and cares. He *listened*.

When I was feeling down, he was there to uplift me. When I was feeling sad, his sense of humor cheered me up and helped me forget my problems. When I felt alone, his caring and assuring words gave me comfort and a sense of safety and security. I've never felt so much love and concern.

When he passed away all of a sudden in 2014, I was heartbroken and devastated. But from the shattered pieces of my broken heart came a certain kind of light: it was David's love. It gave me strength to move on and follow my bliss. It lives in me. I am so thankful to have met such a wonderful, one-of-a-kind human being.

I would also like to thank these equally wonderful people--the real perfect strangers--who were there for me in times of desperate need and assistance. The world deserves to know about their outstanding kindness and what it really means to be a "good American".

First, I would like to thank the wonderful elderly white lady at the Macy's parking lot in Sunnyvale, CA back in 1996, who went beyond--and back to her car--just to lend me a wire hanger. I locked myself out of my car and left the keys in the ignition switch. Being that my 1975 Volkswagen Super Beetle had manual door locks, I had to find some creative way to pull it up.

When I saw this elderly white woman walking towards Macy's, I flagged her down and told her what had happened and asked if she had something in her car that I could use to pull up the door lock in my car. Luckily, I managed to leave a tiny opening in my car window.

The elderly lady and I walked back to her car, looked in the backseat for something that I could use and *voila*! There was a wire hanger lying somewhere! "Here, maybe this will help," she said.

I twisted the top part of the wire hanger and made a small knot out of its tip and very gently aimed at the car lock's tip and to my amazement and relief, it worked.

I reshaped the hanger back in its original form and handed it back to the elderly woman and gave her my most sincere and heartfelt "Thank You".

"You're an angel," I told her. She smiled and walked towards the department store.

So, you see, Joan Crawford, wire hangers have an important purpose! They are not for hitting children!

Next on my Thank You list is this twenty something white guy by the payphone outside Tower Records in Mountain View, CA. Sometime in August 1997, my Karmann Ghia had stalled in the middle of the parking lot outside Tower Records and as I started to push it to the side, this nice young man on the payphone abruptly put the phone down, walked towards me and helped me push my car to a corner. I said "Thank you very much! Sorry I interrupted your phone call."

"Nah, it's okay. Take care," he said.

Related to this Karmann Ghia incident is that of a very nice and helpful Mountain View, CA Denny's restaurant employee.

Instead of calling a friend or relative on their home telephone or cellular phone (which was considered a luxury back then), I decided to call the Denny's restaurant manager for assistance. At the time, I did not have AAA roadside assistance coverage. I was only twenty and did not think about such things which now that I am in my forties, I consider an everyday necessity like food and water. Having a AAA Roadside Membership is so worth it!

So, I used the few remaining coins in my pocket on the same payphone the nice young man was using earlier to call Denny's, hoping to speak with the lady who works the cash register whenever me and my friend Lucy would visit. I was taking a chance, big time. Fortunately, it was my lucky day. She answered and I introduced myself, telling her I am a regular customer and that she would be the one helping us and serving our food whenever I'm there. I told her my situation and she was understanding and helpful enough to dial Lucy's landline for me. I gave her my location so she could relay the information to Lucy.

One smart move I made during this critical moment was the decision to call Denny's instead of Lucy's cell phone directly. People are busy or they're asleep or doing something else and therefore unable to get to the phone all the time. Not a 24 hour Denny's restaurant! I know 110% that someone *will* pick up the phone on my first attempt. The fact that I did not have enough coins to make two phone calls was a deciding factor as well. Luckily, the nice Denny's manager was able to get a hold of Lucy's husband, Jeffrey, and twenty minutes after I hung up, Lucy arrived outside Tower Records.

Sadly, on my next visit to that particular Denny's, a new employee was manning the register and she had no idea what happened to the kind lady who helped me.

That Denny's off of Moffett Field has since closed. Wherever you are dear, kind, classy lady, you are a lifesaver and I owe you a lot.

I bow to you and may God bless you with a long, happy life. I hope that one day, on one of my visits to a Denny's somewhere, we'll meet again. Thank you!

I would also like to make a special mention of Denny's Santa Clara employee, Leslie, and thank her for her kind, understanding heart during those times when I was struggling financially and did not have enough money to pay for my restaurant bill. I am forever grateful to her unique act of generosity when she'd charge me less for the actual price of my meal. This was in the early 2000s. Money was tough then and whenever I'd go to Denny's to hang out a little bit and grab a bite to eat, Leslie and I would have short but meaningful chats. I'd tell her about my situation and she'd patiently stand there by my table for a few minutes and listen. Later on, when she'd hand me my bill, she'd whisper in my ear that she only charged me $3 for my Grand Slam meal; my drink--Raspberry iced tea being my favorite--would be "on the house."

Leslie, wherever you are now, I hope you are reading my book and if I ever see you again, I'd like to take you and your family out to dinner, to a restaurant of your choice, just to let you know I appreciate what you did for me many years ago. Thank you!

I really believe that angels aren't only found in that popular TV series from the '70s; they are also found at Denny's!

MANILA MOMENTS (A CHRONOLOGY)

I could never ever repeat these moments nor do I think they will ever happen again. The people involved--friends, relatives, school mates, neighbors and perfect strangers--have moved on, moved away, passed on or I simply don't know where they are now. But, the memories live on. I close my eyes and reminisce. Some events make me smile, some make me cry and some I wish never happened at all.

The 1980s and early '90s

1) 1980: My very first peek at a porno mag, with lots of good looking, hung naked men.

2) 1980: My Grandmother beat up her underage niece after she eloped with a man that my grandparents did not like. My Uncle Manny, who was visiting the Philippines from the US at the time, stood by and watched.

3) 1982: Unforgettable songs, "The One That You Love" by Air Supply and "Tell Me" by Filipino singer Joey Albert.

4) My Dad would surprise me with a *Matchbox* toy car once in a while. My parents didn't have a lot of money back then, so I considered it a luxury.

5) Cosmos: The best Chinese restaurant in the Ongpin district of Manila. I love their special *pancit*.

6) 1983: My Uncle Mario's estranged wife--Cynthia--instructing her sister to grab Marvin, my cousin, and "discipline" him after he threw a bottle at her during our visit to La Tondena Distilleria.

7) 1983: My Grandma telling my Uncle Mario to "discipline" Marvin after he had just thrown a bottle at her. Uncle Mario chases Marvin upstairs with a *walis tambo* (broom) in hand.

8) My Grandma asked me to dance in front of her and her cousin, Leandra or "Lola Andra", along with another *amiga*, Kumareng Leony. I slipped and fell on my butt and they all burst into laughter.

9) 1983: My Grandma put a yellow chiffon dress on me and asked me to twirl like a ballerina. I happily obliged.

10) I remember our maid, Brenda, a nice young woman from the province of Masbate.

11) My Grandma took me to see the blockbuster movie *Ang Panday* starring veteran Filipino actor Fernando Poe Jr., widely considered as the "King of Philippine Movies".

12) 1984: I remember our maids, Esther and Lorna. Lorna was accused of theft by my Grandmother. Allegedly, she got caught stealing some of my Grandmother's makeup products from the US. She was immediately fired.

13) 1985: "Careless Whisper" by Wham! gets major airplay in the Philippines. I mean, don't you just love the saxophone part in that song? Iconic.

14) The cartoon series *Rainbow Brite*: Indigo was my favorite.

15) 1986: Waking up very early in the morning and heading to my childhood friend Didit's house to play with her and her Barbie doll.

16) Watching Japan-bound dancers train and rehearse at the Garcia Dance Studio near my house; with songs "Rico Mambo", "Body Dancer" and some dance hit with the lyrics "sose ne bebe" playing all the time.

17) I remember my cute neighbors Levi, Julius and Allen, as well as brothers Reggie and Roderick.

18) 1986-1987: Playing with the caterpillars on the terrace at my grandparents' house as soon as I got home from school. It was filled with beautiful plants and flowers (roses and sampaguita); then watching cartoon shows *Thundercats* and *Duck Tales* afterwards.

19) A relative beating up his wife and later on throwing their TV set from the second floor of their rented apartment, out of spite.

20) 1987: A relative would carve Disney characters out of styropor material (carve and apply color) and would sell them to whoever might be interested. Very creative!

21) Three Sisters stationery store along Juan Luna St. selling the cutest little things: note pads, colorful pens, scented paper and stationery, Hello Kitty and other Sanrio merchandise, etc.

22) 1988: Mabuhay Playground Dance-a-thon.

23) Weekend pa-*merienda* (organized by the Garcia siblings).

24) My first taste of *sangria*.

25) Hanging out with some friends in the Mabuhay Playground one night. The teasing begins.

26) Richard, my grandfather's first cousin, walked into our living room one evening unannounced, crying and ranting about something, obviously inebriated, making his case to my grandfather (who promptly told him to go home and rest and settle his issues with his wife when he's back to his normal self).

27) 1989: Hanging out with the Brolio Sisters.

28) The elder Brolio sister, Mary Ann, cussing out Jinny Rose (adopted child of the Brolio relative, Roza): *"Jinny Rose, animales ka!"* ("You animal!"); cracks me up everytime I'd recall how Mary Ann was *not* too fond of the newest member of their family.

29) Mayleen Brolio feeding me hamburgers from Burger Machine while she meets up with a boyfriend. A "bribe" of some sort, so I wouldn't squeal. Her parents had strongly disapproved of her having a boyfriend, They were grooming her to become a nun.

30) My very first *Penshoppe* T-shirt, in soft mint green shade. I love it.

31) Tiffany's album cover is on display in every major "record bar" (store) in Manila; she's wearing a white top and had large hoop earrings on, and, of course, her gorgeous red hair. Iconic!

32) Mid-1989: My cousin Marvin gave me my first cigarette and later, my first taste of *gamot*, or cough syrup.

33) My cousin Marvin cussed out my Grandmother after she refused to give him money.

34) Marvin's friends--including Christian--having sleepovers in my grandparents house. I would join them sometimes. They'd be talking about girls and pussies and be watching porno movies.

35) 1989 hit songs: "Promise Me", "How Can I Fall" and "Hands to Heaven". While Christian and I would make out.

36) A photo session with relatives Marvic, Edwin and Azon outside my parents' house.

37) Hanging out with an older lady friend, Nessy Evora.

38) Hanging out with Ana, Nang-Nang, Rochelle and Alona, my girl friends from childhood.

39) My unique friendship with Nestor "Ron Ron" Balattas, who was straight. I felt we had a connection. He was nice and respectful.

40) My friend, Ana, ran away from my classmate, Raymond, when I introduced the two to each other. I was in stitches. He was *not* her type!

41) Hanging out with other girls from the neighborhood and inviting them to my parents' house and how my grandfather found out about it, made a surprise visit and scolded me; while the girls were hiding in different rooms. So funny.

42) Me cussing out Jinny Rose from my living room window when she started mocking my singing of "Poor Unfortunate Souls" by Ursula in the presence of my good friend, Joverni. JR was hanging outside my house, playing with other kids, but she apparently heard me imitating Ursula and decided to pause for a moment and express her unsolicited *critique*. When she heard my "rebuttal" she wasn't able to utter a single word and never ever spoke to me again nor did she make eye contact whenever we'd cross paths with each other. JR was a bitch even from a very young age. But, I was a bigger bitch. I made sure she *got* that.

43) *Palaisdaan* (swimming pool resort) visits back in 1988 (with relatives Boy and Carol Martin along with their 3 kids), 1989 (with Mabuhay Playground folks) and 1991 (with high school friends, and meeting good looking Tau Gamma Fraternity members).

44) Neighbor Grace Tomson revealed that she had a major crush on my cousin Marvin. She even wrote him a letter. She once confessed that she wrote his name on a piece of paper and put it under her pillow before she went to bed.

45) Did an impromptu dance at the Aryola residence in front of Rowena A. and Grace Tomson. Rowena seemed very surprised, but just gave me a smile.

46) Watching Madonna perform "Express Yourself" live at the 1989 MTV Awards; a rainy night in the Philippines. I had an epiphany: I would become a very good dancer. From that point on, I wanted to dance, dance, dance.

47) 1989: Participating in the religious ritual *Akyat ng Birhen* (The Virgin Mary's Visit); my friend Ana singing Karyn White's "Superwoman" instead of reciting the sacred prayer. Aling Nena, the octogenarian homeowner, a *catolico cerrado* (devout Catholic), giving her a dirty look. So funny.

48) The same religious ritual, this time at my parents' house. Although not required, hosts would normally provide some snacks or *merienda* after the service. My Mom bought 2 boxes of pizza. As soon as the service was over, the guests or participants--mostly young people from poor and impoverished families in our neighborhood--

-converged around the two boxes of pizza and consumed them in less than a minute. I don't even remember getting a slice for myself, but I didn't care. They were meant for the hungry.

49) My grandparents and I would drive to San Ildefonso, Bulacan (a province north of Manila that is steeped in history) to visit a relative, Lola Amor, and how the latter would prepare a sumptuous *handa*: some of the best Tagalog dishes like *sinampalukang manok* and *inihaw na dalag at buro*, and carabao milk or *gatas ng kalabaw*, over white rice. Makes my mouth water every time I think about it.

50) I remember my nice Chinese neighbor, a quiet gentleman and his Filipino wife, Aling Viring, and their three daughters, Emily, Evangeline and Elsie, who were very nice and friendly to me. The father was a traveling businessman and whenever he'd come home he'd give the kids in the neighborhood small presents of all sorts. I wish them well, wherever they are. They were actually tenants of my Grandmother. My grandparents used to rent out two medium sized living quarters within our compound.

51) I remember accompanying my Grandmother to Meycauayan (outside Manila) to collect rent payment–she owns an apartment complex in that town. My Grandmother and I would have *merienda* (mid afternoon meal) at the nearby *panciteria* (noodle house) afterwards. You won't believe the ridiculous excuses some tenants would come up with just to skip payment or not pay at all! Some could even pass an audition or screen test for a dramatic role!

52) 1990: Me playing messenger between my paternal cousin, Marvin, and my maternal cousin, Esang. They were both madly in love with each other. At one point, I had to personally pick up a love letter that Esang wrote and hand it to Marvin.

53) March 1990: A family trip to Baguio, the "Summer Capital of the Philippines".

54) July 1990: A massive 7.8 magnitude earthquake hit the northern part of the Philippines. My Grandmother and I were at the town market at the time. Such a terrifying experience. Did major damage in Baguio, the "Summer Capital of the Philippines".

55) After doing the *pamamalengke*, or trip to the market to buy food and other goods, my Grandmother would treat me to a *merienda* at one of the food stalls within the market. We'd have *lugaw* or *palabok* and the delicious *ginatan halo halo*.

56) My grandparents and I would have early morning breakfast--*lugaw* and *siopao*--at the popular Chinese restaurant Ling Nam on Ongpin Street in Manila.

57) A dead relative's wake, 1990: Cousin Esang, daughter of the deceased, teasing another relative, Arleen, telling her "*Uy, dalaga na si Arleen*" ("You're a teenage girl now, Arleen"; suggesting that she's reached sexual maturity).

58) Tess, Cousin Marvin's wife at the time, invited a gay friend over who then gave us an impromptu dance performance to the tune of Bonnie Tyler's "Faster Than the Speed of Light". I loved it. Decades before the stars of *POSE* came on the scene, that gay guy was *owning* it!

59) On my way to purchase a SwingOut Sister cassette tape: walked along Tayuman St. to reach the LRT (Light Rail Transit) station, hopped on the train and got out in front of a department store called UNIWIDE. I was barely a teenager, but I knew my way around, walking mile after mile.

60) November 1990: Brought a bunch of high school classmates--mostly female-- back home to join in on my grandfather's 59th birthday party. It was a grand affair. The girls enjoyed the *lechon* and spaghetti. We had beer, too.

61) Tess, Cousin Marvin's wife at the time, did all kinds of jumping and leaping while pregnant and when I asked her why she confessed she didn't want to have that child. Thankfully, the baby came out fine.

62) 1991, Gagalangin, Tondo: Religious routine--Sunday mass and coffee and donuts afterwards at Dunkin Donuts.

63) 1991: Early evening "rampa" (evening walk) with Tess and another relative, Orra, on neighborhood streets S. Trinidad, Raxabago and Clemente.

64) 1991 fashion trends in the Philippines: "Preggy Look" dresses and tops; the "Demi Moore" bob cut (from *Ghost*).

65) 1991: Lunchtime melodies (songs regularly played on Philippine radio): "Mr. Lonely", "Unchained Melody", "From A Distance", "*Sasasaddami*", "*Humanap Ka Ng Panget*" and the number one dance hit "Wiggle It".

66) Cyndi Lauper at the 1991 Grammy Awards: "Oh my god! It's Living Color!". Did an imitation of that the following day at school to the amusement of my classmates, especially Lulette.

67) 1991: My *yoyoy* (grandfather) caught me doing an impromptu "runway show" in our living room. The whole time I thought he was in bed already. I wore a

pair of long palazzo pants (that I pulled out from my Grandmother's leftover merchandise stock from the 1970s, when she used to run a clothing store) and wrapped a chartreuse colored table runner around my head as a turban. I strutted like supermodel Linda Evangelista.

68) At the movies, 1991: My friend Joverni and I saw the following movies: *Naughty Boys*, *Nightbreed* and *The Secrets of Pura*.

69) 1991: Cousin Marvin and Cousin Esang talking in my parents' living room as Tess, Marvin's wife, passed by outside; completely clueless when it came to Marvin's whereabouts and what was *going* on. Marvin, only 16 when he got married, was still very young and at the peak of his youth; still very "adventurous" when it comes to girls.

70) 1991: My grandfather's aunt, Purita Barrientos, or "Lola Purita" as I would call her, passed by in front of my parents' house as I peeked through the window. She was the original *mestiza* (fair skinned, with classic Spanish features). She was visiting the Philippines from Canada at the time where she and her husband, Timoteo or "Tio Titong", were based. Lola Purita was very *posturyosa*, or well dressed; and not a single hair out of place.

71) My grandparents abruptly got up from the dinner table and left the birthday party honoring Lola Purita Barrientos, my grandfather's aunt. Apparently, my grandfather felt disgusted by the sleazy dance performance of the scantily clad daughters-in-law of his uncle, Kom Peping. That "Conga" number was part of the program.

72) My grandfather threw his thick slippers at a relative who was chasing his wife to beat her up. The wife burst into our living room one night while we were sleeping, screaming for help, begging for my grandfather to intervene. Crazy scene.

73) 1991: A sleepover at a relative's house in Mabuhay Playground. My grandfather, who probably heard about it, sat and waited outside another relative's house not far from where I was staying. He was probably waiting for me to come out. I did not. I waited until he decided to leave. I've been a Taurus from early on--patience and *waiting* are my fortes.

74) Played The Bangles' *Different Light* CD on the afternoon that Christian flew to the United States, in late 1991.

75) My friends and I visited Marlyn Mora at her aunt's house in Caloocan City where we found her good looking cousin, Alain, sleeping on the couch with only his white briefs on.

76) Marlyn Mora's birthday party at their rented apartment unit in Blumentritt, Manila. Awesome music (Tone Loc's "Wild Thang" and C&C Music Factory's "Gonna Make You Sweat" stood out).

77) Harrison Plaza, Manila, 1991: Where I purchased my Karyn White cassette tape, *Romantic*.

78) December 1991: The wedding of Uncle Tony to his fiancee. A minor controversy, a *faux pas* of some sort: My Grandmother did not like the bride's relatives taking home the entire wedding cake; when the wedding guests haven't even left yet. She found it tacky.

79) Itzel Gaviola's birthday party, 1992.

80) My May 1992 birthday treat for my friends Joverni, Neptune, Kathy and Cecille: we all went to see a movie at SM Centerpoint and ate at Jollibee afterwards.

81) Classmate and friend, Lulette, invited me back to her place to have lunch. Her mom cooked pork *sinigang* for us. Yummy! It's Lulette's favorite dish. She and her family were in the "Magbobote" business (bottle recycling).

82) 1992: Worked for the ADC (Airmail Distribution Center) as part of the Philippine government's Summer Youth Program. I loved it.

83) Attending two grand 50th wedding anniversary celebrations with my grandparents: The old Fernandez couple and that of my Grandmother's cousin, Lola Lucing and her husband, Shahong Vino.

84) Became the sort of "bridge" or messenger in helping a relative, Tita Edna, move into my grandparents' compound when she and her family fell on hard times and got kicked out by their landlord for non-payment. I was only 12 and made the case to my Grandmother who later gave her approval.

85) Went to see *The Crying Game* by myself, at the SM North Edsa Cinema. Love the theme song!

86) Went to see *Chaplin* a month later, at the same place, with classmates Obey Domingo, Cecilia Uy and others.

87) Visited my maternal great grandmother, Fausta, in Pajo. She was staying at my aunt's house at the time. It was my last face to face meeting with the octogenarian

lady from the northern province of Pangasinan. She passed away seven years later, when I was already living in the US.

88) January 1993: The beginning of my close friendship with Bobby. He'd regularly invite me to his place to do whatever, mostly watch movies and play video games. He'd also show me his collection of Swatch watches.

89) March 1993; Graduated from high school.

90) Kuya Edgar, my Dad's first cousin, taught me how to drive. I was 15 years old.

91) May 1993: Edith Simbiling, my Grandmother's niece, and her family, moved into my grandparents' house after losing all their possessions--including their house--to creditors. Crazy times. All of a sudden, the house felt like a dormitory. Every room was occupied, not by one person, but 2 or 3 sometimes, considering the number of family members Edith had (5 children and her husband).

92) Spin Doctors' "Two Princes" playing on the radio as people were moving stuff in.

93) August 1993: My regular gallivanting at the mall and other shopping centers: Robinson's Galleria, SM Megamall, Isetann Recto. At Robinson's Galleria, I came across celebrities like Ian Veneracion, Helen Gamboa, Ella Mae Saison, Tweety De Leon and Abby Viduya.

94) Tess, Cousin Marvin's wife, ran away with their two year old son, Marco. She wanted a legal separation from Marvin. My grandparents fought for legal custody of the child on behalf of Marvin; taking Tess to court. It was a very stressful time for the family.

95) Participated in *Gift Gate's* Dress A Troll contest. I had a wedding gown custom made for my Troll doll *a`la* Princess Diana. My seamstress neighbor, Aling Chedeng, made the dress. My friend Bobby joined, too. Former high school classmate, Gen C, was one of the judges. Bitch didn't pick my Troll.

96) Went to see the *Ang TV Concert* at the Folk Arts Theater. Came across Erica Fife, said "Hi" to her and she smiled and said "Hi" back. I drove myself to the venue. I was 16 years old.

97) Cutie Rameel Ballot hanging out with my cousin Marvin and his friends.

98) 1993 FEU (Far Eastern University) Days: My friends--Gina, Dan, Lissy--very nice people—accepted me for who I am and welcomed me to their *clique*. Handsome student with the last name Espinoza would always sit next to me so I could take a whiff of his cologne--*Eternity* by Calvin Klein. Weird, but I loved it. He looked

so good and smelled really good. Crossed paths with a relative, Jonjon Barrientos. Hit songs of the day: "One Last Cry" by Brian McKnight, "The Right Kind of Love" by Jeremy Jordan and "I'll Never Get Over You (Getting Over Me)" by Expose, plus the remake of a song called "Zoom".

99) More FEU memories: Pinky Pop restaurant; a bookstore across the street where I bought a book about Prince Charles and two magazines (French *Elle* with an article on Collette and *Cosmopolitan*, with Karen Mulder on the cover). A Jesus del Pozo *Duende* perfume ad also included in the French *Elle* magazine.

100) October 1993: Beloved relative, Lola Amor, passed away. Attended her funeral with my Grandmother and my grandfather's aunts, Lola Puring and Lola Purita Barrientos.

101) December 1993: Received a phone call from Cousin Marvin's estranged wife, Tess, telling me she wanted to make peace with the Mateo family. Marco, Marvin's two year old son who at the time was in Tess's custody, spoke to me briefly on the phone. I cried.

102) Feast of the *Kambal Na Krus*, March 1994: Had some friends over--Bobby, Joverni and Joverni's neighbors. Their visit was captured on video by my cousin, Marvin, using his Sony video camcorder. I remember the church band, or *mosiko*, who would be part of the parade, performing 4 Non Blondes' "What's Up" in front of our house. So cool. My friends and I watched them play from the balcony of my grandparents' house. It was the last time I saw Joverni before I flew to the US.

103) April 1994: My grandfather dies all of sudden from a heart attack. Very traumatic and devastating for me, as I was the first one to hear his cries and come to his aid. We were able to rush him to the hospital but it was too late.

104) June 1994: The television broadcast of *The Three Tenors* concert. My Grandmother and I watched. She liked Placido Domingo's voice better than the rest. An aging Frank Sinatra in the house.

105) "Selfish" by The Other Two dance remix was a major hit in the Philippines. I love it. The dance group Streetboys would perform it on local TV shows and I'd be all over the television set. They were so cute!

106) July 1994: Purchased my very first pair of Guess? jeans at Robinson's Galleria in Ortigas; with the image of Anna Nicole Smith on the shopping bag. She is so gorgeous! The store even gave me a complimentary mini telephone/address book

which is still in my possession--twenty seven years later. Smith would visit the Philippines that same year during a worldwide promotional tour; was interviewed by Filipino celebrity and comedian, Jon Santos.

107) August 1994, A Farewell Duet: A couple of weeks before I flew to the US, my gay friend, Neptune, paid me a visit. Before he left, we sang "Let Me Be Your Wings" from *Thumbelina*. It was the last time I saw him in person. Nowadays, I'd see him on Facebook. He seemed to have been living as a "straight" male these days.

HIGH SCHOOL LIFE IN THE PHILIPPINES

It's not really the high school *life* that I treasure but the memories rather: the things I did and the things I did with my close friends, Joverni, Bobby and Neptune as well as classmates who I got along well with. There's also the crushes I had and, of course, the mischief.

I feel sorry sometimes for the high school kids these days in America--there's the home schooling due to the pandemic and all those crazy school shootings and massacres. I'm just thankful for the fact that I *never* had to deal with any of that shit back in my high school years both in the US and in the Philippines. Life was relatively simple, peaceful and normal back then.

The only worries I had back in high school were being called by my mean teachers to answer a question and…my zits. Not to get shot at by some deranged loser with a semi automatic rifle!

No, I do not miss my teachers! They were strict, conniving and mean. My PE teacher even gave me a failing grade just because my Mom had confronted his wife--who is a Religion teacher--about the urgency of participating in an out of town religious excursion commonly known as a Retreat. Apparently, that Religion teacher did not appreciate my Mom's being inquisitive and straightforward about the matter, thus falling victim to the classic retaliatory tactic that Filipinos are notorious for. The Religion teacher probably informed her husband about the encounter, so when the school report card came out at the end of the semester, I got an F in his class despite my regular attendance and class participation. It was so cruel and unfair--and traumatizing.

One would think that school teachers in a religious institution like a Catholic school run by nuns would practice empathy and compassion. Apparently, it's the opposite. My advice to Filipino parents in the Philippines: Enroll your kids in regular public schools.

It's the same thing! It doesn't make a difference whether or not your kids would get better treatment or education. It's the same thing! If the teacher is evil, you can't win anyway. If the teacher decides to maliciously give your child a failing grade just because, then at least you'll have that feeling of consolation that you didn't have to pay a ton of money to enroll him or her in a private school.

As for me, the only consolation I had was meeting and knowing some very nice people, like my best friend Bobby and not so serious teachers like Carina Guerra. Carina Guerra or "Mrs. Guerra" was my Social Studies teacher. She was cool. She had a sense of humor. I like that. She was not the traditional stiff and strict type of a teacher. She died a few years ago. I wish I was there (in the Philippines) to attend her funeral and pay my last respects. But, she will always be in my prayers.

Once, she told me she saw me and an older woman in Pritil (town market) and asked who that person was. I told her it was my Grandmother. "*Ako po ang lagi nyang kasamang mamalengke,*" I explained. ("I accompany her whenever she goes to the market to buy food and other goods.")

Mrs. Guerra had the "human touch". She was not all teacher business. She set her limits alright, but when she disciplined her students she did not act like a Nazi general. She joked around with her students.

Another teacher I liked was Mrs. Manalang. She was cool, too. Once, she caught me using her last name so I could sell raffle tickets for my younger cousin who, coincidentally, had the same last name. When she confronted me about it, I apologized and told her I was only doing it to help my cousin earn some points for a prize raffle at her school. In the end, she said yes.

Music was a major curriculum in my school, St. Joseph's. I once participated in the church choir, but oftentimes I would be asked to sing a song during school parties and other festivities. I remember my Religion teacher from my freshman year, a nun, asking me to sing a song. I did. I sang The Bangles' "Eternal Flame". On a separate occasion, my English teacher who was gay, asked me to sing, too. I chose James Taylor's "You've Got a Friend" for that particular occasion. It turned out we weren't meant to be friends, nor was he ever a friendly person. He was friendly with the good looking male students alright, but not towards me. He was a bitch. He probably saw in my future that I will be a guy magnet and that the only person who he will end up in bed with was himself.

March signals the end of the school year in the Philippines. Around that time, my friends and I would have a weekend getaway of some sort in provinces not too far from Manila: Bulacan and Pampanga. Being that we didn't have a lot of money back then, we would economize our expenses and *improvise*. During one of these trips, me and my friend, Joverni, went to a nearby pond to catch fish. We then looked for a kamias tree because kamias would give the *sinigang* the traditional sour flavor that is most sought after in that particular dish. We found one. Luckily, we also found some tomatoes not too far from the pond. Back in our vacation pad, I started washing and cleaning the ingredients and Joverni started cooking. After some twenty minutes, *voila*! Lunch! For our lodging, we were fortunate enough to have my classmate's relative lend us a couple of rooms for the night, free of charge, provided that we clean up after ourselves.

In December 1992, I ended up acing the school-wide Spelling Bee competition and was lucky enough to represent my school at the Regional Spelling Bee competition along with two other Josephians, Juan Allan and Manoel. We competed with other students from other schools in Manila. We ended up in second place.

I clearly remember handsome classmates, Christofer and Jovanz, along with other good looking school mates, Ferdie and Jerikko, doing a dance number to the tune of "How Gee" during the contest's Intermission.

Christofer, a member of the prominent Cruz clan in Tondo, was a very good looking *mestizo*. He and his friend, Jovanz, with *moreno* (brown complexion) good looks, along with Tau Gamma fraternity brothers, Jerikko and Edson, were the school heartthrobs of the day. They were quite a tease, too, if they chose. One time during class, when our teacher had stepped out for a minute, Jovanz and Christofer pulled my chair closer to them only to give me an impromptu come hither gaze; puckering, biting and licking their lips as if they were showing their *libog* (lust). It was such a total turn on.

Christofer lived not too far from St. Joseph School and the small street leading to his house was actually visible from my classroom window. He had a very good looking older cousin named Boyett who'd park his car out by the street. Occasionally, Boyett would wash his car wearing white tank top and a pair of cargo shorts. He was a vision: tall, fair skinned with *mestizo* good looks and a nice build. He was the original "sexy daddy" for me. He had a striking resemblance to American singer Kenny Loggins. It was a treat to catch a glimpse of him. Sometimes I really didn't care about the classes. I just wanted to see sexy daddy Boyett. It made my day.

Lakwatsa or gallivanting during school hours, has always been part of high school life. You've never really *experienced* high school unless you did the *lakwatsa*. Whether it's near the school or at a mall somewhere, a high school student should at least try it once. It's a coming of age ritual in high school. I loved doing the *lakwatsa*. My favorite destinations were Gotesco Grand Central, SM North Edsa and the back alleys of my high school.

In late 1992, my friends Majo and Neptune and I ditched school early so we could see *Bram Stoker's Dracula* at the theaters. I had a major crush on Keanu Reeves. After seeing him in *My Own Private Idaho*, I got hooked.

Aling Ne's *carinderia* located in an alley near my school was also a favorite spot. I've been a food lover all my life and I couldn't get enough of the *merienda* that Aling Ne sells, mainly *lugaw*, *tokwat baboy* and *palabok*. At one point, I had to ditch class just to get something to eat and unfortunately got caught red handed by my teacher, Ms. Deecho. I just ignored her and walked back towards the school.

I had a prideful habit of ignoring teacher scoldings and berating and just walking away as if I didn't hear a word they said. I knew myself and my self *worth* from early on. I am *a* Mateo for crying out loud! I don't submit to other people's rules easily or fall for their bullshit.

One time during my P.E. class at MVHS, my teacher kept insisting that I do more push ups; that the push ups I was doing weren't enough. To piss her off some more, I got up, gave her the "Fuck you!" look and just walked away. Call it arrogance, but for me, it's just my simple way of making a statement; to let them know that you can *not* play Major Payne on me. I've set my own rules in life from early on. I never let anyone dictate how things are going to be for me or what I must or mustn't do.

MOUNTAIN VIEW MEMORIES

Mountain View, CA was the place I truly called home as soon as my family and I arrived in the US. Before the advent of Google, Mountain View was a fairly unknown, quiet suburb of the San Francisco Bay Area, with its mom and pop shops and family run cafes and restaurants. People would ask me, "Where is Mountain View?". Nowadays, it's in every tourist's destination list.

Amazing how Mountain View has evolved and developed: condo complexes and restaurants and other businesses started popping up like mushrooms left and right. The streets had gotten busier, too. You couldn't even jaywalk on El Camino Real anymore like I used to back in the early `90s.

On my last visit to downtown in May 2021, while having lunch *al fresco* with my Mom, I couldn't help but notice how the atmosphere had changed. It's just so damn busy!

"This is not the Mountain View that I know," I told my Mom. "Too many people. I hate it. It's lost its homely feel."

What irks me is the attitude of some. They were acting like "This is my town. I pay a sky high amount for my rent! So, I'm going to have an attitude whether you like it or not."

I could just smack people in the face and tell them to shut up. I'd tell these nomads "Bitch, Downtown Mountain View was my backyard when you were still getting laid in the backseat of your Pinto with your legs way up in the sky, so high that God peeked through the clouds to tell you 'Bitch, stop poking my balls!'."

I love my Mountain View circa the 1990s. Downtown Mountain View was just a stone's throw from my apartment. It literally became my front yard. Some afternoons after getting home from school, I'd step out of my apartment complex for a little bit to get some fresh air, walk a couple of blocks and *voila*! I'm in my most favorite downtown in America. I gave Downtown Mountain View lots of business from early on.

A nice Mexican-American lady, Connie, used to run a barber shop there with photographs of Cesar Chavez and other icons in Mexican culture hanging on the wall. She'd cut my hair, we'd have some short but meaningful chats and it felt like you were dealing with family, not a strange acting, robotic, non-English speaking entity.

Crystal, the Asian-American lady who ran a small store that sold all kinds of stuff from jewelry to home decor by Villa St., became a friend. She'd call my number to inform me in advance that she was having a sale at her store; that way I'd be able to pick up stuff that I like way ahead of the other customers. It was like Bergdorf shutting down for an hour just so Britney Spears could have the store *all* to herself.

Bookbuyers Printers Inc., now replaced by some boring bookstore, was a Downtown Mountain View landmark. The amount of good, vintage, old books you'd find there I don't think I'd find in any other bookstore. Their vast collection of books including monster size coffee table books and vintage magazines was impressive.

Ninety percent of my coffee table books and other kinds of books and biographies were purchased from Bookbuyers. I am so glad I did it before it closed down abruptly a few years ago--a casualty of sky high rent prices and most likely, easy access to various kinds of information through the internet. People simply weren't buying books anymore like they used to.

Ross, my favorite department store by San Antonio Road, also closed down. I was shocked one afternoon in 2018 to see an apartment building standing on the spot where it used to be. It was a WTF moment. Who are these people? Ruthless landlords and foreign nomads invading my city!

Now I am able to piece together the puzzle of what I call "21st century exodus"--friends and ex lovers who have moved out of California in search of a better, quieter and not so chaotic place to live in--that took place a few years ago. At first, I was like "What the fuck is going on? My white friends are moving out of California?"

That one drive to Mountain View in 2018 and my most recent visit in May 2021 explained it all.

But, as the saying goes, "We have to go with the flow."

We are well into the first quarter of the 21st century. These are modern times. Times are changing. Change means starting fresh. New buildings, towers and other structures symbolize adherence and adapting to change. If it works for my most beloved city in California and it states "We are up to par with the other best cities in America", then so be it.

Now that Mountain View's structural dynamics have changed, so does the interaction among its people or lack thereof. With the advent of the work-from-home system meant less face to face meetings and almost non existent human interaction; unless you work for Google. I heard there's an entire community in their compound.

Back in the day, there was a completely different kind of vibe and it was a positive one. You know your neighbors--you say "Hi" and "Hello" or "How are you?" and they'd respond graciously, with a smile. People were *paying* attention to each other, not their iPhones. People smiled at each other, not giving you a blank stare.

Also along Downtown Mountain View was a Chinese restaurant, whose owner--a friend of Crystal--would give me and my Mom complimentary dishes whenever we'd visit. It just shows you that some business owners will treat you not as a customer, but a friend or family rather--in the *old* Mountain View that I know. I miss that, but I am happy that I got to experience that before this Me!-Me!-Me! Generation took over.

Mountain View's facade and foot traffic might have changed significantly, with all the unrecognizable buildings and the influx of new residents but in my heart, these precious memories will remain for as long as I'm around.

1) Late 1994: Weekend family bonding time in our apartment unit along Ehrhorn Ave: Dad would be watching football while my siblings played with their dolls in the living room and Mom was making the sumptuous beef *nilaga* (beef broth with vegetables). I would be in my room watching an episode of *Style with Elsa Klensch*.

2) A *Cosmopolitan* magazine ad featuring a male model with chiseled good looks and a muscular body--and the smoothest armpits. This signaled the beginning of my *magazine* collection.

3) Fall 1994: Made it a habit to walk along Downtown Mountain View; familiarizing myself with the stores, places to eat, etc.

4) During one of these afternoon walks I crossed paths with my Dad--who was a mail carrier for the city of Mountain View--on Church Street. I waved and smiled at him. My Dad really worked hard for his family and for their welfare and the betterment of their lives. I miss him so much. Some ten years ago, long after he passed, I drove to Mountain View, sat on a park bench near that spot where I saw him and reminisced. I visualized my Dad. It was a poignant moment. Without his hard work and perseverance, I wouldn't be sitting on that bench, in the beautiful city of Mountain View, in this great nation of ours. Most likely, I'd still be in the Philippines. Maybe even dead by now.

5) Spring 1995: Worked for Happi House Japanese fast food restaurant. The Filipino manager, Joselito, would let me take home leftover teriyaki chicken and brown rice during closing time. Nice guy.

6) Summer 1995: Disney blockbuster Pocahontas debuts in theaters. Loved it! Love the theme song, too!

7) *To Wong Foo, Thanks for Everything! Julie Newmar* was released and I *released* myself from the grasp of Happi House and its mean manager Ana, and headed straight to the Shoreline Movie Theaters. I loved seeing Patrick Swayze, Wesley Snipes and John Leguizamo in drag, but wasn't too fond of my manager at Happi House, a Serbian bitch, who herself looked like a drag queen. She was as strict as a Nazi general. She used to fuck the other manager, Fernando.

8) *Clueless*: Iconic movie during my high school years in America. As if I'm going to leave it out of my book!

9) A Smash Hit: "1979" by The Smashing Pumpkins: The theme song of my high school life in America.

10) Oasis, baby! "Wonderwall" and "Champagne Supernova" were the other soundtracks of my youth.

11) My very first visit to Goodwill on El Camino Real; and the first time I saw a drag queen, shopping in the costume section.

12) Late summer '95: Freedom! Got my driver's license.

13) November 1995; Bought my very first *Playguy* magazine. I never looked back--at *Playgirl.*

14) Battle of the Bands at MVHS: My friend Robert played. He was happy to see me after the show. I told him "You are good!" He was blushing, with an ear to ear smile.

15) Mountain View High: First time getting a glimpse of the beautiful W.K. on the school grounds. He was a vision. Aside from Robert, Johnny, Missy and Kevin, he was the only other important reason why I went to school every day. That's right. Just to see B. He was gorgeous.

16) Winter 1995: Saw W.K. driving along Grant Road *en route* to school, in his charcoal colored VW Jetta. So beautiful. Those eyes! What a total turn on. I was obsessed, I guess.

17) Early 1996: Ran across Tyler, another MVHS cutie, at the KFC on El Camino Real.

18) World Lit Class, MVHS spring 1996: I'd bring boxes of chocolate candies and share them with my classmates. They loved it. Especially the guys: Jeremy, JJ, Jared, Ergin and Omid.

19) Same class: A nice Mexican girl, Elena, gave me a glowing compliment with regards to the essay that I wrote. I'll never forget that. I thanked her on the spot.

20) Riveting!: *All Quiet on the Western Front* by Erich Maria Remarque

21) Take A Picture: Ben C's beautiful face as he drove next to my car in his red VW Jetta, letting me know that I had left my Adidas sneakers on the roof of my car. So nice of him. An overall nice guy. We were classmates in my Photography class. Bryant St., the road leading to MVHS, was a two way residential street. Amazing how it worked out.

22) Smoke Break: My friend, Missy, a transfer student from Guam, was my sidekick--
and smoking partner. We'd smoke cigarettes in the parking lot, in my car, on school
grounds. Smoking cigarettes, as well as talking about boys, happened to be our *other*
favorite curricular activity.

23) Spring 1996: My friendship with Robert; we were in the same Spanish 1 class.
Very nice guy. Didn't matter if you were gay or straight, you *are* his friend! Very rare
for a young man his age. Plus, he was the cutest thing.

24) Summer 1996: My Dad bought me a 1975 VW Super Beetle Fuel Injection. I love
it. It's so fun to drive.

25) June 1996: Graduated from high school.

26) A cruise along Alma Street in Palo Alto, CA one evening. Bush's "Machinehead"
was playing on the radio. Bush, one of my all time favorite rock bands. Gavin
Rossdale's got the sexiest voice.

27) My Grandmother bought me a round trip ticket to San Diego so I could have a little
post graduation vacation. I ended up staying for over a month. I had a fantastic time
with my relatives there, particularly my cousins. Plus, the 1996 Summer Olympics
was going on. Very memorable, especially when Muhammad Ali lit up the Olympic
Flame. My Grandmother and uncle and I would go to Sycuan casino every other
day. There were some good looking valet boys and Concessions employees there.
One guy in particular who I was very fond of had the most beautiful piercing blue
eyes and a toned body. He reminded me of gay porn star Joe Landon.

28) Fall 1996: Enrolled at Foothill College. At Foothill College, I would frequent the
library. I love reading their books on European History, particularly the British
Royal Family, and some about myths, legends and folklore including vampire
stories. I got to surf the internet for the first time. Ran into some article about
homosexuality called "Kabaklaan". Very fascinating.

29) The Spice Girls!: These Britches caught the world by storm.

30) Early spring 1997: Lost and found. A young guy (in his mid 20s) pulled in front of
the post office as I was about to hop in my car, telling me he used to own my car, a
'75 VW Super Beetle; asked me where I got it. "Bought it from a guy off of Bush
Street," I said. "Enjoy!", he said with a smile and drove off.

31) Good looking Walgreens coworker Brian Lunna asked me for a ride home. His
mom bailed on him. Or she just dozed off and forgot to pick him up. Cell phones

were a luxury back then. Not everyone could afford it. It was midnight. He used to live at a house off of Bowers Avenue in Santa Clara. He was so thankful.

32) Samoan coworker Lyka Eseka asked for a ride home, too. She lived in Sunnyvale. Nice girl. I liked her. We got along well. Probably because we were about the same age--about twenty. She got knocked up early though.

33) My time working at Walgreens would be very boring without these coworkers who were so fun to be with and so full of life: Jenny Samoa, Tina Lesbian, Sheila S, Mama Dawn, Tamara Pharmacy and Sister Bernie. Thank you, girls!

34) Around this time, Lucy and I had gotten very close. We were like Laverne and Shirley. We'd go spend hours at the Denny's near Moffett Field after we got done with work at Walgreens around midnight. We'd stay till the wee hours of the morning, having Grand Slams and drinking dozens of cups of coffee, talking about just anything and anyone. One time I got home around 6 in the morning.

35) Summer 1997: Lucy hosted a birthday party for her young daughter, Steffany, at their home in Moffett Field; everybody got up and danced to the Village People's "YMCA". Lots of fun.

36) Wept as I drove home from Tower Records after learning about Princess Diana's death on the radio.

37) Fall 1998: My good friend from Japan, Tess, and I would go clubbing downtown. We had such a blast.

38) In the early 2000s, when I was already living in Milpitas, I would visit Walgreens Mountain View from time to time late at night, just to hang out with Sister Bernie and her gay nephew, Neemo, for a little bit. Neemo was fun to be with, but he still had reservations and insecurities--hang ups perhaps--when it came to being totally out and *out* there. Poor thing. You only have one shot at life--celebrate your being gay to the max!

39) 2001: Lucy and I would be hitting the bars and clubs often. I love it when the bouncers at some of these clubs would let us in for free. Maybe they were thinking "Fuck the cover charge! The dancing queens are here!"

40) Took Julia, my cousin Marvin's wife at the time, out clubbing. We had a great time. I wore a short tight blue dress that Julia had given me a few days prior. Some guys went *crazy*; danced with me nonstop and I got tons of compliments, especially on my long legs.

41) I once saw former MVHS friend and classmate, Jeremy C, drunk and cussing out the drive-thru cashier at the Jack In the Box on El Camino Real and Calderon. A couple of years ago, I ran into him on Facebook and am happy to see him settled down, with his partner and two kids. I'm glad he's turned his life around.

42) Funny Granny: I still can't get over laughing every time I recall Manang Lea's facial expression when she confided in me that our Walgreens coworker, Mama Dawn, had a young lover. I did see the young man visit Mama Dawn at work a couple of times. I didn't care one bit. She was nice to me. That's all that matters. Filipino women can be very *chismosa* sometimes; would gossip behind your back about you and other people. I gave Manang Lea a free pass though because of her age. I just can't get over her facial expression the minute she mentioned about Mama Dawn's dalliances. "*Friend lang daw!*", she said with a very funny--almost distorted--facial expression. Cracks me up every time that encounter comes to mind.

43) There is beauty everywhere: Of course, my time at Walgreens won't be as fun and exciting without some very good looking male customers. There's this very sexy white guy in his early 20s who is just a tease. He'd come in wearing nothing but a pair of denim cut off shorts and a tight tee. He had a gorgeous chiseled face and beautiful rosy complexion. His bulge could feed an entire nation. I fucking loved it! He reminds me of one of the hot models from *Playguy*. MVHS grad Tyler A would also frequent the store as well as this young guy in his late teens who'd come in wearing white A shirt and a pair of cabana shorts all the time. He won't buy anything but would stand near the sunglasses rack and check himself out, give me a quick glance, smile and walk out. Baby boy, if I find you on Tinder you are mine!

44) Cover Boys: Love my *magazine* collection! Torso, Mandate, Playguy, etc. Thank you, Tower Books!

45) Wigstock Forever!: Wigstock: The Movie DVD, one of the best purchases (Rasputin Mountain View, 2006) I ever made, in life! A total stress reliever and a riot!

46) Lastly, Mountain View won't be as fun and exciting without some of the good looking and good hearted men I met. Thank you, Brian, Chris S, Ramon, Adam, Mark Tropical, Don S, Mike T, Sam, Lee, Avi, John and Andrey for accommodating me.

Chapter 5

SANCTUARIO DE VANESSA

The house that Vanessa built may be small in size and minimal in square feet, but the value and appraisal of its precious and pricey contents make up for it, I believe. Think of the Ark of the Covenant.

The house that Vanessa built is merely a sanctuary--a museum of some sort--that holds and keeps evidence of my many years of hard work and sacrifice. I am so fucking proud of my collections!

My passion for art and other beautiful things is hereditary. Thanks to my paternal grandparents and great grandparents, they filled our ancestral home in Tondo with a phalanx of interesting stuff, from musical instruments like the accordion to rare ephemera like a whip made out of a stingray's tail, said to have belonged to my great-grandfather, Emilio, or "Lolo Kalbo" as he was affectionately known in the family.

I was about three months old when Emilio passed away in 1977, but my Grandmother, from early on, would tell me stories about how his father would check on me periodically despite the gravity of his cancer. He'd summon what's left of his energy and make that difficult climb upstairs where my bedroom was. My Grandmother would then reprimand her father because of the fragile nature of his health, but the old man would insist on having his way. He had to see his great-grandchild! "*Gusto ko lang makita ang apo kong negro,*" the old man would say, as told by my Grandmother.

Also on display in our ancestral home was the miniature tea cup set from the early 1900s said to have belonged to my great- grandmother, Teofila. I remember my Grandmother showing them to me with a sense of pride and nostalgia. It brought a smile to her face. That miniature tea cup set definitely stood the test of time, considering the many decades that they had survived; silent witnesses to two world wars and several natural calamities.

Old and vintage family photos left a great and lasting impression in my psyche as a young child. I am very fortunate to have seen photographs of my long gone forebears and relatives because now that I am a full grown adult and uncertain of the whereabouts of those old photos, there is a sense of consolation and satisfaction with the fact that I was lucky enough to have had a glimpse of such precious memorabilia. One particular photograph that stands out is that of my paternal great-grandparents on my grandfather's side, Antonio and Leonila, burying their infant son in the early 1930s. My great-grandmother, young and petite, wearing the classic Philippine *terno*, inconsolable in her grief.

My bedroom is the ultimate treasure trove. It's not surrounded by water like Ariel's treasure trove, but rather filled with mouthwatering baubles and other nice pieces that would make the Duchess of Windsor salivate had she been around today. Also in my possession are rare pieces of art and artwork that would excite any museum curator and entice antiques dealers and collectors.

I am notorious for having men from all walks of life in my bedroom. Lately I've been seeing a lot of Georg--Georg Jensen, that is. I love his big, hard pieces--his pewter and silverware. I have a few of his creations lying around somewhere in my room. I also have works by Judie Bomberger, Eugene Kingman, Pablo Picasso and William Sidney Mount.

If a painting or piece of art speaks to me, I buy it. It has to have some kind of significance though. For example, the William Sidney Mount print of his *Dancing in the Barn* that hangs in my bedroom wall *tells* me "Vanessa, take a break from your day's work and dance a little bit."

Just like with cowboys and ranchers, horses are an important part of my life--my collecting life, that is. Why I collect horse inspired pieces is simple: Horses, aside from being some of the most hardworking creatures on the planet, are also some of the most beautiful and magnificent looking. No wonder they are always present at grand parades and coronations. They symbolize a powerful combination that I hardly see in people: strength and elegance.

It adds an extra kick to my day whenever I open a jewelry box filled with my pieces in galloping form: brooches, pendants and necklaces.

I also started collecting Japanese lacquer recently. I'm particularly fond of those fashioned as jewelry boxes; more special if they double as a music box. As the old adage goes, "They don't make them anymore."

These lacquer boxes have become a significant part of my growing *chinoiserie* collection--jewelry and other *objets d'art* from the Orient. Just like McDonald's, I'm loving it!

My Asian inspired jewelry collection has significantly expanded over the years. Something about Chinese design, craftsmanship and symbolism fascinates me. I find myself in a state of peace and calm every time I wear--or even peruse--my pieces of Asian origin: my jade and South Sea pearls. Maybe it is Buddha simply channeling his zen towards my direction.

I've also started collecting hand painted plates--both large and small--from different parts of the world. I'm especially fond of this plate of Persian origin with its intricate enamel work. It features a wonderfully detailed wedding scene of some sort. How mesmerizing.

Also part of my plate collection are some jasperware by Wedgwood. I particularly adore the one made especially for Elizabeth II's Silver Jubilee in 1977, the year of my birth. I found it at Goodwill and paid $3 for it.

I like capturing the sparkle in the eyes of my nieces and nephews when they enter my bedroom and gaze--with awe--at my art collection, trinkets and other treasures. My room is, in essence, a treasure trove of fabulous, unique and interesting pieces.

None has seen a major upgrade from ten years ago than my jewelry collection. Just like the orange tree in my backyard, it has kept on growing. And within this fabled and fabulous collection are the fruits of my labor and hard work. "Work hard for the gold, bitch!" I'd tell myself from time to time. Yes, I fancy myself as an Olympian sometimes: constantly aiming for the gold.

I prefer estate jewelry because there is a ninety percent possibility that those pieces are rare and are not being made anymore.

Some of my new favorites are crafted in solid 22 and 24 karat gold; some in vermeil and sterling silver. Included in this high karat gold collection are coin pendants from England, Iran, Saudi Arabia, Switzerland, India, Austria, Greece and China. Also part of this new batch of baubles is a Ceylon sapphire brooch with an Etruscan design. I am also crazy, madly in love with my 3 inch carved jade pendant from the Art Deco period. A 34 carat Amethyst cocktail ring in gold from the Retro period also took up space in my enormous Lady Buxton jewelry box recently. A couple of golden South Sea pearls found their way in there, too.

I have yet to find a fish tank for my golden treasures from the sea, namely my gold fish enamel brooch with rubies and diamonds in solid 18 karat gold as well as a Krementz necklace with a 3 inch long articulated fish pendant. Don't forget about my estate marlin ring, also set in 18 karat gold.

But, of course, my critter collection isn't limited to sea life. There are also whimsical jewelry pieces in the form of lions, tigers and bears. Oh, my collection is such a diverse one! In my "Animal Kingdom Collection", one would find pieces in reptilian form. My favorite is a snake brooch in solid 18 karat gold, with blue and green enameling and ruby eyes. In Chinese Astrology, my birth year falls under the symbol of the snake; hence my partiality and affiliation towards serpentine jewelry. Others might find it bizarre and revolting, but who cares. I'm more worried about getting attacked by snakes with two legs walking among us than those sitting pretty in my jewelry box.

Oakland Zoo beware! There's a new topiary in the Bay Area!

I buy jewelry not to put them in a safety deposit box at a bank somewhere, but to put them around my neck, fingers and other parts of my body rather--the way they were meant to be. More importantly, I buy jewelry with the pure intent of enjoying it for all the days of my life.

Each precious piece has a sentimental story behind it. For example, the white gold diamond cocktail ring with F colorless diamonds that I bought many Christmases ago reminds me of my ex lover, Chris Flanerty. The money I used in purchasing that ring came from him--Christmas and birthday gifts. I could not afford to simply spend them on stupid, insignificant stuff. At least with jewelry, I know I'll have them on me and with me for the rest of my life. Even though Chris is not with me anymore, his spirit shines through the sparkle of the diamonds in that ring.

Another piece of jewelry that I treasure so much is my magnificent Ceylon sapphire brooch crafted in solid 22 karat gold. Like Chris before him, my current lover, the buff and gorgeous Andy Baby, would shower me with monetary gifts every Christmas and on my birthday. Instead of spending them on nonsense stuff, I use them to purchase fine, fabulous jewelry. This 22 karat gold brooch is part of it. I'd put it near my left breast; also Andy's favorite spot to put his head on during our down time.

In my sterling silver collection jewelry box lies a pair of pearl earrings with white zircon in them; in essence, a gift from my good friend, Kevin C. He is a handsome fiftysomething "daddy" type, very successful in life, manages his own business and a total gym rat. He works out every day. He reminds me of news anchor Ken Bastida. We'd hang out once in a while. In May 2017, he gave me a couple hundred bucks as a birthday gift and I spent it on jewelry.

Kevin, like most of the silver fox type of men that I know, is fully committed to taking care of himself; number one by going to the gym every day and second by eating healthy. He even suggested that I try these protein bars called Laura as a nutritional supplement.

I have a habit of purchasing fine pieces of jewelry using the monetary gifts my male friends and lovers give me; that way I have something to look at and hold on to when the time comes that I'm old and bedridden and I've got nothing to do but reminisce about the precious past. Hopefully, I'd still be wearing my precious pearls from Kevin.

Jewelry--gold jewelry in particular--is eternal. Roses wilt overtime but gold lasts for a lifetime. Plus, it's a smart investment.

During my Facebook years, a "friend" named Kongpa living in the Philippines would outright scrutinize and criticize some of my gold pieces, particularly my 14 karat gold pieces. Apparently, eighteen karat gold is the standard in the Philippines, hence her partiality towards it. No big deal to me. I have my fair share of eighteen karat gold pieces in my private collection. But, criticizing *my* gold specifically is a big deal to me. Once you venture in that territory of mine, you have to be very careful especially with your choice of words. So, when the time came for me to evaluate and *appraise* individuals lurking in my Facebook friends list like Kongpa, she automatically fell in the mystery metal category--not even 10 karat gold or gold plated brass. Worthless! I have since unfriended the shady bitch!

Gold is gold whether you have fourteen or eighteen karat gold in your jewelry collection. They are all precious! What's not precious to me are Filipinos acting as if they are the top connoisseurs of the best and finest jewelry in the world. I call them garbage and they have to be treated as such. They need to go! Mind your own business and I'll continue to mine my own gold through hard work and sacrifice.

I hope future generations of my family will guard my beautiful treasures the same way I do. Jewelry is meant to be worn, enjoyed and celebrated, but they also need tender care.

Chapter 6

THE GOOD LIFE ACCORDING TO VANESSA

I am no lifestyle expert. I'm not even an expert on life and living. But, I do what feels right and feels good. In life, that's the only thing that really matters. Follow your heart!

LIVE DELICIOUSLY

No matter how bad or tragic things are, don't forget to *live* and breathe. Make time to do the things that make you happy. Forget "eat, pray and love". Just eat, fuck and shop! The world is a buffet table full of delicious things. Pick your poison!

Gorge on goat curry and chicken tanduri at your favorite Indian restaurant! Indulge in chocolates, ice cream and tiramisu! Make afternoon sex a regular routine with your lover! Have trysts and affairs and always include an awesome orgasm on your to-do list! Open your eyes to beautiful art and works of art! Wear your fabulous clothes and precious jewelry every day! And never underestimate the importance of coffee, tea and pastries!

As we all know, once things turn for the worst--a debilitating disease for example--the only thing you can really do is sit on a wheelchair for the rest of your life and punish yourself with endless guilt: why didn't you do those fun things while you still could.

Regrets are like Best Picture awards on Oscars night--they always come last!

BEAUTY REGIMEN

For my skin care, I swear by Neutrogena beauty products and daily naps (mostly in the early part of the afternoon).

There was a time in my young adult life when I grew Godzilla-size zits. Then I discovered Neutrogena Rapid facial wash. Within a few weeks, the persistent pimples perished and my self confidence level went to the top of the pedestal.

Other beauty routines I practice religiously:

1) Take a shower everyday especially before leaving the house. A clean and good smelling person is an attractive person. Your attitude might stink, but not your body.
2) Never forget to do a touch up on your hair's roots once the whites appear. Whoever said gray hair is beautiful must be shot by firing squad. I say "Nay" to gray! It makes people look twenty years older than their actual age.
3) Always--always--wear red lipstick!
4) No time for a nail salon session? Make your toenails ready to go with an instant pedi. A quick touch up of red nail polish does the trick.
5) Never leave the house without any jewelry on. People are judging you the minute you step out of your house. I love the compliments I get regularly on my jewelry. Girls think I'm a wealthy lady. Guys think I'm a rich bitch with cash to burn.
6) Don't forget to splash some perfume on before you leave the house. A good smelling woman is an unforgettable woman!

HOW'S MY OUTFIT?

Oh yes, clothes do make the man--and woman! Clothes definitely play an important role in our lives. What you put on in the morning will define your outlook and attitude for the rest of the day. It will also leave a lasting impression among those you meet.

I never leave the house without being properly dressed, whether I'm going to the grocery or the DMV. People are looking and they *are* judging!

I'm more of a designer top and blue jeans kind of woman when running errands on a regular day. Even when making a quick trip to the grocery store for some bread and eggs, you'd find me donning clothes by some famous designer out there--Missoni and Versace, to name a few.

On cocktail parties and other evening events, one would find me wearing a sheath dress by Calvin Klein or Ralph Lauren. None of that over the top, occupy-the-entire-football-field ball gowns! I always take into consideration how I am going to be able to *use* the restroom when picking a party outfit. Again, I use common sense when it comes to these things.

Someone told me a long time ago that people won't be able to tell if you're poor and struggling as long as you have nice clothes on. For some strange reason, she is right.

Rich or poor, it doesn't really matter as long as you choose to adorn yourself with rich fabrics and some jewelry. Remember the old saying "First impressions last"? It doesn't matter how much money you have in your pocket; it's the nice clothes you have on that will get you noticed!

Even while lounging at home and watching *Breakfast at Tiffany's*, one would find me wearing a Dior caftan and a humongous cocktail ring, reeking with a Yves Saint Laurent fragrance. Hey, at least if I happen to have a heart attack that day I'd *go* looking fabulous.

Emily Failenson, you are not the only well dressed bitch in town!

FANCY FOOTWEAR

Like former Philippine First Lady Imelda Marcos, I am a huge fan of Salvatore Ferragamo. His shoes are the best! Not only are they well made and elegantly designed, they are very comfortable, too. It's almost as if they were custom made for tall, wide footed women like myself. Like Imelda's husband Ferdinand, Ferragamo *knows* women!

I was at my sister's wedding a few years ago and I chose to wear a pair of Ferragamo pumps. My feet never got sore, considering I was on my feet for hours. I danced the night away in my Ferragamos at the reception.

I love my Birkenstock sandals, too. They're so comfortable.

ROUTINE CLEANING

Twice a year, I do a general life edit. Here's what's on my check list:

1) Let go of the toxic, lazy and bitter people in my circle.
2) I donate or sell clothes that I don't wear anymore.

3)   I attend some kind of religious service on some Sundays. It's so good for the soul.

4)   I make it a regular habit to sing and dance.

5)   I never forget to spice up my sex life. I'm always excited to try new things. Hey, this is the 21st century!

SUNDAY MORNING

After a hearty breakfast on an easy Sunday morning--one that includes some eggs, bacon, sausages, toast with jam and butter, sliced fruits, pies, a glass of orange juice and of course, several cups of coffee--it's time to lay out my jewelry boxes and peruse the gold, gemstone and silver treasures inside.

Recently, I've been obsessing on coin jewelry--Lira pendants, Elizabeth II coin charm bracelets and other solid gold pieces depicting European kings and other rulers. There is something fascinating about owning gold and silver coins. It's the allure! I feel like Hernan Cortes sometimes.

But, of course, as you may well know by now, my passion for jewelry--fine or costume--does not begin and end with gold coins or gold plated KJL pieces.

Everybody knows I live and breathe jewelry. Just take a peek inside my fabled sanctuary--my bedroom. In there, you'll find jewelry box after jewelry box, each containing a certain, organized group of gems: "Purple Passion" for my amethyst collection, "Hearts on Fire" for my diamonds and "Green with Envy" for my emeralds.

I think feeling rich and living in luxury is a state of mind; a case to case basis. It's how you'd analyze the concept and apply it in your daily life. There are filthy rich people out there who do not bathe and have the worst manners; people with cash to burn who look like they've gone through hell with their appearance. I don't care if you're a Rockefeller or a Rothschild. If you don't look or act the part, you're a hobo in my eyes.

Same thing with "rich" people who are accused of theft and plunder.

Imelda Marcos has the finest rubies in the world. But, do you think she really enjoys wearing them *sans* the guilt? Without her keeping an eye on her back? I mean, she walks in a room wearing those monster size rubies and what do half of the people in the room think? That she and her deceased dictator husband, Ferdinand, pocketed millions of dollars from the US Government (that were meant to aid the poor). Allegedly, Imelda, who had an "edifice complex", spent them on expensive jewelry, rare works of art from Europe and high rise buildings in Manhattan.

I cannot be like that! I'd be happy and content wearing a skinny sterling silver ring. At least I know deep in my heart that I worked hard for it, and did not steal it from the Philippine treasury.

Going back to my idea of Sunday morning bliss, I'd wake up in the morning thinking of two things: what's in the news and what jewelry to wear for the day.

One great advantage of having a vast collection of jewelry is that it adds a little excitement to your day. It's like doing an "eenie meenie miney mo" on a box of Godiva candies. That itself is luxury by my standards!

My jewelry doesn't have to be worth thousands of dollars *all* the time and be in a safety deposit box 364 days a year. As long as it is well made and it *speaks* to me, I'd buy it.

I've repeatedly talked about my jewelry but somehow failed to mention my jewelry provider. Beladora of Beverly Hills, the online jewelry retail store partly owned by former Christie's VP Russell Fogarty and one of my jewelry providers since 2008, has achieved significant status in the industry over the years. I've purchased some of my equally significant baubles and other precious pieces from them.

Nowadays, I often see Beladora pieces being featured on a variety of fashion magazines, worn by fashion models and fashion mavens alike.

Beladora truly has some of the finest pieces in the vintage and estate jewelry category. Like the old adage goes, "They don't make them anymore." Some pieces in my personal collection worthy of a spread in *Vogue* or *Elle* include a pear shaped onyx cocktail ring with diamonds set in eighteen karat gold, a mid century sapphire, ruby, diamond and emerald dome ring also in 18k gold and a Middle Eastern inspired high karat gold bracelet with cannetile design.

I also purchased a pair of gold earrings by jewelry designer Simon Alcantara from Beladora. A similar pair were worn by Cynthia Nixon in an episode of *Sex and the City*.

There is an added sense of pride in my smile every time I see Beladora jewelry in the magazines that I read while having a sip of coffee and nibbling on pastries. I'm proud to declare "That's my jeweler, too!"

2017, THE YEAR OF LIVING FABULOUSLY

2017--the year of my fortieth birthday--was in itself, a very special gift. Well, I consider all the years of my life a gift, but there's something especially noteworthy about 2017; one that's deserving of a spot in *W* magazine.

For the very first time, the fashion world's most notable brands convened in my closet: Versace, Escada, Saint Laurent to name a few. They now join the old time greats like Ralph Lauren, Christian Dior, Gucci, Fendi and Balenciaga.

Other pieces that get me excited include a Nine West brocade coat in a Yves Klein blue shade with fur trim collar. I wore it during a Christmas service last year and had gotten many compliments.

A Marrakech inspired fuschia pink caftan with dark blue knit embroidery is also a lot of fun to wear especially while lounging and relaxing at home. It's so rich and luxurious.

Sometime in the summer of 2017, I snagged a Michael Jackson inspired sequined jacket by BCBG at my local thrift store and wore it at the club one Friday night. I received many compliments, particularly from those who were on the dance floor with me. Finally, for New Year's Eve 2017, I got to wear an '80s inspired shiny silver lame top with Joan Crawford shoulder paddings and partied the night away. What a fun and fabulous way to welcome the new year!

Chapter 7

RECENT TRIPS AND NEW DISCOVERIES

CACHE CREEK CASINO

Life is *really* a cabaret at Cache Creek Casino. Have a drink! Have a double! Dance the night away, but don't get yourself into too much trouble!

I recently rediscovered Cache Creek Casino. This time around, it was a 180 degree turn. No more wasted hours standing behind a friend seated in front of a slot machine gambling away her cash and maxing out her credit card, contemplating when it would end and eventually going home tired and unhappy.

In August 2017, my Mom--sixty but looking much younger--and I decided to visit Cache Creek Casino in Brooks, CA as part of our Labor Day weekend fun.

My Mom and I have not been there for almost ten years. The last time we were there--on Mother's Day 2008--we crossed paths with Amalia Fuentes, a veteran actress from the Philippines, known for her timeless beauty and the moniker "The Elizabeth Taylor of the Philippines" due in fact to her striking resemblance with the legendary Hollywood actress.

For me, personally, my history with Cache Creek goes farther than 2008. In the early 2000s, my friend Maude would tag me along with her whenever she felt the urge to get lucky--in a gambling sense--and place a ton of bets. When things do not come her way and the actual money's gone, her debit and credit cards would be her last resort and eventually, the final casualties.

It was a somewhat terrible experience for me. Some nights--and occasionally very early mornings--we would drive home tired and broke; sore losers, literally. Eventually, I had gotten tired of the same old miserable scene and decided to focus on the other aspects of my young life; one that involves hitting the sack early and getting some good sleep and being productive the following day instead of hitting the slot machines for winless plays.

Fast forward to 2017, it was a totally different story. I finally discovered the real purpose of Cache Creek--for me and me alone. This time around, it's all about great food, good music and dancing the night away. It's really all about *living*.

The gambling part has always been insignificant to me. I am not a gambler. I don't even know how to play poker! Who knows? Maybe after writing this book I'll get lessons from James Holzhauer.

Aside from having awesome servers, Cache Creek's Harvest Inn Buffet has, in my opinion, one of the best intercontinental cuisine selections in the country. There's never a shortage of Alaskan King and Dungeness crabs and other kinds of seafood. The fishermen from the TV series *Deadliest Catch* would be jealous.

The sumptuous steak and lobster combo is a must have. And don't even get me started with the dessert selection. Contestants from The Great British Baking Show, eat your hearts out! Harvest Inn has the best pies, cakes and pastries in the world. Just leave me a slice of Paul Hollywood though. That man looks good enough to eat!

After the buffet, I head to Club 88 which is a few steps away to dance the night away.

There's a variety of bands that play the best live music at Club 88. I particularly love cover bands who play disco music from the late '70s and early '80s. My Mom--who's also my dancing partner--and I have such a blast. Move over ABBA! The real dancing queens are here!

This time, for the very first time in so many years, I came out of Cache Creek Casino feeling like a true winner. The valet boys are not bad either.

2018 DISNEYLAND AND SAN DIEGO TRIPS

I have not been to Disneyland in almost a decade. I have been a very busy woman lately that I barely had time to see Mickey and Minnie.

By February 2008, I decided it was high time that I sojourn to Southern California and visit Disneyland, the happiest place on earth.

This particular trip was extra special. Driving along Interstate 5 near Paso Robles, CA, with the vast almond plantations in plain view, my curious Mom cheerfully recording the scenery on her iPhone, she captured my humor filled annotations that went something like "This is the cherry blossoms, in America!", spoofing the typical *manong* Filipino accent and with the characteristically incorrect grammar.

We hardly noticed the length of travel time in that Interstate 5 phase of our trip. We were never bored at all. Occasionally, we'd gorge on boiled eggs and PBJ sandwiches and sip on coffee to keep us up and energized during our six hour drive. Also, to quell boredom during our long trip, we'd gossip about friends, family and other people; typical girly stuff.

At Disneyland, there was no shortage of people: young kids, the young at heart, Gen X-ers, baby boomers, baby makers and baby daddies as well as millennials and Gen Z-ers. People from all walks of life seem to have converged in the "happiest place on earth" that Thursday morning.

The classic rides--Space Mountain, Indiana Jones and Pirates of the Caribbean--never cease to amaze. It was almost a ritual: your Disneyland experience won't be complete without those rides. After the fast and wild rides, it was time to slow down and settle down literally, on the seats of the It's A Small World ride.

What made this particular visit more exciting was the influx of the Gen Z crowd. For some strange reason, their presence amped up the energy to a higher level. Sure, I ran into some who gave me weird, curious looks, but thankfully, the entirety of my Disneyland visit went scot free.

I also ran into some very good looking Gen Z-ers whose young strapping bubble butts could smother the life out of you. What is up with the Gen Z-ers' diet routine these days? Is it in the milk or formula? A lot of them seem to grow big butts these days. No complaints here. One particular teen tease who's probably eighteen or nineteen was walking a few feet ahead of me just outside the Mark Twain Riverboat area. I couldn't help but notice his beautiful bubble butt. He reminded me of my one time "hookup" from Hayward, CA, twenty year old Dylan O. He's got the stocky varsity wrestler build and the face of an Abercrombie & Fitch model--very all-American. I love it.

As I walked behind the teen tease, naughty thoughts came to mind: "How does it smell?" and "Is it smooth or a little hairy?" were some of the questions I had. I was waiting for Maleficent to smack me in the face with her wand so I could return to my senses and wake up from my daydreaming.

At any rate, Disneyland has lost its *innocence* during my visit.

Disneyland has become not only a playground for the young and young at heart, but also a haven for those with very *playful* minds. It's the truth! Believe me. It's the truth! Just like Walt Disney himself believing that he will be risen from the dead through cryogenics.

The following day--a Friday--it was time to head further south, to sunny San Diego: my most favorite city in the world. Destination: Coronado Island.

There was a bit of a chill in the air when we arrived in San Diego that Friday afternoon. But, I came prepared. I wrapped myself in my luxurious Saint Laurent rabbit fur coat.

We arrived a little after twelve in the afternoon and immediately took a quick stroll downtown to look for a place to eat. We ended up having *aperitivo* at Brigantine; they serve the best spirits and cocktails and their seafood appetizers are really good.

After our late lunch, it was time to visit Hotel del Coronado, that famed San Diego landmark which was featured in the blockbuster movie *Some Like It Hot*, starring Marilyn Monroe, Tony Curtis and Jack Lemmon. Hotel del boasts some of the quaintest little shops including an ice cream parlor that serves some of the best. It also has a fabulous little jewelry store that I enjoy visiting whenever I'm in town.

After my stint at Hotel del, it's time to drive to inner San Diego--El Cajon in particular--and visit my favorite thrift store, Barras.

Barras Thrift Store is a treasure trove of old and vintage hunts, from designer clothes to sterling silver and costume jewelry. They even have old furniture from the Victorian period. I love that place.

Locally, Savers Thrift Store does it for me. It's where I purchased some of my significant, brand name pieces. They include a Tiffany & Co necklace, a pair of Gucci sunglasses, a Longines watch and a fabulous pair of Chanel earrings that I only paid $2 for but resold online for $200. Can you imagine? Brings me to repeat the old saying–with a little upgrade–"One man's trash is another tran's treasure."

Whoever donated those Chanel earrings probably thought they were trash--maybe the ex boyfriend or ex husband of some stylish woman out there.

You'd have to bring a lot of patience and a good eye though. Being well equipped with a fair amount of knowledge on fashion and fashion designers helps a lot because you'll be able to spot those brand name items easily.

THE POWER OF NAPS

The word "nap" may be short and simple but its effect no doubt plays a significant role in our health especially in the hustle and bustle world that we live in today. Naps--20 minutes tops--help recharge our mind and body in the most unexpected way. When most Americans don't get the required eight hours of night time sleep, you'd be surprised with how good you'll feel after taking even the shortest of naps. Put that laptop or iPad to the side for a moment, turn your cell phone off and doze off.

I don't have to be Dr. Quinn Medicine Woman to prescribe you a daily dose of naps. I practice it religiously and the results are nothing short of miraculous. As soon as I wake up, I feel recharged and revitalized. I feel more inspired and energized--to write or draw. I'm ready to do more household chores! I'd probably be singing, too, like Snow White, as I perform my scullery maid duties at home. I don't care! I feel good doing it. Thanks to my nap.

Take it from a woman who has done a lot of cleaning and a *lot* of men in her days. As soon as I arrive home from my morning errands and shopping, I fix myself a quick lunch and take a nap. The results are better than Melissa Miner's freshly botoxed face. I have a fresh looking face from Mother Nature. My body is also re-energized, so I'm ready to take on my day--and my armada of lovers. More importantly, I have a clearer mind and a more positive outlook.

Maybe after reading this you'll consider including naps in your daily routine the way Joy Behar and Megan McCain do their daily bickering on *The View*. Do it! It makes people feel good.

OUT IN THE OPEN

Life's too short. The clock is ticking nonstop. Time is one of humanity's greatest enemies. Time never waits on anyone unlike the doorman at The Ritz. Before my time runs out, I'd like to take this opportunity to let my family--especially my Mom--know that I love them so much.

The past few years of my adult life have been filled with love and joy. That's all that really matters--and a fat bank account if you're lucky. My family and a few good men-- friends who really care--have made it possible.

Give love to get love and *be* loved. Show people you care and that you are sincere. If you don't practice these things, your life is meaningless. Practice them and good karma will always pay you a nice visit.

I want my Mom to know that in the event of my early passing--on my funeral--anyone who tells her that they feel bad or sorry for her because I lived my life a certain way should be reprimanded harshly. Kick them out of the chapel! They're full of crap.

I've lived a happy and content life. I was surrounded by people who loved and accepted me for who I am and gave me utmost respect. Showing respect is a rarity these days, you know. People are so full of themselves. That's why I've unfriended a bunch of people not too long ago.

My family should also know that there was never a day--never a day--that I did not pray for them. Prayed for their safety, prayed for their health and prayed for their peace of mind. May God protect them through the days of their lives.

My family should also know that there was never a day in my life that I did not think about Dad. No words can express the longing in my heart and how I miss him so much.

Aside from my Mom and siblings, here are the names of the few good men in my life who have been there for me through thick and thin: Don, Stewart, Steve, Mike, Roy, Keoni, Richard, Arthur, Alfonso, Jeff, Andy and Tony. *Besos!*

Chapter 8

SEX, ANYONE?

"This ain't no *Sex and the City* bullshit, bitches!"

I've said this before and I'll say it again: sex is the cure. Sex is my preferred kind of high. It's like Prince Charles circa the 1980s and '90s when he was cheating on Princess Diana with that wrinkly old drag queen with a vagina named Camilla: he just can't live without it! I *can't* live without sex. Ordinary guys can't live without sex! Your dad, brother, cousin and uncles can't live without sex! Even your 80 year-old grandpa can't live without sex! Welcome to the real world!

If sex is like gasoline—to get our bodies and *engines* running—then fill me up! It gets me going. It gets my brain cells going. It helps me become more creative and productive.

I like all kinds of sex and doing it with different men; men of all ages and different racial backgrounds. There's the old, the young and those belonging in the "middle ages": mid-40s, mid-50s, that sort of thing.

Variety is the spice of life. For me, variety means twentysomething heartthrobs, DILFs in their forties and fifties and of course, frisky senior citizens with lots of spunk.

My plate is always full, so what! If Paula Deen could eat all kinds of meat in one sitting, so can I! Now, just like a three course meal, there are varying levels of satisfaction in every *entree*.

For my bedroom appetizers in bed, I prefer the company of jalapeno hot Latin men in their twenties and early thirties. They give my libido a certain kick and their macho qualities are a perfect match to my uninhibited feminine wiles in the bedroom. It's like taming a wild buck--in the bedroom. It can be rough at times but it's exciting.

For my main course I prefer the solid meaty stuff; the kind of meat that has been seasoned to perfection and not overly cooked like George Hamilton. No! We're not in the senior category yet. I'm talking about my daddy-licious lovers in their prime. Yes, Virginia, those in their forties and fifties. Now, these studs are the kings of the stables; with glorious behinds that you can hold on to, tap or even spank a little. They have the right amount of speed and control, too. The minute I mount them or vice versa, you know it's a match made in bedroom heaven. Forget Churchill Downs! I tell my lover, "Let's get down!"

Senior citizen guys are like desserts--go easy on them. Some of them are fragile like jello, so be gentle with them. None of that reverse cowgirl crap, please. No, we're not in a redneck pub in Texas with a mechanical bull inside. That's for the cheap, drunk broads out there. Plus, you don't want to break grandpa's hips. Grandma will be furious and her kids might sue you! So, be careful with an older lover.

My other favorite "dessert" in bed is called "Justin". A gentle giant with the strongest hands and a firm touch; perfect for my night time massage. The bodyrub he gives me sends me to Dreamland instantly. It's the perfect icing to the cake. And don't even get me started with cakes!

I love all kinds of *cakes* and *buns*: vanilla, chocolate, even some Filipino--and I'm not talking about cakes from Goldilocks bakeshop.

You know what they say, the best buns are the ones from Asia. Hello Keen on tumblr!

Some mornings I wake up with--to quote my long time lover Mark R--"bubble butt breakfast in bed." Now, I'll leave that to your crazy ass imaginations!

Sex makes us healthy and happy--unless you do it with ten men at the same time, then it'll make you hemorragey.

Sex is also, like my Baby Ronnie once told me, "the best form of exercise."

So true. Once, we role played as gym members and personal trainers. Oh, the trouble we got ourselves into. And the fun! I loved him hovering over my face.

I like to say "Have your husband take care of you and your family but keep a sexy, hot personal trainer to take care of your pussy."

I once had a personal trainer for a lover. DJ was the sexiest thing. I don't think our workout "routines" would be legal and acceptable at 24 Hour Fitness though.

I've probably done almost every role play sex scene in the book. Role playing is a bedroom must!

ROLE PLAY

(DIARY OF A LONELY DIVORCEE)
"Dear D,   January 2016

This is an entry about some guys who *entered* me not too long ago. It's our little secret, okay? You're my only trusted friend.

'Fremont is not sleeping tonight' is what comes to mind when I'm in the mood for sex that involves role playing. I'm such a nasty bitch in the bedroom sometimes. So nasty that some nights I give people a hard time sleeping, with all the noise and sexual cacophony me and my lovers create. It's my call of the wild. It also means the bitch is back in town. So, I tell Fremont residents "Get your earphones ready and make sure your walls are thick enough because you will definitely *hear* from me!"

My next door neighbor once complained about my bedroom noise. He was furiously banging at my door one night. I'm a Taurus, so naturally I increased the volume of my moaning and screaming to further annoy the son of a bitch. Never provoke or annoy a bull. Never! End of discussion.

I wanted to tell that jealous bitch, "Don't blame me. Blame the idea of role playing! It's a wonderful thing!"

I had a threesome not too long ago. It was my own remake of the Clinton Prison jailbreak in Dannemora, NY back in 2015. I wonder if people remember that. It was an absolute head scratcher. How in the world did two inmates--not one, but two--manage to escape from one of the most secure prison fortresses in the world. That incident rocked the prison system in America--and rocked my queen size bed not too long ago.

In Dannemora, two not bad looking inmates broke out of prison with the help of a nasty and neglected housewife slash prison employee: a fat, middle aged white woman with tons of insecurities in her bones. Now, in my book, that's the stuff fairy tales are made of. Things couldn't get any better than that, one would assume. But, as fate would have it as well as Murphy's Law, it was doomed from beginning to end: the fat lady sang--and fretted--and her fugitive lovers got caught.

But for this other nasty bitch from the West Coast, your friend, May, that prison break theme was a wonderful recipe for sex for three.

After seeing the breaking news on TV that fateful July day in 2015 involving lover boys on the lam David Sweat and Richard Matt, my burning desire to get double teamed by two *fucking* fugitives reached a breaking point: I had to have it. I needed to make it happen--in my bedroom.

Luckily for me, I didn't need to travel to Dannemora to pick up some fugitive finds. My handyman friend, Brendan, and his buddy, Steve, were *handy*. These men are some of the Bay Area's most handsome and horny fellas. I could *cum* just by looking at their faces, let alone have their giant cocks working my orifices. Their magnetic charm and masculine appeal were undeniable. They have that "tradie" look: rugged and Wrangler-wearing roughnecks. One can outright say "That's a *real* man right there!"; you know, the Tom Selleck and Mark Harmon type.

A few months after the Dannemora prison drama, my fugitive fantasy plans of fornication came to fruition. In November 2015, I managed to make my own fugitive fucking role play fantasy become reality. November was perfect: the weather had become chilly and my hot blooded lovers, Steve and Brendan, were ready.

The cold temperatures also warranted my wearing of furs and other luxurious garments such as my mink coats and chowchilla jacket.

I love getting fucked while wearing my fabulous furs and expensive jewelry in the fall. Again, it's a luxurious state of mind. Decadent!

To some, it might be cheap filthy sex, but at least it's done *with* taste. That's what exactly happened when my hot and hung "lovers on the lam" came by for role play sex night.

I instructed them to "break in" to my back door--no pun intended--and work their way through the kitchen headed for the fridge; then when I hear some noises, I'd come down from my room in my red negligee and white fox fur acting surprised and eventually seduced by my *mentruders*.

They would then convince me that they weren't going to hurt me; that they just needed some food and a place to sleep in. At the same time, Steve would be fondling my breasts and Brendan is kissing the back of my neck while rubbing his boner on my plump ass.

Alas, me being a lonely and lusty divorcee, welcomed them with open arms and open legs; succumbing to their charms.

After letting the famished fuckers raid my kitchen pantry, I led them to my bedroom and let them *raid* my pussy.

Christmas came early for me last year. Santa brought me what I really wanted: not joy to the world but joy in bed. I had two pink cocks hard as a candy cane to lick and fuck the shit out of me. Priceless! And I'm not talking about those boring TV commercials from *MasterCard*.

My "fucking fugitives" really let loose that night; not only by beating up other inmates who stood in their way during their "escape", but beating up my horny, needy pussy as if it's their last night on earth. Think of the Japanese Army in the Philippines back in World War II as they retreated; just destroying everything on their path.

I let Steve eat my pussy like it was his last meal and I *ate* Brendan like he was my last meal. Never die on an empty stomach!

"Save some appetite for tomorrow, bitch," Brendan reminded me while he was on all fours on top of my queen size bed.

The one major difference in this scenario was the fact that the escaped convicts were in a much nicer and more comfortable bed; clean and dressed in satin sheets. And the cigarettes are free!

From news reports and video footage at the time of David Sweat's arrest, he really looked like he'd gone through hell and lived in pure filth and squalor during those sixteen days of evading capture. For my own Dannemora role play scenario, I vowed to pamper my fucking fugitives the best I can.

I'm a true believer in good karma: you treat others well and they'll treat your pussy--or ass--right.

Naturally, I had to provide first class amenities to my lovers on the lam. At one point in the night while we were doing the nasty, I even let them enjoy my queen size bed all to themselves. I had them both in doggystyle position while I was kneeling on the floor, giving those solid meaty glutes the best pleasuring only a lusty lonely divorcee could give. I even wore DIORouge lipstick that night. Tell me how many luscious lips in this world you know that's covered in expensive lipstick do *that* these days?

Many years ago, I hooked up with a rising "director" from Los Angeles, a big and tall handsome guy of Arabian descent--code name director-of entertainment--who prefers his "models" do regular touch ups on their makeup, especially their lips, because "it looks so good on video", he said.

I've also dated real life jail wardens in the past: Mario from Salinas Valley Prison, Daniel from the Santa Rita Jail and Alex from the San Jose Main Jail. No arrests involved. Just plenty of frisking and fucking.

Going back to my "fucking fugitives", Steve and Brendan, and the moans and groans they made that night, they seem to have thoroughly enjoyed the oral pleasures that I gave them; a time honored classic bedroom routine of mine. A man will remember you not for the meals and dishes you prepared for him, but how you tossed his salad.

He loves his mom's cooking, not his wife's!

Steve and Brendan "left" in the wee hours of the morning to avoid "capture". They may have left my luxurious bedroom in total filth and disarray like their bunkers, with all the sweat and sperm stains and spilled beer and cigarette butts on my carpeted bedroom floor, but in hindsight, they left me with a brand new outlook in life: some "criminals" have good intentions...in bed.

In the ensuing days after my "fucking fugitives" have left, I had to hire a cleaning service, had to swallow a bunch of Tylenol pills and had to order a wheelchair from Kaiser. I couldn't walk for days! Sometimes in sex the classic rule applies: No pain, no gain!

Another memorable role play scene I've "produced" and performed in includes my handsome lover from the USMC, Peter. In it, I requested that he'll be my pimp and that I was not able to give him his share of my earnings the night before, but did promise to come up with some cash the following day. When I failed to keep my word, he showed up in my "hotel" the following night, ransacked my room, slapped me silly and sat on top of me while yelling repeatedly "Where's my money, bitch?!"

He only stopped when he realized I had an orgasm. He dismounted my face, put his uniform back on and bolted out of the room as fast as an F16 out of the USS Enterprise. He yelled out 'See ya next time, bitch!' on his way out with a naughty grin. How could you not *love* a man in uniform?

Okay, diary. Time to put the pen down and start grabbing on some penises. It's getting late and I've got another date. See you next time!

Your friend,
May Ligzaratvu..."

HIGH SCHOOL LIFE

Filipina singer and actress, Sharon Cuneta, once had a hit song back in the late '70s called "High School Life" in which she sang about crushes and other exciting things teenage life could offer. Well, I'm not one to dwell and dabble on boring stuff, so fast forward to the new millennium, there is a new kind of "high school experience" going on in my life: sex and its pleasures only a horny jailbait would know and appreciate. Move over, Britney! I'm gonna do *it* again, too!

Nothing gets a grown up man *going*--especially those in their late thirties and up--than a sex scene depicting teen sex. It instantly reminds them of their fucking days in Pussyville High.

As a "student" during these modern times--certainly not those fast times at Ridgemont High--I like going all the way and doing more nasty things: things that would surely give my evil teachers back in the Philippines--Lolita Poposen in particular--a sudden heart attack had she caught me doing it thirty years prior.

When I summoned my luscious lover, Miguel, to my house back in October 2017, it was not to do homework together but rather as the song goes, focus on makin' whoopee together. Miguel, a half white, half Mexican stunner, was not stunned at all after hearing my roleplay request. Are you kidding me? Ninety nine percent of my lovers are "yes" men. Their prime objective in life aside from having great careers and a nice car is to make their girl Vanessa happy and give her a great orgasm. Thus I am the luckiest girl in the world. You don't need to get a Ph.D to figure that one out; maybe a trip to the D to get tested instead.

I advised Miguel that during sex, I will be acting like a curious girlfriend cautiously trying new and different positions and eventually enjoying them wholeheartedly. The results, as you can imagine, were, unlike my final grades in Math and Geometry in high school back in the Philippines taught by my evil teacher Lolita, a success.

And of course, no babies involved. Unlike those stupid and slutty knocked up skanks from that reality show on TV, I learned from early on that if I were to become a teen slut on a rampage, I'd have to invest in condoms as well, not just wild color eye shadows.

I WANT SOME PAPA RONNIE

One fine Saturday afternoon this past summer, I stopped by my neighborhood Little Caesars on my way home from a shopping trip. While in line, I whispered to myself "I'm having papa Ronnie." Apparently, the cashier had heard me and asked me to clarify.

"I'm sorry, did you say you wanted pepperoni?", he asked.

Why I mumbled something like that I don't know. I suppose that's what true love--for a man's big strong body--does to a lustful lady like me. You just blurt things out from out of nowhere.

In traditional gay lingo in the Philippines, "papa" means boytoy or male lover; almost like a term of endearment. Hence my use of that word preceding "Ronnie"--or any of my young lovers' names.

On a more serious note, I think I really am in love with my Baby Boy, my one and only papa Ronnie.

We've been seeing each other for fifteen years now. "If you don't call it love, I don't know what else you'd call it, baby," I told Ronnie one time while licking the tip of his cock.

"Yesss nasty mamahh," was his breathy reply.

That alone gives me satisfaction and affirmation, along with the fact that I know I'm giving my Baby Boy the greatest kind of pleasure only a genuinely nasty mature woman can give her lover.

I met baby faced Ronnie back in the summer of 2005, much thanks to the now non existent Craigslist Personals. My Indian-American lover, Mike, and I wanted to get a little adventurous in the bedroom so he decided to invite a third party. Ronnie showed up. All three of us had a nice time together that evening. Before we parted ways, Ronnie asked for my phone number. The following week he was back in my bedroom giving me what I regularly require from men: a good orgasm.

I think I've had more sexual encounters with Ronnie rather than with Mike. We were so into each other. Ronnie couldn't refuse my man pleasing skills and I couldn't resist the way he'd tease and please my body, eventually sending me into fits of ecstasy and ultimately, a loud orgasm.

It's still crystal clear in my mind how he'd put his elbows behind his head, revealing his beautiful armpits and the few specs of hair in them and the certain way he'd close his eyes at the peak of the pleasure he is experiencing which I find so arousing. It makes me want to please him more and make him very happy in bed.

Ronnie, along with my other lover, Chris, came to my life around the same time some fifteen years ago when I was recovering from a broken heart caused by my break up with my previous lover, Mark. Chris and Ronnie were the remedy, and slowly but surely, became the cure for the pain and depression that plagued me after Mark left me.

But, the pain and loneliness are gone and everything is behind me now, except Ronnie's beautiful behind, which I love putting in front of me and on top of me during his delicious visits.

On Ronnie's most recent visit, I surprised him by wearing one of my short and tight dresses by Express. Men just go crazy hard and horny when I have it on; as expected, it had the same effect on my Baby Boy. I even danced a little bit in a slow and sensual way, shaking my hips and ass like Stormy D when she was young.

Ronnie excitedly moved towards me and started groping me, kissing me on the back of my neck, whispering in my ear "You're running around in that short dress with that sexy lil ass of yours hanging out."

I felt like a hot and horny housewife teasing her husband who had just got home from work, getting him all pumped up and ready for some bedroom fun before dinner. I know, I'm "such a tease" (to quote the dozens of men who fell victim to my feminine wiles).

I tell you, if only wives and girlfriends would dress and act this way every time their man comes home, divorce rates would go down. But, of course, if the wife or girlfriend is a genuine hardcore evil bitch from the get go, that's a totally different story and it belongs in the Dr. Phil show.

As for my Baby Boy, I have one simple message for you if you happen to read my book: I love the hair on your balls and the soft fur on your ass crack. I'm glad you make no effort in shaving them off. Leave it like that, please. So natural. So beautiful. Mama loves you!

LET'S HAVE A THREESOME!

A threesome is fun if it's done right and with the right people. It's a big plus if the men you're going to do it with are comfortable with each other. This saves everyone involved from having that awkward, uneasy feeling while the bed is rocking and shaking. Luckily for me, everything went smoothly as I was getting *lucky* with my lover and his buddy.

I sometimes ask my friend and lover, Mike, if he side hustles as an "event organizer" of some sort, considering the fact that he had arranged, organized and planned half of my menage-`a-trois encounters with some men out there: divorce' Steve by Downtown San Jose, college hottie Shane from Union City and my very own Baby Ronnie.

I do my "homework" and "research" for my own "projects" as well.

First, I ask for a photo. I am a visual person. There has to be physical attraction before any physical *connection* or "connecting" takes place.

Once I have the players submit the photo requirements, the interview process begins. I make it a habit to first get to know and have a "feel" of who I am meeting: a week-long email exchange or text messaging would be smart. That way, there will be a "warming up" period; plus you get to familiarize yourselves with one another. I'd ask questions and would likewise tell them what I'm into and how I visualize our upcoming bedroom activity for three. I want the three of us to be comfortable with one another before heading to the Comfort Inn.

I also ask for their input before I let them *put* it in me: what they like, what turns them on, what limitations they have.

I am so detail oriented when it comes to almost every aspect of life and that includes my sex life and the things I enjoy doing in the bedroom. I want things to go smoothly and scot free as much as possible.

Once the stage is set, all we need is a bedroom set. That should be easy. Good old Krobel Inn is the place to be!

Some of my memorable threesome experiences were with buddies John and Zach from Fremont, Palo Alto resident Frank and his roommate and Livermore daddy Gary and his friend, Jeff.

Another encounter, one that I consider extra special and spicy, happened back in 2005 with Texas native Robert Valenz and a local UPS driver he met on a chat site. Robert and I "acted" like husband and wife and when the UPS driver knocked to make a delivery, we invited him straight to our marriage bedroom to bring us the *package.*

That UPS guy was sexy AF; tall and handsome, with an athletic build and a meaty, big dick that could feed an entire residential neighborhood. Suffice to say that Milpitas "couple" Robert and Vanessa were pleased and satisfied with the package *delivery.*

At one point, on a separate occasion, I had three guys rocking my bed, which automatically became a foursome–or a gangbang of some sort. Mike felt a little extra adventurous and decided to invite a third guy. It somehow backfired when he noticed that one of the younger guys–about twenty–was enjoying himself a little too much and was getting more attention from me. "Baby, mama is an equal opportunity employer," I told Mike. "No need to be jealous."

After the other two had left, I gave Mike a "bonus" for all his efforts and for doing such a great job: another *service* before he went home. I wanted to give him the assurance that he was still my favorite no matter how hard the hot twenty year-old Middle Eastern stud tried to get my full attention.

A more recent encounter happened back in the fall of 2019; this time with my friends Jeff and Ken acting like my step "uncles". The three of us enjoy role playing as nieces and uncles in the bedroom. A common scenario would have something to do with my "dad" and "stepmom" being out of town and that I'm left in the "care" of my two step uncles ("brothers" of my dad's new "girlfriend") who are both single. They'd check on me in my room from time to time, making sure I'm doing my homework, etc.. But me being a spoiled little brat from the get go, I have a tendency to break the rules and just be naughty: look at dick pics on my phone and exchange *sext* messages with a bunch of guys. That's when the "disciplining" takes place. Uncle Jeff, the "strict" one, confronts me and lays out the rules. Uncle Ken overhears the commotion in my room–with Uncle Jeff scolding me–and he intervenes, telling Uncle Jeff there could be an alternative *way* to "discipline" me, one that involves less words but more *actions* instead. I suppose you know where this is going.

Being literally the center of attention is a wonderful thing, especially if the men you're with love spoiling you rotten in the bedroom. Plus, the fact that these two gentlemen are comfortable with each other makes the entire occasion a lot of fun.

THE WHORE FROM OLONGAPO

Once, in the Philippines, I had a flirtatious and frisky middle aged neighbor named Melly who sold *merienda* (afternoon snacks) and also had a penchant for sharing raunchy tales of her shady, checkered past as a prostitute in Olongapo, Philippines where the US Naval Base once stood.

Melly worked as a whore from the dime a dozen bars in the naval mecca of Asia– Olongapo–back in the 1980s. She's now in her 70s and her golden days of whoring--which included *golden showers* sometimes--is way behind her. Or so the neighborhood thought. Melly was unusually proud about sharing her bedroom stories--the adult kind.

Out of the money that came from her days of "putting out" as a Pinay *puta* , she was able to put up a *sari sari* store (small store in front of a house). She also sells fried golden bananas on a stick, or *bananacue*, a favorite Filipino *merienda*. Ironic when you think that two decades ago she was the one doing the "eating" of the dozens of "bananas"--with different shapes and sizes--and getting *sticked*.

Melly the Puta has some stories to tell and they're not exactly the kind you'd read to your child before bedtime albeit hers certainly involve lots of beds and sleeping...with Prince Charmings with crispy American dollar bills, not beanstalks, in their pockets.

One popular anecdote this former cock-doting woman likes to share with the townsfolk was an incident back in the mid-1980s when local police raided the motel room where she and two American servicemen were staying. Melly was *servicing* the servicemen that moment. She was getting double penetrated when two Filipino cops blasted in her room yelling "*Raid to!*" ("This is a raid!")

Melly fondly and funnily recalls how her moans and groans changed in a blink of an eye:

"*Putang ina! 'Ahh ako ng ahh' habang tinitira ako nung dalawang kano hanggang biglang naging 'Ahhy mga putang inanyo! Magsilayas kayo!*'" ("Son of a bitch! My 'ahh' moans turned into 'Oh, you sons of bitches! Get out of here!'")

Some things never change. Melly the former puta, like any other whore, is still as foul mouthed as any sailor she's *anchored* herself with back in her Subic Bay days. I wish her well and hope her banana business thrives for a second time.

Chapter 9

STDS (SEX TRUTHS AND DISCLOSURES)

MY DADDY ISSUES

Now I understand why men--regardless of age or status in life--need and crave the company of another woman--or transwoman--outside his marriage. He is the eternal Peter Pan, curious and adventurous. Likewise, there is a Hugh Hefner *in* every man. Sex for him is a major life rule, a forever must. He lives and breathes women…or women with male parts.

Looking back at my early teenage years, when my paternal grandparents would fight and argue about issues of infidelity, I now have a clear sense why.

For a man, his libido is his baby. His car is his other love. He has to nurture both, making sure they are running fine and ready to *go* anytime.

This might sound like a cliche`, but men need to fuck constantly. And men in their 60s are no exemption. I realized this first hand many years ago because my paternal grandfather apparently had a mistress.

Coincidentally, he and my Grandmother weren't sleeping in the same bed during the time that I was living with them. I never saw them together in the master's bedroom.

Almost thirty years later, the puzzle has been solved. My grandfather, like some of my older lovers these days--my "daddies"--was in his early 60s at the time, and believe me when I say my "daddies" could still fuck like rabbits. It even makes some of them blush every time they hear me say "Damn, daddy, you fuck like a twenty year old."

My great, late 63 year-old grandfather, god bless his soul, was just like any other older gentleman I've dated: a prisoner of his unflinching sexual desires.

CALL ME "DADDY"

Why I do what I do--calling an older lover "Daddy"--is simply beyond me. All I know is there is a sexy, mature and confident man lying next to me, taking care of me and never leaving my bed without satisfying me.

Sometimes being a high strung, demanding bitch can also be tiring. Sometimes I just want to sit back--or lay on my back--and have a guy over fifty dominate both my senses and sensitive parts.

"Come on, Daddy. Punish me! I've been a naughty girl" would be my favorite line when I'm doing the nasty with a single, married or divorced "Daddy." Daddy likes it!

Conversely, he is so turned on and empowered by it, especially if his "baby girl" is as kinky as me. I come once in a million years, you know. With all my creativity and natural talents in and out of the bedroom, there will never be another one like me. Men will never find another one *like* me. Some men might disagree, but their dicks won't. My longtime lover, Martin, recently confessed that "there will be no one else" like me. He even suggested I make a video of my pleasing skills and sell them online.

I love how men's dicks would stand in full attention the minute I walk in a hotel room. It happened to my ex lover, Mark, many times. "Sorry, Vanessa, I get an instant hard-on everytime you walk in," he'd say.

Sometimes I think of myself as a walking Viagra pill.

"Vanessa, look what you did! You got my dick hard already!" would be the common line I'd hear from one of my "daddy" friends. It's like a long playing album: I hear it over and over again!

Viagra aside, I can make five or more daddies achieve amazing orgasms in one night as evident in my December 2017 trysts with seven men. And these are men over 50, mind you. Not a lot of men in that age range could orgasm properly--some have a hard time, some don't orgasm at all; until they meet the one and only Filipino transsexual Vanessa.

Amazing how some of my "daddies" would be so dumbfounded and in a state of disbelief after I make them have an orgasm--loud and hard.

"Vanessa, what did you just do to me?" is what I'd often hear.

I just give them a smile.

Some would simply call me a "miracle worker".

I suppose that's the reason why those "daddies" love me. They can survive five years of nagging and bullshit from their wives and girlfriends but they can't live without the five seconds of intense pleasure and earth shaking orgasm they get from the one and only Vanessa.

There is a certain kind of devilish grin on my face every time a daddy of mine gets out of the shower and towels himself dry in front of me. I have a penchant for asking how his family is doing, particularly his adult son. I wonder how junior would react once he finds out that his old man is having way better sex than him, getting laid nonstop like there's no tomorrow.

My train of "threesome with father and son" thought would be abruptly derailed by the beeping of my phone, signaling another text message from another daddy that typically says "Call me. Daddy."

AT FORTY

When I turned 40, I realized that all the riches in the world can't compare to the rich love and pleasure my lovers--especially my Baby Ronnie--give me. Our time together is more precious than gold, sweeter than honey and spicier than *habanero*.

Life is really worth living when you're with someone who treats you well and makes you feel extra special.

I also realized that the true meaning of luxury does not depend on the expensive cars in your garage or the exotic places you visit. Luxury is also a special kind of feeling--when you are being pleased and pampered by a gorgeous, sexy man with no abandon. And you don't have to spend a single dime for it! No! I am not one of those desperate housewives who are into pay for play. I have plenty of men to play with, for free.

Only at that point will you discover that you won't have to ask for anything more.

I realized that I prefer having a hot and handsome stud wrapped around my body rather than the dozens of high karat gold jewelry and other precious gems I possess. These days, nothing excites me more than a glistening hard cock in my hands.

YOU'RE SO COCKY!

Guys love the way I suck cock. I mean, men of all ages--18 and up--think I'm a cocksucking champ. Ask me how I do it or why I do it so well and your guess is as good as mine. Maybe it's an inborn talent. A learned skill perhaps? Who knows? All I know is if you love to eat--food--then you're likely destined to enjoy eating cock as well.

If Beyonce is the ultimate performer on stage, I could be most likely the ultimate performer in bed.

All praises aside, I really think my true forte lies in the art and act of fellatio. Maybe I am really a cocksucking champ. After all, a one time lover from Petaluma, CA commented "Damn, girl. You suck dick like a champ!"

GET A ROOM!

Anyone who says Krobel Inn is not synonymous with all things seedy--and sexy--is a big, fat liar. Just like its regular tenant--the one and only Vanessa--it has a reputation. Having stayed there religiously for almost twenty years, the experience is one for the books. At the Krobel Inn where I stay, I've seen and heard almost everything and anything: gangbangs, police shootouts, beatdowns, and of course, loud sluts and whores. There are also lighthearted moments such as family members hanging around the barbecue pit on a warm July afternoon while unruly little brats run around the courtyard.

But forget the seedy and shady stuff that has been going on at the Krobel Inn that I go to. Everywhere you go, there will always be seedy and shady stuff going on! Think of the White House before President Biden took office.

It has been, for nearly two decades, my second home. At the Krobel Inn that I go to, I find peace and calm as well as pleasure and joy; thanks to my armada of lovers and all the masseurs I've hired over the years. As one song's lyrics goes: they "put my soul at ease."

Life is not perfect at the Krobel Inn. There was also pain and heartache. At the Krobel Inn I call my second home, deals have been brokered and ties were severed; not to mention me tying up one of my guests using a pair of nylon stockings.

Now we're talking.

Many a Tuesday night I met rejection face to face.

People would just walk out on me as quickly as they had entered my room; men who did not approve of my looks. That or my appearance did not meet their expectations. They were probably looking for a Barbie tranny. I could've cussed out those jerks, told them "Go to Toys 'R Us, motherfuckers!"

For a time, I considered that act--walking out of a room just because you did not like the appearance of the person you're meeting--part of the holy rosary: the elusive sixteenth mystery!

I used to ask myself "Why? What went wrong?"

Nowadays, I just say "Fuck it and fuck you! Go to hell! Get outta here!" with a Bobby De Niro accent.

I've learned to let go. I cannot be bothered by all that ridiculousness anymore. Life is too short and I've got bigger fish to fry.

When I turned 40, I learned to let go of the assholes--but kept the nice *ones*. There is no point in holding on to something not worthy of a single second of my precious life. If you let the bad and hurtful memories linger, pain will continue to reign over you. At some point in your life, you really need to follow the *Frozen* character Elsa's advice: Let it go!

Because I consider Krobel Inn my second home, I only let good things happen when I'm there. No more awful people and awkward scenes. And when I'm home--particularly in bed--my pleasure is of utmost importance.

Yes, I've stayed in other hotels, but nothing beats sex in my queen size Krobel Inn bed. It's so cozy and comfortable and you don't have to worry about it getting dirty and stained because the clean sheets are unlimited; at least for me. Maids and even front desk receptionists have extra clean sheets handy for me the minute they see me.

"Here comes the nasty bitch" is what they probably whisper to each other.

"Here are your extra sheets, Miss Vanessa. Enjoy your stay." is what I actually hear when I check in.

Just by looking at my queen size bed, my blood turns green. Maybe because I can't help but think and reminisce about the many kinky sex acts I've done on top of it with my willing lovers; not to mention the upcoming encounters I'll be having. The possibilities for being creative while in bed are endless.

One of my regular visitors, Jon J, once told me "I can only imagine all the sex you're having in your hotel bed. Must be a lot of fun. You must have some crazy stories to tell."

Once, the Filipino front desk receptionist jokingly told me *"Bendisyunan mo na yung bagong kama! Ha ha ha!"* ("Be the first one to fuck in the brand new bed! Ha ha ha!")

I like trying different positions and scenarios when I'm with my lover or lovers. Remember, creativity is key. I let my imagination run wild while the hotel maids are busy running up and down the corridors, constantly in a hurry to bring me fresh new sheets and clean towels.

Some of my favorite "scenarios" include "My husband just left for work and I'm having my mystery lover over" and "I'm a horny divorcee wanting some hot new stud with a nice body to satisfy me". My number one favorite is "I'm bringing this hot guy I met at Starbucks this morning back home".

But, at the Krobel Inn that I go to, the maids are not the only ones working. In order for these naughty fantasies of mine to happen, I have to do some work, online work, that is. And no, I'm not one of those Facebook addicts monitoring other people's photos 24/7 and the stupid shit they post on social media websites.

Once in a while, I would put up an ad on Craigslist inviting potential guests and companions to satisfy my bedroom cravings. You'd be surprised by the number of applicants who are interested in filling up--and *performing* certain "positions".

Once, I had a "new hire" come over and informed him on the spot that not only was I his boss, but I will be the same person giving him a physical as well. This petite and handsome 40 year old guy with a not so petite penis happily obliged. I like that in a man. A "yes" man is a hired man!

Mike initially confided that he worked for the utility company and I immediately suggested we do a role play scene of him acting like some sort of a water bill collector and me a sexy stay-at-home mom whose husband missed out on our monthly payment and that I would have to "pay" using my pussy. Mike happily obliged.

After this encounter, he was never the same man again. He confessed afterwards that no one else had made him orgasm so quickly the way I did; that and the fact that it felt so good.

Utility companies with hung and horny bill collectors should also have the payment option "pay-by-pussy" available. Makes life easier for everyone involved, as long as both parties agree.

At the Krobel Inn that I go to, love is also a possibility, not just lovemaking and other bedroom activities.

At the Krobel Inn I know back in 2005, my former boyfriend, Jon Drissom, declared his unconditional love for me. It was around the time that a strong and powerful hurricane named Katrina was wreaking havoc in Louisiana.

Jon's love for me, it turned out, was twice as powerful as Katrina. For the next three years, he showered me with monetary and material gifts, took me out dining at the best restaurants and shouldered every major expenditure that came my way. He really *took* care of me. I am so thankful for that.

Jon would check on me every day, asking me how my day was and if I needed help with anything

Three years later, it was a totally different story. Jon broke up with me and I was completely devastated. It nearly ruined me. But, just like the citizens of the great state of Louisiana, I eventually recovered, with great optimism.

I remember driving home in my Mercedes and thought it was raining hard because I was having a hard time seeing what was in front of me; only to find out seconds later that it was actually the tears in my eyes blurring my vision.

Jon leaving me for a selfish, opportunistic, separated middle aged woman from the Philippines nearly destroyed me.

But, as soon as he handed me a $5,000 check--a "severance pay" of some sort, I quickly wiped off the tears, retouched my makeup and headed straight to Nordstroms and Ben Bridge Jewellers. I told myself "Fuck being sad and fuck that user bitch! I'm going shopping!"

In a letter he had sent me many years after we broke up, Jon said that he fell in love with me "on the very first day" he met me.

I've weathered many storms in my life. Nothing scares me anymore. You really need to be one tough tranny bitch in order to survive in this world. People will stab you in the back, stab you in the heart and will even fuck with your head, but it's how you come out of it that will define your true character as a person, as a fighter and as a survivor, and of course, what you're really made of.

Chapter 10

THE JOKES ARE ON ME

If medical mariuana is the rumored cure for many pains and illnesses, one thing I can assure you is that laughter *is* still the best medicine. Now, I'm not here to aspire to become a great comedian like Steve Martin or Robin Williams, nor do I aspire to surpass the comedies of Dante, but out of the innumerable pains and tragedies I had in life, I find relief and revelry in humor.

911 MEN TO THE RESCUE

When I was living in Manila back in the late `80s, I used to watch *Rescue 911* (hosted by William Shatner) on TV a lot. In 2003, after almost fifteen years, never in my life did I imagine that I would be riding in the back of an ambulance myself. Thankfully, my injuries weren't serious and I came out okay. A fat woman in a minivan rear ended me at 40 miles per hour. Bitch was probably paying attention to the Big Mac in front of her instead of paying attention to her driving.

My days of watching *Rescue 911* are long gone. Nowadays, whenever I'm at the local bar, I do enjoy watching and observing hot First Responders horse around and be themselves--boys.

First Responders--the men in particular--are some of the hottest and sexiest heroes around. There is no denying that I've always fantasized about being in bed, not in a gurney, with some of them. Luckily, I've dated a few of them in my lifetime. Suffice to say that they really helped in putting out the fire...in my pussy.

Let me share some para-men-dic tales that might require immediate attention.

Once, at a local bar in Sunnyvale, CA, I told a couple of sexy off duty paramedics that a much better way to find out if I'm still alive is not to pump my heart with CPR moves, but rather pump my ass with a big, hard dick. If I scream that means I'm still alive.

I always have 9-1-1 on my speed dial especially when my big assed lovers come over because there is always the possibility that their big, beautiful behinds would smother and suffocate me, eventually causing a heart attack. Actually, sometimes I feel as if I'm having a heart attack every time I see a hot guy with a bubble butt. So, yes, I *always* have 9-1-1 on my speed dial! It's a must!

Sometimes, after I post an ad on Craigslist's Casual Encounter section, I get confused after getting a bunch of responses--and eventually, visitors. In the wee hours of the morning, I begin to wonder if I'm still in my hotel suite at the Marriott or I'm at the Playboy Mansion on a Sunday morning: there's just too many naked bodies lying around.

THE JOCKS ARE ON ME

I love Buster Posey--one of the greatest athletes in history. I love his body, too. Look at those thighs! And just his name alone--Buster--it sounds like my ass is up for a wild, fun and crazy ride. One can only imagine how he *is* in the bedroom.

Below is my personal tribute and show of appreciation for my imaginary slugger lover boy, Buster.

1) It's *the* good life. Let go of the stress and let Buster in!
2) I told my soon to be ex husband to replace our toilet bowl with a larger one before he packs up and leaves because as soon as he exits the door, I'll be inviting Buster in.
3) How I'd love for Buster to join this other sexy slugger named Anthony in the dancing and twerking on that popular late night comedy show on TV a couple of years ago. What a great way to die--getting teased in the face by two of the sports world's meatiest butts.

KINKY KIKI MALACHITE IS BACK!
LISTEN TO WHAT SHE HAS TO SAY:

1) Sometimes I feel like a foster child: So many daddies abusing me and abandoning me afterwards: "Daddy? Daddy? Can you be my Daddy? Daddy, please?"

2) A typical bedroom banter between me and a "daddy": Daddy: "Thanks for the awesome blow job, baby." Me: "You're welcome, Daddy. Wish I could do more, but I'll be late for school." Daddy: "It's okay, baby. It's the throat that counts."

3) An afternoon with ALEXIA: Stay-at-home dad: "ALEXIA, talk dirty to me while I jack off. Tell me you want to eat my ass." ALEXIA: "Can't. Wife will be home in a couple of minutes."

4) Once, my ex boyfriend, Guy Lozero, noticed the dark spots on my knee cap, suggesting that people with such marks tend to kneel a lot. Well, you can imagine the Ursula-esque smirk on my face the minute he mentioned it. In my mind, "Yes, honey. I kneel a lot in your living room while you're at work and my lunchtime lover is on top of your couch, getting *eaten* by me."

5) Back in the Philippines in the early `90s, I was so into clothes by Company B; these days I just want BB's company--my super sexy "daddy" friend.

6) Either you eat ass or you eat pussy. What's your poison?

7) My innate talent when it comes to accurately weighing silver and gold pieces must have come from my many bedroom experiences, particularly guys of different shapes and sizes sitting on me.

8) A Starry Storyline: A brief exchange from my imagined film, *Star Whores*, with the alleged father meeting his estranged child for the first time at the immigration holding facility in Texas: Dad Vader: "Bitch, I am your father." Loca Skywalker (an undocumented trans teen of mixed race being pimped out by some shady characters, starving): "*Yo quiero Taco Bell papi, por favor.*"

9) If I were to produce an online ad for a potential pornographic flick titled, *SleepTrain Mistress,* I'd probably hire two macho studs (in a box truck), making a drop at the home of this lusty, jeweled up middle aged divorcee in full makeup and short tight dress, waiting in the master's bedroom. The marketing slogan would say "Pull a train on your new SleepTrain mistress" or "When you see the SleepTrain truck across the street, expect your slutty neighbor to sleep good tonight!"

10) White Meat Only: You know the saying that goes "White meat does good for the body!"

11) Cumcast: My lover, Ricky, playing as a broadband installer: Horny housewife: "From the moment I saw your ass I knew we had a connection." Ricky (on the floor, fixing cables, bubble butt sticking out): "Oh yeah?" Horny Housewife: "Yes, baby. I wanted to plug my tongue in you."

12) The truth about men's love affair with tits: A guy would fuck a quadriplegic broad or a dirty blond--and I mean *durrrty* like Stormy D--as long as she has big tits. That's just the way it is. A man doesn't even care if she's in a wheelchair; as long as she's got the bazumas. That dick has got to go somewhere!

13) My zits are like bad tenants from the projects. They're just so fucking hard to evict!

14) A Bitchin' Exchange: Bitchy Gen Z: "Look at you! You're so fucking ugly!" Kiki: "I can't wait to see the look on your face once I start fucking your dad. Let's see who's gonna be the ugly one. I'll tell your dad to give me your allowance money after I have sex with him and you'll end up eating toilet paper in the girls' restroom during lunch. Broke ass bitch!"

15) I'm really not into Carrie Underwood or Taylor Swift. I'm just into dicks.

16) When I was young, I was into fairy tales. Now that I'm older, I'm into furry tails: "Looks like my Prince Charming's got a hairy bubble butt. Can't blame him. Who shaves their ass in the Middle Ages anyway?"

17) The very first time my gorgeous lover Ricky rubbed his ass on my nose I got hooked. I was hooked like Tom Cruise got hooked on Scientology. I never looked back!

18) I sometimes go on a mindset that my asshole's name is "Porsche" whenever I'm at the local bar on a Saturday night to pick up a bunch of guys and bring them back home with me in my diminutive European sports car. My libido level goes on overdrive when one of the boys would curiously ask "How are we gonna *fit* in your Porsche?"

19) No More Stress: Before, when someone gives me the dirty look or say something smart I might punch them in the mouth, but nowadays I just yell out "Fuck off!". I'd rather spend my energy scrolling down on hot ass pics on tumblr than pay attention to some asshole who doesn't really mean anything to me.

20) "Eau Daddie" is what I'd name a fragrance brand that I would especially create in honor of the silver foxes in my life. It would have a strong, woodsy scent. "Eau Bebe" for the young studs. It would have a fresher, fruitier scent.

21) A Street Whore Named Desire: Desire: "Hey, Mr. Arseteen, I'm an actress now and I got a role for an upcoming play!" Mr. Arseteen: "Is that so? And what's the title of this play, my dear?" Desire: "His Glorious Body" Mr. Arseteen: "Interesting. And the part you're going to play?" Desire: "Hisbatt. An exotic looking transgender teen working the streets at night."

22) I keep telling my daddy friend "Daddy, you might have the libido of Justin Beiber, but remember, you have the ligaments of Joe Biden. No more moshpit diving at concerts!"

23) Once, I got pulled over by a big, beautiful bear-ish cop in Danville, CA and my initial response as soon as he approached my driver side window was "Please don't beat me up, officer! Please don't beat me up!" I wanted him to use his *baton* on me though. He was gorgeous!

24) People ask me if I ever went to college. Naturally, such rude questions deserve a ridiculous answer: "Yes, I did. It's called Noe Reed University." And when they act skeptical about it and further inquire about the campus location I just follow up with "It's on Enny Street in California."

25) Sometimes being a mature whore is like being a used car in a car dealership lot. Guys want to ride you but they don't want to pay a lot of money.

26) One time I texted a bunch of white fuck buddies and not one responded. I was so depressed and disappointed. It was like organizing a KKK rally and not one guy showing up.

27) "Come on, baby! Wrap those thick thighs around my neck like eczema!"

28) Hey Sexy Daddy from Kentucky: "You have more thighs than a bucket of KFC. I love it!"

29) Legos and Play Dohs are for kids and their kiddie activities. Dildos, nipple clamps and anal beads are for horny daddies and me during our *fucktivities*.

30) My tongue has more viruses than Anthony Weiner's laptop.

31) I had more asses sit on me than the men's locker room toilet at Penn State.

32) Mean Old Lady at the Bingo Hall: "Don't sit next to me ya filthy whore!" Kiki: "You're the ringleader of DAR (Daughters of the American Revolution) and you're

still alive, bitch? You must be 150 years old now. You must've fucked Abe Lincoln, too! Mean old nasty bitch!"

33) Once a male friend asked if I ever ate pussy. "Why, yes, of course," was my enthusiastic response. "It's the kind of pussy found on a guy's asscrack. It's called *manpussy*."

34) Having sex with a senior citizen fella is like dealing with an ovulating wife or girlfriend, I'm sure you guys--you guys--have experienced it before. You have got to put up with the *cycle*. Sometimes he'd have an orgasm, sometimes he won't. Sometimes I have to wait for a couple of days before his balls fill up.

35) Elderly Care: I sometimes feel tempted to ask the following questions to my octogenarian lover as he orgasms: Old Man Cummings: "Yes, yes, yes!" I'd ask him: "Do you need a walker? A wheelchair? Am I in your will?"

36) A Short Play/Musical: Dolly, Pardon The Late Night Banging: Dolly, a retired madam who manages a rundown apartment complex in Detroit and a transsexual tenant and her horde of late night horse-hung hunky humpers honkering down in Apartment H regularly. Dolly's opening line: "Sweet Jesus! She's a HO-le new kind of deal!"

37) My fellow students in high school didn't believe in me too much. They voted for Tammy Lynn as Most Likely to Succeed. They should've put her in the Most Likely to Suck Dick category, judging her notorious reputation as campus slut.

38) Now that the Corona virus is spreading and health officials have issued precautionary measures and stores are running out of face masks, should I start using Buster Posey's jock for a face mask?

39) Martha Talk: "Hi! I'm Martha and I will control your lives and everything you do and I will boss you around, bitches!"

40) More Martha Talk: "Now that you know how to clean and cook vegetables, leave me the fuck alone!"

41) Even More Martha Talk: "My strawberries and peppers are clean and fresh. I make sure my Mexican pickers wash their hands with...*voila*! My very own hand soap--the Martha hand soap, made in the Hamptons, in the beautiful United States of America!"

42) I'd sell my pussy so I can buy me some Gucci.

43) Yes, these are my terms!: 1) Nikka Teen (one of my bedroom nicknames): So addicting! 2) Lateeno: A hung 18 or 19 year old lover of Hispanic descent.3)

Sexiopath: A person who's a sex addict and commits crimes in order to achieve sexual gratification; like stealing dildos and nipple clamps from adult stores. 4) Men's Names in Alpha-booty-cal Order: From the stud with the biggest ass to the one with the skinniest. 5) Proper Men-agement: Scheduling your trysts and sexual encounters properly, so meetings and appointments with different men do not clash. 6) Fantascene: Sexy scenes in my mind that I eventually turn into reality or make happen in the bedroom. 7) Homme Improvement: A former lover who's improved his looks after not seeing him for 5 years. 8) Whor-king Girl: You get my point.

44) Sir Ernest Shackleton, Pay Attention: I have the endurance...in bed.

45) There's a new police headquarters in Allmenda County. It's located in Jasmine Abuslan's pussy.

46) Kiki Policy: No Money, No Entry; "Oh no, no, no chile. I treat my pussy like a masonic lodge. Only rich white guys can enter!"

47) My imaginary TV show (title and characters): The Sextons (The family that *sex* together stays together): Starring Kiki (as the Naughty Niece), Maurice (the Grandpa who loves Viagra), Will (the sinful Stepdad), Andrew (The biological father, or so I thought), Al (my Cousin Al...we have a *history*) and introducing, my naughty uncles--Jack, Kent, Franky and Donny. No mother figure. She left the house and never came back after seeing me on top of the coffee table doing a burlesque-like performance one afternoon when she arrived home from work; the men in the family were all sitting, watching me, with their hard dicks out. It was too much for her.

48) People these days are so fucking senstive! They're like my nipples.

49) Merry Christmas: A kiss under the mistletoe? Forget about it! How about I kiss Tommy's toe?

50) Bitch, you know more positions than my yoga instructor!

51) Now that my next door neighbor, Kevan, is a divorced man and the wife has moved out, it's just him and two other single guys–his adult son and brother in-law–who are left in the house. I imagine there's a lot of jerking happening in the evening. Maybe I should give them boxes of Kleenex and a few bottles of baby oil as Christmas presents.

52) Smash and grab thieves at Walgreens and other stores in San Francisco with their cohorts waiting in red Chargers and Mustangs outside: Little Red Riding Hoodrats.

53) You wanna swipe that cock up my ass? Remember to pay the anal fee.

54) You wanna enter my pussy? Enter at your own risk. I can't tell you what's inside.

55) First Impressions: The first thing that comes to mind everytime I see a hot guy is how his ass smells and tastes.

I GIVE YOU SOME VAGEENA MANLOG

We all have an alter ego--something or someone that we've always wanted to *be* or *become*, but we can't at the present time because of work, family and frankly, we're apprehensive because we feel a little embarrassed about it and unsure how others will receive us. We see him or her all the time when we're alone: We talk to ourselves when nobody's looking or we talk to our reflection when we're in front of the mirror. One of my greatest fantasies is to perform at a comedy club somewhere–with the alter ego Vageena Manlog–and share my jokes. It stays on the backburner for now. For now, that fantasy is just...a fantasy. Regardless, I'd like to share with you my precious Vageena; her jokes, I mean.

"You know, I was a big fan of Wilson Phillips back in the day. I still am, actually. Who could forget Carnie? That big bitch. I love her! I could totally relate to her. I was a big girl once. And, oh, how I love their song "Hold On". As a matter of fact I still sing it every morning when I wake up and look in the mirror to check on my bad teeth. I sing "Hold on for one more day!"."

"I used to give people a ride home when I was working for Walgreens. Yeah. I'm single, so why not. One evening, I gave this cute young co-worker a ride home. He's alright. Nice guy, you know, But, not my type. The next day, a senior citizen co-worker asked me if I could give him a ride home. I kinda felt sorry for him, so I was like, sure, why not. You know, you gotta respect old people, right? But as soon as he hopped in my car there came a weird funky smell. And as I continued driving the smell had gotten worse. I was like 'WTF?'. The next day, I mentioned it to my other co-workers. They laughed at me. "That's why we don't give Rodger a ride. He stinks!" one co-worker confessed. So, that same night as I was leaving work, Rodger asked me if I could give him a ride home again. I politely declined and drove off. 'Where's that young cute co-worker of mine?' I asked myself. I'd rather give my boy with a fresh smelling bubble butt a ride home than a stinky old man who pees in his pants. I wanted to tell Rodger in a polite way "You can't always depend on others to give you a ride home, Rodger dear. You need Depends!"."

"I once dated a gorgeous Latino grocery clerk. He's about 20, 21. Absolutely stunning. I think women--and some men--went shopping in that store just to get a glimpse of him. He had a very

nice body. This guy was packin meat! And I'm not talking about the rib eye steak and pork chops that I bought. Over time we've gotten friendly and later on friendlier. To the point that he'd hang out with me in my bedroom some nights. To keep me company. To let me taste the other meat he's packin'…inside his pants. While my boyfriend's out of town. One day, I saw him at the counter and when it was my turn to pay for my stuff he gave me a wink and asked how I was going to pay for my meat. 'You only take cash all the time anyway, right?' I shot back, with a wink."

"Once, while having lunch at a nice restaurant overlooking Monterey Bay, a relative of a friend kept insisting that I check out the otters swimming in the water. She probably mentioned it three times. On the third time I had to shut the bitch down. 'I know what an otter looks like! I see them all the time. In my bedroom!'. The woman gave me a confused look and I just continued chomping on my steak and baked potato. For those of you folks who are new to gay lingo and shit, an "otter" is a cute guy in his 20s with some beard and mustache."

"One time at a birthday party, some friend of a relative rudely commented on my teeth. He said they looked like the New York Skyline. Yeah, I know I have bad teeth. I love to eat. I love sweets. I can't get enough of cakes and candy. So, when this motherfucker mentioned it again, I shot back with 'Oh yeah? So, what are you gonna do about it? Pay for my dental plan? Or crash a 747 on it like the Taliban?'"

"Many years ago, I visited Louisiana and during a boat tour on the bayou I became very uneasy. The guy operating the boat was giving me such a mean look I really thought he was gonna throw me overboard and feed me to the alligators. I told myself, 'Just stick to the Mardi Gras Parade next time, V. Just stick to the Mardi Gras Parade. You get to take the beads home and add them to your jewelry collection'. Hey, you gotta at least try to make negative things turn into something positive, right?"

"For my second life, I wish to return as the University of Michigan's Wolverines locker room. Can you imagine seeing beauty all the time for the rest of your life? No, not Penn State. I'd be fighting with Jerry Sandusky all the time."

"I asked my one time lover, Nick: "You believed in me once. What happened? What changed, my love? Is it because of my chronic whoring? I can't help it. I'm stuck to it like Jesus is stuck to the cross. So hard to break free!"

"What? Pay for a ticket to see that wannabe comedian Dave? That sorry ass mothafucka?!? Hell no! I'd rather give my money to the homeless guy at the intersection. At least he's got something nice to say to people like me like 'God bless you!' and 'Have a nice day!'. I ain't givin' that mean ass homophobic mothafucka shit! Na-ah! He a thug! He a thug! Na-ah!"

MORE VAGEENA MANLOG TALK (IN TAGALOG)

Vageena Manlog, critic and comedian, has something to say, too, in her native tongue.

1) Mosang Bugakels (Nosy Neighbor): *"Bakla, ano trabaho mo sa Amerika?"* ("Bitch, what kind of work do you do in the US?")
   Vageena: *"CPA."* Mosang Bugakels: *"Ano yon?"* ("What's that?") Vageena: *"Certified Puta in America."*

2) *"Sex muna para alam ko kung happy ako with him, right? Test drive muna, ika nga. Ok ba ang kambyo mo?"*

3) *"Putang ina! Nag remburak sa kama!"*

4) *"Putang ina! Nag sirko sa kwarto!"*

5) *"Sa kwarto lang ako nag be bending body eh."*

6) *"Titi ang torotot ko. Happy New Year madlang people!"*

7) *"Massage Titirapist ka ba?"*

8) *"Hindi ko naman na kailangang makipag relasyon. Dami ko nang ka relasyon eh."*

9) *"Ano ka ba? Templo ng Muslim sa Quiapo? Dami lalaki pumapasok sayo, a?"*

10) *"Ano ka ba? Altar? Dami nakapatong sayo, a?"*

11) *"Ano ka ba? AIRBNB? Paupahan?"*

12) *"Paano sabihin sa wikang Bumbay ang "before" and "after"? Bapur and apdar."*

13) *Nasa Amerika na lahat. Masarap na pagkain. Malamig na klima. Magagandang tanawin. Magagandang lalake.*

14) *Post ni Lola Choochie Serano Villa sa Facebook tungkol daw sa "pecking order" ng mga amiga nya. Baka "puking" order siguro yon. Simula sa kung sino ang me pinakamalaking kepyas hanggang sa me pinaka makipot.*

15) About Neggi: *"Putang ina! Mukang kakainin ka nyan ng buhay!"*

16) *"Tang ina! Bali na nga balakang ko sa dami ng mga lalake ko, lalo pang mababale dahil sa bigat mo!"* (Complaining about helping an elderly relative who's having mobility issues at home)

17) *"Hindi naman sya kasing gwapo ni Ian Veneracion pero maganda naman ang wankata Inocencio."*

18) *"Putang ina! Hindi na utot yung lumalabas sa puwet mo eh. Atomic Bomb na yan eh!"*

19) *"Namputa Adwina haba ng nguso natin a? Abot hanggang Ostralya!"*

20) *"Meron akong kapitbahay na ang mga pangalan ng mga anak ay Ivy Ross Ann, Ivy Monikka pero nakalimutan ko yung pangalan nung pangatlo kaya tinanong ko yung nanay 'Ano nga uli pangalan nung bunso mo?' 'Hulaan mo!' sagot ba naman ng bruha! 'IBM?', tanong ko."*

21) *"Putang ina! Para ka palang That's Entertainment pagdating sa mga lalake mo. Merong Monday Group, Tuesday Group, Wednesday Group."*

22) *A relative from the Philippines a long time ago: "Mak, walang bakla sa Mattio."*
Mak: "Eh di ngayon meron na. Ha-ha-ha!"

23) *"Bawas bawasan nyo ang pagiging chismosa. Siguro intindihin nyo muna ang kakainin ng mga anak nyo at mga buhay buhay nyo bago nyo pakelaman ang buhay ng iba!"*

24) *"Puro na lang imbestigasyon, wala namang solusyon! Lantaran pa din ang korapsyon!"*

25) *"Hello, ako po si Pat O. Chada! Yung iba senyo matatalas lang ang dila pag nakatalikod ako no? Pero pag kaharap nyo na ko para kayong mga titing supot! Urong!"*

26) *"Pat O. Chada po uli, nagbabalik! Yung ibang tao mga pakitang gilas lang pero pag harapan na mga urong naman pala ang mga bayag. Matatapang lang pag me hawak! Pero pano kaya kung walang hawak at puro kamay lang? Eh di enjoy sa Kamayan restaurant! Sarap kaya kumain ng nakakamay! Ay teka, yoko nun. Baboy yun. Waitor, pengeng kutchara at tinidor!"*

27) *"Hello, it's me again, Pat O. Chada! Comment ko lang sa mga nasa Pinas no, bakit kasi ang hilig nyong kumain ng baboy jan. Cheez Escudero Wiz afford naman pala! Hindi na lang kumain ng isda o gulay. Marlin Mora na, masustansyasha Padilla pa! Kayo talaga! Lagi nyong iniisip ang sasabihin ng mga kapitbahay nyo! Eh kung talagang tag hirap eh! Eh di walani Mercado! Ganern? Kaya buy na lang ng gulay sa talipapa! O kung talagang tag giraffe eh di bagoong na lang. With rice. O diba? Sarap pa! Busog na sa rice, me pauso ka pang bagong klase ng rice, o davao? Introducing--bagoong rice! Ang pumalit sa adobo rice! Bow! Baho! Pwe! Yoko nyan!"*

28) *"Dati rati ang hilig kong mag shopping sa Syvels, Kadiwa at Cherry Foodarama!"*

29) *"Inday, bili mo nga ako sa Mercury Drug ng Katialis, bilis!"*

30) *"Sinumpa daw ang mga Mattio? Katarantaduhan! Mga ulol! Paano nyong nasabi yon? Ano bang masama ang nagawa ng mga Mattio para sila maisumpa? Meron ka bang alam? Meron ka bang katibayan? Testigo? Pruweba? O baka lumabas lang sa malisyosang dila ng matriyarka ng pamilya Halimau? Dahan dahan kayo sa mga pinagsasasabi nyo lalu na kung puro naman kasinungalingan! Me galit ba kayo sa mga Mattio? Nagka kanser ang*

karamihan sa mga miyembro ng Mattio! Ang kanser o ano mang klase ng sakit ay parte ng buhay! Lahat ng tao mamamatay oy! Baka nakakalimutan nyo sa pamilya Halimau meron ding namatay sa kanser diba? Correction Talits! Hindi sinumpa ang mga Mattio. Namatay ang karamihan sa kanila dahil sa kanser at iba pang karamdaman! Mga ulol! Kung ano ano ang pinagkakakana nyo dyan! Ang dudumi ng isip nyo! Di bale nang mamatay sa kanser ang mga Mattio wag lang dahil nalason ang pag iisip dahil puro tae ang laman ng utak! Mas gusto ko na ang kanser kesa mamatay ako dahil puro tae na pala ang laman ng utak ko! O ano? Kayo siguro yon! Baka yun naman ang titira sa pamilya Halimau! O kung sino mang pamilya herodes and nagsabing sinumpa ang mga Mattio. Sumabog ang utak dahil puro tae ang laman! Maghunos dili kayo sa mga pinagsasasabi nyo oy! Tandaan nyo! Ang karma laging nakamasid sa inyo!

31) *"Move on na kayo oy! Tatanda nyo na hanggang ngayon pinoproblema nyo pa pamilya ko lalo na si Ulo. Tagal nang patay nung tao oy! Kawalangya nyo naman talaga. Mag let go na kayo! Iilan na lang ang buhay nyo. Kaya ganyan mga buhay nyo. Bulokes hanggang ngayon! Kasi ang dudumi at sasama ng mga ugali nyo! Ayan tuloy, tinitira kayo ng karma. Mahiya kayo sa mga sarili nyo oy! Kakapal ng mga mukha nyo!"*

32) *"Mas gusto ko si Ronnie Alonti nung medyo malaman pa sya. Kaya ke Papa Zeus na lang muna ako ngayon. Yumminess!"*

33) *"Sardinas pagkain ng aso? Pano mo nalaman? Natikman mo na? Baka ikaw yung aso? Aso ka siguro no? Tang ina ka, aso ka nga siguro! Ikaw yon! Hayop ka talaga! Sabi ko na nga ba eh! Hayop ka nga! Hindi ka tao! Tang ina ka, pakakatay kita jan eh! Gagawin kang pulutan ng mga lasenggo sa kanto!"*

34) *"Pintas ka ng pintas sa kapwa mo eh bakit hindi mo sya gastusan para masiyahan ka sa itchura nya? Pa Belo mo sya! Bigyan mo sya ng lifetime supply ng Papaya soap! Afford mo ba? Eh kung hindi naman pala eh di tumahimik ka! Dada ka ng dada jan eh! Punyeta ka! Pataygutom ka naman pala! Tumahimik ka nga jan, hampaslupa! Mag pagpag ka na lang! Bugak!"*

SCENE AND READ: THAT'S SO RACIST!

SCENE #1: A white male employee talking to an Asian co-worker.
White Guy: "What's for lunch, Lee? Ramen noodles?"

SCENE #2: A white guy in line at the checkout counter joking with the black guy who's in front of him; black guy carrying 3 packs of chicken meat.

White Guy: "You people love barbecuing on Sundays, huh?"

SCENE #3: A white guy at the bar talking to his buddy (who's also white).

White Guy: "You lookin for a wife, dude? Go to the Philippines. They'll be all over you like *adobo* over white rice."

SEX ADVICE ANYONE?

Treat sex as something that you know will make you very happy, like a Christmas or birthday present. Get excited for it! Then eventually, you'll be good at it. They say sex is "America's favorite pastime". Well, why not make it your favorite form of exercise this time?

Sex is good for the mind and body, unless of course, you're doing those brutal sex scenes by underground pornographers and actors which include pain, fisting and torture. That's called live human slaughter! That's not pleasurable sex. Maybe to some it is, but not for me. I am not Dr. Frankenstein's patient! I don't want someone or some people tearing my body apart and inserting all kinds of garbage inside it. I just love a good old dick. Not that old president with a funny nose who got impeached back in the '70s.

Make sex fun. If it's not fun for you, then most likely something's wrong. I can't tell you how many women--some men, too--have told me that sometimes they do it just to please their partners and "get over it." That's not good attitude! You might as well hire a stripper to make your evening more exciting.

Sex should be a happy experience and you should be very happy--with a big smile on your face--after doing it.

Make sex a two-way-street thing. If you want to get good sex and receive satisying intimate pleasures, be ready to give the same thing to your partner. Don't just lay there like a corpse. Move, *crawl* and slide around his or her body! Channing Tatum is so good at it. He's *got* the moves! I'd hire him in a New York minute.

In addition, be passionate about it. Show your partner you are serious about it. Make him or her feel you're *there*. The human touch is a wonderful thing; especially if it's done right. Not too rough and abrupt, please! You are *not* Chris Brown beating up Rihanna! We're not slaughtering chickens at a farmhouse either.

"Don't choke me too hard, please," I'd tell my lover sometimes.

I can't tell you how many times my lovers have given me compliments with regards to how I use my hands on them. They say my touch is "like velvet" or it's "the best." I don't know. I wouldn't know! I'm not the one on the receiving end. But, what I know is this: I give my best to make my partner or lover feel really good. I want him to *feel* me. I want him to have the best experience in the bedroom.

Now, for the novices:

1) You really don't have to go all the way on the first date. Leave room for some kind of mystery. Unless you're Stormy D. There's no mystery left in that bitch anymore. Even the flies know she is *done*! They don't buzz around her anymore. They'd probably pass that bitch and say "Nope. It's just a carcass." Going back to leaving some mystery--keep your man's imagination running wild by using small but significant sexy hints that would eventually make his engine go into overdrive mode. Make him *excited* for other possibilities. Make him look forward to his next trip to your bedroom.

2) Make every intimate moment a night (or afternoon) to remember. Spice things up! Play it up! Dress up! These routines will keep him *up*. Take a cue from Guns N' Roses: use your illusion.

3) Play an important role--initiate a role play scene if you can. Creativity is key. Try being a lady in red this time instead of a slutty high school skank in bubble gum pink. That shit is *passe*. Honey Lynn's done it before. It's old. She's old! I ran into her at Safeway a couple of years ago. Instead of asking her "How are you?" I opted for "How are your face creams working for ya?"

4) Never underestimate the power of a potty mouth. Take it from the new sex therapist in town, Miss V. It works big time! Your man will surely enjoy it. Not to mention the big orgasm he'll have when he reaches his climax.

5) Lastly, your brain will always be your biggest sex organ. Nope, it's not your big dick or your big loose hanging clit that looks like a rooster's wattle. It's your brain! Use it! You'd be surprised by the many fun things you'll come up with for your next bedroom activity. Unless, of course, you're not that creative and kinky-minded like me. But, never lose hope, my friend. Try and try until you achieve that big, fun and oh-so-good orgasm.

Chapter 11

A TESTIMONIAL
FROM THE HEART

"Wala namang nagturo sa akin kung paano mabuhay at mag survive. Lahat ginawa 'ko-- pakikisama sa tao at sa mga taong nakasalamuha ko. Kahit pagod ang katawan ko at ang isip ko, tuloy tuloy lang ako sa pagtatrabaho para kumita ng pera at para maging maayos ang buhay at makakain ng tatlong beses sa isang araw. At syempre, para makatulong sa mga pang araw araw na gastusin, at makatulong din sa mga kaibigan at kamag anak na nangangailangan ng tulong pinansyal."

Did somebody tell me 'This is how life's going to work out for you!'? No one! Absolutely no one! I had to figure it all out on my own.

There were a lot of roadblocks and obstacles, for sure, but I persevered and worked my way through. Remember, each day for me was a struggle. And I'm proud to say I did not beg Uncle Sam for welfare checks or food stamps or any kind of government support. I didn't need any of those because all I needed was the drive and determination to earn some money, get my ass out of the couch and do some work out there. I didn't even get a single penny from that stimulus package. I made my money through hard work and *diskarte*.

So, there is an extra spring in my step and my chin and head are held up high every time I'm out in public. I'm proud to say I am not a welfare check recipient nor am I ever part of the government's stimulus program!

You have no idea the pile of shit life's going to dump at you, so you better be ready and you gotta be strong. Be strong always! Even if you think you're not. Just keep telling yourself 'You can do this, bitch'. And don't forget to pray. Miracles come out of prayers. God has a strange way of responding. He listens!

Chapter 12

THE TAKEAWAY

It's been close to fifteen years since I published *Naughty and Nice: The Colorful Life of Transsexual Vanessa* and a lot has happened since then. Reality star Donald Trump became president of the United States, a united Black Lives Matter made their voices heard through countless rallies across the country and the LGBTQ Community is slowly but surely becoming part of mainstream America, thanks to the hard work and perseverance of those who continue to fight for our most basic human rights and those who keep the fight alive. They are the ones who keep the *fire* burning. There's still a long, bumpy road to trek for transgender individuals in order for them to achieve unconditional equality and total freedom from bigotry, harassment and assault. Transgender people must be aware of their surroundings all the time and be vocal as well. If you see or hear something that is insulting or disrespectful, you must speak out.

Let the public know you *exist.* But, try to exist with decency and respectability. Move with grace and dignity. Don't be like those two tacky trannies I encountered at the Great Mall in Milpitas a couple of years ago. You act trashy and people will treat you like garbage. I'm pretty sure they are getting *it* somewhere. And please...please put some decent clothes on. When taking a stroll at the mall, do not dress like a stripper or streetwalker. Do not treat the mall as if it's a sleazy bar where you show your skanky ass! Remember, children go to the mall, too!

You act and move like a queen and people will respect you and *yield* to you. I really appreciate it when my fellow Americans hold or open the door for me in public buildings and businesses or stop and let me pass first on tight alleys at the supermarket or grocery store. I thank them from the bottom of my heart. Thank you for the respect!

Conversely, I'd like to tell those who are not so kind and respectful that transgender people are here to stay! Love us or hate us, we are here to stay! Learn to *live* with us! If cats and dogs could coexist despite their differences, so can straight, gay and transgender people! Get on with it, America!

Let's try our best to live in peace and harmony. I know damn well I do my part all the time.

Sadly, there are the neverending mass shootings and massacres brought by gun violence and reckless--reckless and irresponsible--gun ownership. The recent school shooting in Oxford, Michigan is a classic example.

That rifle won't be in your son's hands had you stored it in a place where he won't be able to find it--the lake! Bury it under the ground! Put ten locks around it and throw the keys off the Gulf of Mexico or the Atlantic, for crying out loud! Or better yet, just donate those guns to your local police department. You are not participating in a civil war unless you're part of the January 6 Capitol siege. Or are you? That's the question I'd like to ask these people straight up. Why do you need to own a semi automatic rifle in the first place?

Another important question I'd like to ask those January 6 rioters and insurrectionists: Were you trying to destroy America's peace and democracy? Let's also ask Donald Trump, Kevin McCarthy, Josh Hawley, Mitch McConnell and other Republicans who played deaf and blind as those modern day barbarians stormed the Capitol, one of America's most sacred and hallowed grounds.

People who defend those January 6 rioters and their actions must be questioned, too. Why? What's your motive? Are you pro America or anti-America?

Joe Biden won the election. Move on!

If you really love America you would protect her landmarks and buildings. They represent our nation's pride and soul. Do not destroy and defile them! If you do, you *are* the anti-America! You are *the* traitor and therefore must face the consequences of your actions. Uncle Sam should put you behind bars for a very long time. You don't deserve to walk the sacred grounds of my beloved America!

Parents and guardians of those mass shooters I've mentioned earlier are partly to blame, no doubt. They, too, have blood in their hands. I hope they are reading my book. Maybe this will help them realize the devastating effects of their irresponsibility and lack of concern for the lives and safety of others.

I am also hoping for the best. America is still the best place in the world for me. I still believe in the "land of the free" and the countless freedoms that I cherish so much. And I still have *faith* in its people. That they will continue to fight for one another, be good neighbors and most important of all, respect individuals like myself.

Despite these "hopes" and prayers, I remain completely alert and I pay full attention to my surroundings all the time. All the time! I've learned to practice caution and common sense more often.

If I really don't need to go to a crowded place (like festivals or fairs) with no visible police presence then I won't go. Forget Outside Lands. I can listen to great music indoors--in the comfort of my home--with my *BOSE* stereo system and a glass of wine. I'm sure I'll still have a great time.

If I notice an individual is acting strange--walking and moving in an odd manner or just acting a little off, I'd exit the place I am in immediately. I'll probably mention it to the manager first. Remember the golden rule: "If you see something, say something."

Also, I make sure I have my face mask on wherever I go. In this crazy Covid world that we live in, prevention is key. Protect yourself!

On a personal note, in the small, quiet progressive California town of Milpitas, there have been significant changes--mostly spiritual and emotional--in the life of its first transsexual resident author, Vanessa.

Over the years, slowly but surely I've found my inner peace and have decided to practice what Buddha has taught humanity for thousands of years: incorporate zen in your daily life.

I have more self control these days. I don't get easily riled up or stressed out by small, petty things anymore unlike before. If my two mature girlfriends are bickering about a child's name and they want to slash each other's throats for it, then so be it. Not my problem! If some jerk cuts me off on the freeway, I let him go because I know sooner or later karma will catch up with him. Back in 2006, I once chased a young road jerk in Fremont, CA after he cut me off somewhere along Warm Springs Boulevard. He thought he was going to get away from me but I eventually caught up with him and cornered him near a gas station. There was no escaping for him. I moved my car very close to his car's driver side, looked him straight in the eye and yelled a bunch of obscenities at him for a good two minutes. He couldn't utter a single word. The fear in his face was priceless.

Nowadays, a "road rage payback" is a thing of the past for me. I've learned to adjust and I just avoid bad drivers most of the time.

We need to learn to move on. It's an important armor we must carry all the time in this battle called life.

I tell myself, "Joe Biden and my beloved firefighters have bigger problems to deal with, not you, Vanessa. Tough shit! Move on!"

I've also been very religious in practicing--no pun intended--the solemn act of praying. Prayers are so therapeutic. They are my silent wishes and thank yous that I really don't need everyone to hear. I don't need to post on Facebook about how prayerful I am and that I follow God's words unlike some people in the Philippines; only to post nasty comments about other people after the "Pray for my neighbor" post. That is so fake. What a bunch of hypocrites! A one time neighbor, Rolanda, is notorious for being that way. That bitch is something else.

Included in my daily prayers are those for world peace, my peace of mind and that these deceased loved ones' souls may rest in eternal peace: my friends David and Lucy and more recently, my cousin Marvin.

"People drop like birds," a good friend of mine told me a long time ago. It's a sad realization.

Part of my mental and emotional maturity is the fact that I need to realize that I won't be seeing certain individuals--who at one point became an important part of my life--anymore. I had to drop them from my guest list called "Vanessa's life".

I've matured mentally, but sadly, these former friends have not.

I've said this before and I'll say it again; when the friendship and other relationships you have with others start to create tensions and cause stress to the point that there is nothing that can be done about it, you have to let those people go.

I used to be good friends with these two women (Girlfriend X and Girlfriend Y) who themselves were at one point, best friends with each other--until one of them named her newborn baby "Allen" (which coincidentally, was the name of the other woman's teenage son). This, for some stupid reason, created a huge crack on their friendship.

Stupid, stupid, stupid! Mind you, these are two grown women in their 40s. One would think that they'd exercise some hint of class and maturity and just let it go.

I, on the other hand, did not want to be caught in the middle of this bitch fight. I've said this before and I'll say it again: "The only cracks I want to be involved in are the ones found in a man's behind." Not those found in the relationship of two bickering bitches.

No, sorry! I don't want any part of it.

So, to avoid absorbing their negative vibes, and more importantly, for my peace of mind, I've decided to stop seeing both women.

I am a mature and classy Louis Vuitton-carrying woman in her 40s and playing referee to two immature individuals was never in my vocabulary. I'd rather focus on the chaos and drama found in my drawings and sketches rather than the ones involving two grown ass women fighting over the name "Allen"!

But wait, there is a twist to the story. The "Allen" issue was actually the icing to a really bad, rotting, crumbling cake! Long before the fight over "Allen" began, the friendship of those two women had already gone sour. The prime suspects: envy and ego.

"You pick your battles," the old saying goes. I chose peace--peace in my surroundings and peace of mind.

There's too many wars, conflicts and hatred going on in this world. It would be nice to create and nurture peace around you for a change.

Let go of the drama! In the end, we are really the ones in control of how we'd like things to be--unless, of course, there's an evil president in office. Then we really have to be in combat mode.

Assholes, tragedies and mean, obnoxious people will always be a part of life, but I have two custom made buttons for these things that I resort to before things get out of hand and the situation becomes helpless: "RUN" and "MOVE ON".

I raise my barriers with the words "Stand back, motherfucker! You're bad luck!"

The choice is ours and ours alone to make. We have that kind of power. Use it. I also keep in mind the advice from our brave and beloved men and women of Law Enforcement, "If you see something, say something." On the other hand, if someone says something mean or offensive to you, give them a dose of their own medicine. Never back down. Cuss the motherfucker out!

Once, a handsome police officer from Fremont, CA told me it's totally okay to say what you want to another--"Fuck you!" included. It doesn't matter how mean or foul. "It's your freedom of speech!", he pointed out.

Do not be quiet when the going gets tough and the aggressors get tougher. The more we become silent the more empowered these racists and bigots become. Let them know our voices are as loud as theirs or better.

We are the ones in control not only of our destiny, but also the present day.

There is much work to be done and more improvements to be made; more experiences to have and more men to have some fun with. Hey, you only have one shot at life, right? Aim for the bullseye!

Who knows? Maybe I'll be writing my third memoir fourteen years from now. But for now, I'll put my pen down and do a karaoke number of one of my favorite Beatles songs, "Ob-la-di Ob-la da". Life goes on!

God bless America and the wonderful people of this great nation of ours!

ABOUT THE AUTHOR

Vanessa Mateo, freelance therapist and author of two books, is a full time female transsexual living in the South Bay neighborhood of the greater San Francisco Bay Area. Vanessa has long considered herself a passionate advocate and torchbearer for LGBTQ rights and other causes especially after emerging victorious in her fight to use the women's restroom at a federal facility in San Jose, CA some twenty years ago, long before the issue was brought out into the spotlight. She views that milestone as one of her major accomplishments in life. Vanessa is also a jewelry aficionado and an avid collector of rare pieces of art and pop culture memorabilia. A businesswoman at heart from the very beginning–she used to sell food and other refreshments in front of her grandparents' home in Manila back in the late '80s and early '90s when she was barely a teenager–Vanessa now curates one-of-a-kind pieces of art and jewelry and would, from time to time, present them at local art fairs and flea markets.

Vanessa's other interests include fashion, music, history, science and photography. She also frames and archives old and unique photographs and vintage prints as a part time hobby. Vanessa is also a lifelong dance enthusiast; considers dancing as the best form of exercise.

Also by the author:

Naughty and Nice: The Colorful Life of Transsexual Vanessa
SCANDALOUS! Dark Times in the Life of Kiki Malachite

BOOK DESCRIPTION

"I'm not an expert on life and *living*, but I do what feels good and feels right," Vanessa Mateo once said. "In life, that's the only thing that really matters."

In *SEX and RELATIONSHIPS in the 21st CENTURY: A Transsexual's Point of View*, Vanessa delves into the rich and colorful forty four years of her existence and delivers what could be the tell all to end all other tell alls.

Vanessa takes her readers on an exciting journey back in time--the irreplaceable years of her childhood and youth--and back to the present, with fresh new experiences and remarkable encounters with people from all walks of life, ultimately summing up a life some might not consider ordinary but one that is truly well lived nonetheless.

This latest autobiography, considered both a prequel and sequel to *Naughty and Nice: The Colorful Life of Transsexual Vanessa*, highlights the ups and downs of 21st century life for a transgender individual living in an ever changing and sometimes not so forgiving world. Vanessa, in her classic, straightforward style of storytelling, recalls the fun, the pain, the sex and the triumphs with such gusto and with no abandon. This transwoman definitely knows how to speak her mind! She does it in a most unabashed and unapologetic manner. From Diana, Princess of Wales to that daring Dannemora Prison escape, as well as the dos and don'ts during sexual intimacy, hear what Vanessa has to say. And you'd be surprised to find out what she really thinks of that guy named Donald! Vanessa's got you covered.

www.ingramcontent.com/pod-product-compliance
Lightning Source LLC
Chambersburg PA
CBHW080922190726
48293CB00010B/2654